I0681316

Out of the Park

EVENING THE SCORE

JAQUELINE SNOWE

EVENING THE SCORE

Dedication

This book is dedicated to the one softball season my husband and I coached together. It is filled with memories I'll never forget. Life is always an amazing adventure with you.

To Rebecca Fairfax. It is challenging to put into words how wonderful it is working with you. I am so grateful our paths crossed and I cannot thank you enough for everything you do to make my stories shine.

To Miranda Darrow. It is incredible having gotten to know you through our back-and-forth comments. Your insight and knowledge made all the difference and I cannot wait until we can grab that beer and talk baseball.

And thank you, Nancy, Cheryl and Kacie. I am lucky to have such supportive women who encourage me in the best way. I appreciate you all so much.

Chapter One

Fiona

"Shut the fuck up. *The* baseball-playing star of my fantasies Gideon Titan?" Spit left my mouth and my pulse raced at the thought of that perfect specimen of a man. His poster hung in my room. He had starred in my dreams more than a handful of times. His eyes, abs and smile...I shivered. Wishes did come true. The receptionist at the Los Soles stadium gawked at me and I held up a hand. "Forgive my language. But please clarify. Who will I be coaching with again?"

Her gaze darted to the door as a blush crept up her neck. "Uh, Gideon Titan. He's volunteering for the season for the fourteen and under baseball team. You're paired together."

"Cool." *Ohmigod.* "Thank you." I tried my best to remain calm and smiled while she printed off the schedule. She chewed on her bottom lip so damn much I wanted to smack her. I couldn't be the first person to lose their shit at the chance to meet Gideon Titan.

He defined the term *masculine*. He put all men to shame. For a baseball-lovin' southwest chick, he was it. When he was in full form, he was the epitome of perfection. Even with his injury and slight limp, I would take any invitation he offered. I left her desk with the practice schedule, reading about the forty games within four months, four games a week after two weeks of full practice.

Fucking Jade. Amazing, beautiful Jade. I called my pseudo-boss from the non-profit I had volunteered at for the last four years. She was my best friend, mentor and the version of a sister I'd thought my real sisters would be. She answered on the first ring her voice cheery. "Lo?"

"Gideon Titan."

Jade's breathy laugh traveled through the phone. "Surprise?"

"Hell, yeah. Best surprise ever. When I asked to get involved with youth sports, I was thinking more like pee-wee soccer. Not baseball. How did you do this?" The fresh air hit my face as I barged through the exit and I couldn't contain my grin. November in Phoenix had perfect weather — I intended to enjoy every drop of it.

"Well, I know a guy who knows a guy...plus, you've put a lot of work into our programs that focus on high school kids. You're great with them and this will be a good fit. You can talk about the dangers of texting and driving *and* get to coach one-on-one with Gideon Titan. I see this as a win-win."

The stab of pain came and went — I was used to the wave of grief whenever Justin crossed my mind. It got easier to not react to it. I cleared my throat and wiped my suddenly sweaty palms on my jeans. "Thanks for

thinking of me for this. I'm grateful. And hello? Gideon. Freaking. Titan."

"Yeah. I heard he can be a real asshole, but I want every detail."

My brain wasn't in the right place to fully comprehend her words. I laughed it off. With a face like Gideon's, he could ramble on and on about stupid, irrelevant information and I'd still be happy. "You misheard it. I'm sure they meant to say he's a hot piece of ass."

Jade sighed, ignoring me. *Typical Jade.* "Anyway, crazy. We need to talk about that job offer that is still unanswered."

My throat closed and I let out an awkward grunt. "Mm, yeah. Sure."

"I'll let you go enjoy your moment to think about Gideon, but I need an answer, Fi. See you at the office soon?"

"Yup." I hung up, took a deep breath and started the drive to the shitty two-bedroom apartment I'd moved into a month ago with a former co-worker. I'd made enough the two years before, waitressing at an IHOP, and had saved every last penny to be able to live on my own my senior year. I adored my mom and my childhood home but shit—I needed to cut the cord and live my life. Her meddling personality got in the way, despite her good intentions. I wasn't a bitch, but I wanted to be independent even if it killed me. Yeah—I had a stubborn thing going and I was damn proud of it.

Jade's words weighed heavy on me the entire drive. Volunteering at Texting Too Late had started out small to help me cope with Justin's death. But it had grown into more. Once a month had become twice, and twice a week had become almost daily. The foundation was amazing and it gave me a fulfillment I needed to deal with the guilt, but could I accept a full-time position knowing damn well every day would remind me of him, and my secret?

I gripped the wheel tighter and scoffed at all the couples holding hands. *What the fuck? It's like noon on a Tuesday – why are they just strolling down our shitty street?* I parked in the covered carport, spying Michelle's Toyota, and checked my phone before heading into our modest place.

Jade: You would get to see me every day.

Jade: Diane knows you kick ass with all the money stuff I avoid.

Fiona: Keep the compliments coming. It's good for my ego.

Jade: You could pick the music station?

Fiona: I would choose 2000s R&B and it's still a maybe.

I pocketed my phone and pulled my hair up into a ponytail before walking inside. I was quite proud of the way I handled donations to TTL and that our rating had gone up in the past three months. I allocated about fifteen percent of all donations for maintenance, freelance work and advertising, but Jade had proposed moving it to twenty and keeping me on full-time with pay. Diane – the president and founder – agreed.

It had insurance, great benefits and a good salary for a non-profit. I would work with Jade, who was pretty fucking awesome, and have a job on the table before graduating.

But...*Justin.*

Nah. Not today, grief. I straightened my shoulders, pushing down the negative spiral I was sure to have. I avoided feelings. Tied up, sewed shut. I hadn't had a relationship that amounted to more than awesome, gravity-defying sex since I was eighteen, but that didn't really count, and I was okay with it. Sex was easy. Attention was easy. Feelings were not. Feelings did not lead to happiness. I came across as wild, reckless or cold to most, but it didn't bother me. It was safer, smarter and survival. Light rock music carried from our place and I plowed through our front door. I had news and Michelle Benning needed to hear it.

"Michelle. Get your ass out here right now."

"What is it?" She waltzed out of her room, just to the right of the kitchen. She wore the ugly blue apron and had her hair done up. We both had our secrets, our pasts that defined the core pieces of us. But I hadn't asked her what hers were, nor had she asked me. We enjoyed each other's company and I didn't require much more than that from my first roommate besides my mom.

"Guess who the fuck I got paired with to coach this team. Guess." I plopped onto our long-standing burgundy couch. It had been a family piece and my mom had given it to us. It smelled like an old basement, of stale popcorn with a mix of lemon furniture polish. I loved it. Michelle ran her manicured red nails over her chin, humming in thought.

"My mind is blank. Tell me."

"Gideon Titan." I smirked, pulling up a picture of him on my phone. "*The* Gideon Titan."

"Fuck me sideways." She snatched the phone out of my hands. "I want to sit on his face."

"Girl, join the club. I want him to sit on *my* face." I fanned myself with my free hand. "I have to send him an email, or reach out to him somehow. Practices are four times a week! Then, forty games."

"I hate you." Her dark brown eyes widened, her hand going to her heart. "I'm not one of those jealous bitches. But I could cut you right now."

I snickered. "I don't blame you. Here, will you help me type out an email to him? Or should I call? What do you think?"

She took the schedule from my hands and skimmed the bottom line — *contact me for details*. She pursed her lips. "He left a number and email. What would you rather do?"

"It makes more sense to text, right?" Nerves took over. I would be texting someone whose face was plastered all over our city. *Wow. But what if he's driving?*

"I think so. If this wasn't Gideon Titan but some random person, you would text, right?"

"I'd rather call. I'd want to talk about logistics and division of coaching duties. It'd be easier to talk than type." I wiped my palms on my jeans. "Shit."

"Girl, this is insane. Call now. I want to hear his voice." She grasped my hand, with her face a little too happy, a little too eager. I couldn't blame her, though. My excitement and nerves took center stage and the reality of the situation had me stiff. "Call."

"Okay, okay!" I skimmed the informational sheet the woman had given me and his number sat at the bottom. Gideon Titan's number. I dialed it, hesitating for a second before pressing call. Then it rang. "Shit. Ah!"

It rang three times, each tone causing more sweat to form on my brow. The fourth ring, he answered.

"It's Gideon."

His voice was rough and strangled, but my body reacted to it anyway. My legs clenched together, the deep tone affecting me way too much. Michelle said something to get my attention and I cleared my throat. "Hi, Gideon Titan. My name is Fiona —"

"Who fucking gave you my number?"

His sudden verbal attack made me jump. My tremulous voice gave me away, I was sure. "Los Soles, sir."

"Why?" Something shuffled in the background, the accusation clear as day. "What do you want?"

"We-we got paired to coach the fourteen-blue team." *Goddamn my nerves.*

"Christ." He released a long, aggravated sigh. "I don't need another coach. Tell them you can't do it and never call this number again."

Then he hung up.

The first spark of anger began in my stomach. It worked its way up to my chest, then to my neck. I wanted to *murder* this guy. He was an asshole of epic proportions. Michelle's eyes were the size of small saucers.

"Did he for real just do that?" Her brittle voice matched mine.

"Yeah. The fucker hung up on me." I fisted the paper into a crumpled ball. "Fuck him."

I hit redial, his rough voice answering the same. "Listen, asshole. I'm coaching with you. I want this opportunity. So fuck off. I'll see you at the first practice."

Then I hung up.

"Oh my god. What did I do?" I threw my phone onto the small coffee table. Michelle's face remained unmoving, as though my actions had frozen time. *Whoever cusses at Gideon Titan?*

"When is the first practice?" she asked.

I unfolded the paper, glancing at the date and times. "In five days. That should be enough time for everyone to cool down, yeah?"

"Sure, hon." Michelle got up, shaking her head at me a little bit. "I knew I liked you for a reason. Your balls are bigger than most men I know."

I laughed. "Then you aren't around decent guys. Ball size is everything."

She cackled, shouldering her purse and reapplying lipstick. "Balls are a deal breaker for me."

"Dude, I know." I leaned farther back into the couch, wishing it would swallow me up. Regret and embarrassment would hit me later, with Michelle at work and no one to distract me. "I've said it all the time, *but* balls are weird. Guys have to have them, but where do they go when they ride a bike?"

"Right! Or when they sit? Do they squish them to the side or flatten them?"

"How can they cross their legs?" I added. "And why must they touch them all the damn time? And do the reach-down-then-smell-their-fingers thing?"

"Why do they ball tap each other? I don't mind a titty twister now and again, but I don't greet my friends with a boob grab every time."

I laughed—Michelle had a great point. "I mean, the thought they walk around with a stick hanging out boggles my mind. But add two squishy sacks of skin next to it? Why?" I closed my eyes, thoughts of balls and penises overtaking my mind.

Michelle snickered and headed toward the door. She had to work and the thought of doing homework alone depressed me. "I'll be home later than normal. I might be staying until breakfast."

"Damn, well, be safe. I'll be here thinking about balls."

"God." She shook her head. "I'm glad we're roomies. See you."

She shut the door and I smiled. I liked Michelle as much as I could like someone outside my family. Hope blossomed in my chest that maybe, just *maybe*, I could let her in.

Chapter Two

Gideon

"Uncle Gid, Uncle Gid! Take me to the park. Please. Please!"

I rubbed my temples — the headache from the phone call hadn't gone away. Punching brick walls would be preferable to coaching with that *woman*. "Quinn, not now."

"But why?" Her pursed lips resembled her mother's to a tee. Sassy, loud and with the ability to manipulate me into doing anything — Quinn was the miniature version of my sister.

"I have a headache." Maybe if I ignored her, she would find something else to occupy her time. I ground my teeth. *Someone coaching with me? Fuck. That. Noise.*

"You always have *something*." She sighed as much as a seven-year-old could and stomped out of the living room. *Finally, peace and quiet.*

Recalling the phone call got my blood boiling again. *Who the hell is this chick? Why does she have my number? Why did she sound sixteen? Why do I have to fucking coach?*

Quinn shuffled around her room, making more noise than necessary to get my attention. A slight wave of regret went through me. I hadn't been the best uncle since my injury. We used to do all sorts of crazy activities—fairs, parks, zoos, libraries. She was my favorite little person. Now, when I babysat her, we never left home. The last time we'd done *anything* was go see a new kids' movie. And that had been weeks ago.

"Quinn?" I groaned into the pillow. Her excited footsteps tapped down the hall until she stood right in front of me. Her sly toothy grin told me she'd planned the whole thing out. "Were you trying to make me feel bad?"

"No." She pouted, her wide-set eyes bugging out at her obvious lie. "Why would I want to upset my favorite uncle?"

"*Only* uncle, but I'll accept it." I pulled her into my lap, her giggles echoing off the wood-paneled walls. My sister wasn't keen on decorating, but the few things she had hung up all reflected her life with Quinn. Hell, it showed off Quinn's work and the colors she brought to our lives. My loft had been top dollar, yet it didn't look like anyone had lived there the past five years. *Because my life is sad.*

"What do you want to do? The park? Ice cream? Batting cages?" I tickled her side, her laughter becoming desperate as she squirmed away from me. "If you're going to be a monkey, I'm gunna treat you like one."

"Stop!" she shrieked, the sound not pleasant, but her laughter made up for it. "I'm not a monkey. I'm not!"

"Say Uncle Gid is the best."

"*Uncle Gid is the best!*" she squealed and I picked her up like a sack of potatoes. "Uncle Gid!"

"I don't hear anything. La la la!" I teased and found my mood lightening. *Screw that chick on the phone.* "To the park we go!"

"Can we play monster when we get there?"

Monster. The dumbass game I'd invented when she was little. I'd never live it down. I had to walk like a zombie and pretend to get her while sounding like a *Walking Dead* character. "Please, please, please!"

"Maybe. If you can sing my favorite song to me."

"Hey now, you're an all-star."

"That's my girl. I am an all-star."

We made the short trip to the neighborhood park after it took ten minutes to put on my brace. I despised the mechanical piece, but it let me still do active things—like take my favorite mini-human outside. I sent a quick text to her mom. I spent most of the time away playing ball and another wave of remorse hit me. I hated leaving Quinn during the season. *Hated it.* And I needed to cherish the little moments. I only got to babysit her from November to February, and I wanted her to love every second with me.

I had to make up the time for not being there much because of the injury. *The fucking injury, root of my problem.* I smiled when she forced me to watch her go down the slide, and jump off the swing, and do ten cartwheels...but I did. I smiled like hell and instantly became her biggest fan. Because if a seven-year-old could love me, then I wasn't a total piece of shit, despite what my coach and teammates must think. *Why did I blow up at them? And on camera?* One bad day could ruin my future. "Mr. Titan?"

"What?" My entire body stiffened at the interruption of my self-deprecating thoughts. I had never gotten used to it — the photo requests, autographs, smiling and touching strangers. But I was scolded for not being more *fan-friendly*. This kid appeared to be about ten or so, and I wiped my hands on my pants. I could play nice for a kid. "How's it going?"

"I can't b-believe I'm meeting you. I'm a huge fan. The hugest. Are you feeling better? How's your leg?" He pointed to the wrong one, without the injury, and his entire face paled. I held out my hand, forcing myself to smile.

"Love meeting fans. I'm working on getting better. What's your name?"

"Peter O'Callahan, sir."

"Well, Peter, thanks for rooting for me. I need to hang out with my family so we'll talk later, okay?"

"Sure thing!" He smiled and showcased his missing teeth, and ran off toward a nervous-looking woman, who I assumed was his mom. I diverted my attention back to Quinn, and had to go through five more experiences like that before everyone took off, leaving just the two of us in the park. *Thank god.*

The older carbon copy of Quinn met us there with a wave a short time later. Quinn dangled from the monkey bars from one hand, and I knew a lecture was on the way. In three, two, one. She opened her mouth but I held up a hand. "Cheryl. Don't start — "

"I told you…" and I tuned my older sister out. Quinn and I shared a look. *Here we go again.* Cheryl lectured about safety and Quinn and I disregarded it every time. We all knew I would do damn near anything for Quinn. She was perfectly safe with me. Shit — Cheryl worked as a nurse and spent an insane number of hours at the hospital. Quinn had suffered a life-altering papercut once in my *entire* time watching her. So Cheryl could calm the hell down. "Gid! Do you even listen to anyone besides your own ego?"

"Woah, shots fired." I shook off her comment even though it hurt to hear. My ego—a topic of popular conversation between her and my coaches. They all harped on at me about *sorting out* my priorities. Quinn played the role of obnoxious older sister a little too well. *She has to without having parents around…* My heart clenched.

It irked me because she wasn't the only one who'd said shit like that to me lately. My agent, older teammates—even my recent hookup had said *'I can't believe you're still on the team after what you said to Tate. He's like a living legend here.'* I shook the memory away.

But I did what I did best and forgot about it. More self-critical thoughts would come later, after a drink or two—that was for sure—but I always chose to live in the present. "Come on down, Quinn. *Mother* is here."

"Mother." Quinn mocked and I got a deserved smack to the arm. I hid my chuckle until I got a closer look at Cheryl's face. She had been crying. *Shit.*

"What gives?" I set Quinn down and she took off toward the swings.

"Nothing. Let's just watch Quinn for a bit." She brushed me off, the Titan family trait we all succeeded at. I put my hand on her shoulder and stopped her from walking away.

"Spill it," I demanded. My sister and her spawn might annoy me, but no one messed with them. *No one.*

She rubbed the bridge of her nose for a solid five seconds and a bubble of worry formed in my chest. Thoughts snowballed, one idea worse than the other, and my anxiety took hold of all my senses. "Cheryl, please."

"It's…it's Quinn's father."

"What does that piece of shit want?" *Piece of shit. Scum of the earth. Asshole. Liar. Sleazebag. Any name works.*

She met my eyes, her deep brown ones filling with pure fear. "He wants custody. Vic wants custody and I-I can't l-lose Quinn." Her entire body began shaking and I put my arm around her. *I will kill this guy. Fuck Vic.*

"He can't get full custody, right.? He hasn't fucking been around in seven years. Best-case scenario, he gets supervised visits." I held her tighter. "I'll help any way I can. You know this."

"Rationally, I know he can't. But there is a small part of me with the *what if* and my world crashes down. I c-can't imagine my l-life with her." Her chin met her chest and soft sobs came out. I rubbed her shoulder and kept an eye out for Quinn. My heart ached for her— Cheryl had escaped a bad situation when she left Vic. He would not win this case. No sane lawyer would think he had a chance. An unsettling, disgusting thought entered my mind about his intentions, but I didn't voice it. I would do my own research. Cheryl needed to focus on Quinn and that was it.

"We'll figure it out. Do you need to go pull yourself together somewhere? Get your nails done or a drink? I can stay with Quinn. Hell, she can spend the night if you want."

"I appreciate the offer, Gid, but I think it'll be best for me to be with her. Get as many cuddles as I can." She gave me a small smile and I observed her put her mask on. She straightened her spine, wiped under her eyes and took a long breath before she made her way to Quinn. Pride bloomed in my chest. *Cheryl defines supermom.*

"Want me to stick around?" I yelled to the pair. Their long brown hair, the exact shade of mine, flew in the wind and joy radiated off Quinn. *Good. That girl deserves all the happiness.*

"Uncle Gid. What about dinner?" my favorite person asked in a high voice.

"What about it?"

"You staying? I can show you my doll house."

Cheryl smirked and shrugged. "I brought home pasta. You can stay."

"It's decided." I joined them at the swings and pushed Quinn higher. She squealed with each push and for a brief moment, all negative or worrying thoughts didn't matter. The joy carried over through dinner — that was, until my agent called me with a stick already in his ass. *Typical Billy.*

"Titan. How's the leg doing?"

"Fine," I replied through gritted teeth. He interrupted my dinner and asked the exact same question every goddamn time. *No progress on my leg. Still hurts like a bitch. Still worried my career is over. Still limping like a fuck-stick. Still an asshole.*

"Good, good. I wanted to run some things by you. Got a second?" He spoke with too much enthusiasm in his voice. It exhausted me. I ignored his question and cut to the chase.

"Billy — why the hell am I coaching with some chick?"

His laugh reflected all his years of smoking. "Why the hell were you an asshole who lashed out at his teammate?"

"You're really bringing that up? I didn't do it." *Dick.*

"You asked a question. I gave you an answer. Your coach thought you needed to find your love of the game again. The kids will lose their shit, Gid. Think how much your little niece loves you. These kids think you're the greatest thing since sliced bread."

The kids were the best part of being a professional athlete — but Billy was missing the point. "Why am I paired with someone? Also, a girl who sounds about fifteen years old. I don't need a partner."

"Her name is Fiona Davis. She was recommended by someone close with Los Soles."

"They she probably did this as a favor or some political bullshit. You know, I bet she's some crazed fan." I let out a long string of curse words. I did not need this. "I want her gone."

"Tough tits, man. Chief wanted to pair you up. Not sure why they picked her, but it is what it is. Could be worse — think about that."

"That's shit advice and a shit answer."

"Life's not full of sunshine and rainbows, buttercup." He laughed at his own joke and I wished he was there so I could deck him. "Now, quit your bitching and let me ask you my questions."

"Fine." I snuck a glance back at my sister, but she was making a goofy face at Quinn to get her to eat. "What is it?"

"Sponsors. Agua Chill wants to do a photo shoot and a commercial — you up for it?"

I pulled at the back of my neck. Was I up for it? *Fuck yeah.* I needed money, especially if my ACL didn't pull through. And these days I wasn't sure it would. "Sure. Sign me up and let me know."

"Good. I'm glad you're in an agreeable mood. Let's continue that. I need you to do a visit at the children's hospital, speak at an assembly at a middle school and I'll bring the photographers."

"Billy. No photographers." I seethed. "I'll do those *without* the goddamn press. Not everything I do is for show. *Jesus.*"

"Whatever, Gid, just doing what you've asked me in the past."

We hung up and two things bothered me. Sure — Billy had stuck by me when a big endorsement had fallen through two years ago and he'd always supported my charity work. He had done more good than bad, but he was pissing me off today. The first was his constant jabs at me. I knew I could be an asshole. Sometimes I was. But I always insisted on doing the hospital visits without photos. Those were my favorite moments.

The second was about the coaching. I hadn't lashed out at a teammate. I had called out Tate Monaghan for using a cork bat and the swine had spun it to make me look like a deranged, injured has-been. No one had taken my side. *Now I'm stuck rehabbing from a torn ACL, on the verge of becoming an unwanted free agent, and paired up with some whiney chick for four months.*

This had to be karma for something, because the stars were not aligning for me.

Chapter Three

Fiona

What does one wear to coach teenage boys, while also in the presence of Gideon Titan? Is there a right or wrong answer? I sighed and fell onto my bed. I had tried on five different options and each one felt sillier than the last. *Yoga pants and a baseball top? Shorts and a sweatshirt? Tights and a baggy T-shirt? Fuck this confusion.*

I stormed to my tiny closet and eyed my few options. I didn't have a lot of clothes, but I had staple pieces that could be arranged for numerous looks. Shout out to Pinterest for the help with finding eighteen ways to wear a scarf. A comfy, loose baseball shirt from the Desert Aces popped out. I paired it with black yoga pants and called it a day. If Gideon Titan was as rude in person as he was on the phone, then I wanted to be comfortable. Looking good for him was out of the question. The thought alone had me snorting. Gideon Titan giving me attention? That would be the day. I was a flea in his world.

But the pants hugged me in the right places. It wasn't every day a girl met the star of her fantasy sex dreams. "Michelle!"

"Yeah?" She appeared at my door with raccoon eyes and wild hair. *Looks like someone had a crazy night.* "Going to meet the hot asshole?"

"Yup. We're meeting for coffee before the parent meeting," I sneered at my phone. He'd informed me of the *meeting* in a demand.

Yeah. I wasn't thrilled about it. "Do I look like a tool? A hoe? Normal?"

She sucked her bottom lip and hummed in thought. She often did that and I thought it was endearing. Her crazy black hair fell over her eyes and she pushed it back. "I think you look the part. Do you have a track jacket or a fanny pack?"

"Perfect idea. Yes. I have both." I dug deep into my dresser and pulled out a bright red first aid fanny pack. I had it from a spirit day in high school—lifeguard day—and it was magnificent. "I'm really gunna look the part."

"That's the goal, ain't it?" She yawned and let out a whistle. "I had a hell of a night."

"Yeah? I didn't hear you come in." I wiggled my eyebrows at her and she looked smug as hell. Curiosity had me wanting to ask what had happened, but we weren't quite there yet. "But I want what you're having with that little smirk."

"Hm. I don't share." And she walked out. Michelle was mysterious and I dug that about her. I gave her no more thought while I gave myself one more glance over. My outfit stuck out in the mirror and I grinned. Yeah, Gideon Titan might be an asshole and would try to get rid of me, but he would *not* succeed. I wished I had a clipboard to really embarrass him, but I would have to put that on my to-do list.

With a final farewell to Michelle, I hopped into my beat-up car and blasted Carrie Underwood. She got my blood pumping and ready for battle, because Gideon Titan seemed like a war. Noona's stood on a grungy corner in downtown Phoenix. Vagrants roamed around the white-bricked building but I paid them no attention. Phoenix had a homelessness problem in the winter months because we had perfect weather. I found a free parking place and scanned my surroundings. *Is he trying to scare me away? Is this a trick?*

Suddenly, I wished I carried mace. I chose to jog to the entrance of the restaurant and sighed in relief when it was uneventful. *Don't be crazy. I'm fine.*

"Hi there! Good morning. Table for one?" The over-the-top hostess smiled at me with crazy eyes. My gaze flicked to the extra-large coffee on her podium. She needed *less* caffeine. But I didn't judge.

"I'm meeting someone here at nine. Is there a big guy, awful personality but nice face in here?" I scanned the room and the hostess frowned. I chuckled. My presentation wasn't the best. Clearly, he wasn't here, or she would know who I had referred to.

"I like my face, too." The same rough voice from the phone came from behind me. I instantly stood taller and took my time turning around. I felt no shame in my insult, but my body broke out in goosebumps and my heart raced.

When I faced my *co-coach*, all insults and thoughts left my body. His looks had me damn near speechless. The hazel eyes. The perfectly styled hair. The playful, mischievous lips. The chest girls dreamed of seeing in person. I couldn't look hard enough at this specimen. But then he opened his mouth.

"Take a picture. It'll last longer and you can flick your bean to it later."

And the spell broke. Like a dam breaking in a flood, my attraction went from one hundred to zero and his words slapped my face. "Excuse me?"

"Didn't stutter, did I?" He crossed his massive arms. I briefly realized his arms were about the size of my legs. "You should wipe your drool from your mouth. You have some, right there."

The asshole had the nerve to bring his finger to my chin. I smacked it before he made contact. "You're an asshole."

"Yeah. Not the worst insult in the world." He grinned with malice and clicked his tongue. "Are we done here?"

Then it hit me. *He wants me to quit. This is his plan. I'm surprised he didn't change the meeting time and call me a flake.* I pulled on the fanny pack and gave him the nastiest smile I could. "Ma'am, could we have a table for two, please?"

The bastard's smile fell, and I winked at him. *Point for me.* The hostess looked horrified — not that I blamed her — but she recovered. "S-sure. Yes. Uh, right this way."

I whistled while she chose a booth in the farthest corner of the dining room. Probably the best decision since I assumed she'd heard our entire exchange and preferred us away from the entrance. I thanked her and plopped down in the plush booth. I brought my legs up and crossed them. "I've heard they have excellent hash browns here."

He grunted in response. I refused to look at him and ignored his stare. The silence remained for a full three minutes before I glanced up. "Take a picture — you can beat your meat to it later if you want."

It was brief, but one side of his mouth quirked up before flattening into a scowl. It was a damn shame, because his lips defined perfection. When they were closed, and not making sounds. But he ruined the spell. "Touché."

"Nice place here." I made a point to spend time looking around the rundown diner. It was a local favorite and part of the charm was the grunge, but it wasn't a place I would go after dark. For any reason. But I spoke sarcasm and wasn't afraid to use it.

"I don't want to coach with you." The look on his face told me as much.

"No shit, Sherlock." I cackled. "You've made your point loud and clear."

"Quit," he commanded.

"Yeah...no. I don't answer to anyone, especially not entitled jocks." I set my hands down on the table and narrowed my eyes at him. "I have to say — well done on your part. I almost fell for it."

"What are you talking about?" His eyebrows came together, making his hazel eyes a little darker, and it would've been charming if he wasn't such a fuck-stick.

"The act." I waved my hand in the air. "The *look at me, I'm a douchebag* act. Insulting me, scaring me. Valiant attempt."

He shook his head, the loose strands of his hair moving in the process. "Wasn't an act."

"No one is that much of an asshole. You wouldn't get this far in life if you were." I went into my fanny pack and found lip balm. I applied it, his gaze not leaving my waist. "Jealous of the fanny pack?"

"No," he scoffed and curled one of his lips up. "What's your endgame?"

"In life? For the season? For graduation? Pick one." *Where is our waitress? I need more coffee to deal with this guy. Maybe I should've asked the caffeinated hostess for some of what she's having.*

"Coaching. You're a girl. Too young at that. It's baseball, a guy's sport. How did you get involved?" His tone left no room for argument. He wanted me gone, gone, gone. But my little feminist heart geared up for war. Now, there was no chance in hell I would walk away. Not after that chauvinistic taunt. I'd rather cut off my own arm than admit defeat to him.

"Wow. I'll just add those comments to your list of shitty things about you." I gripped the menu tighter. "Get this through your pretty shallow brain. I'm sticking this out. I'm not here for *you* despite your obnoxiously large opinion of yourself. I'm here for the kids."

"What's in it for you?"

"The experience. The kids. Volunteering. Do I need another reason?" Anger bubbled in my chest. This was supposed to be a *gratifying* experience. No chance that would happen. *No. Chance.*

"How did you get it?"

"Let's turn this around." *Still no waitress.* "Why is it that you, a famous athlete, are stuck coaching with some chick? *Hmm?*"

He gripped the silverware and clenched his jaw. "My coach asked me to. I do what he says. End of."

"I'm sensing more of a story here—but whatever, man." I raised my hand, hoping a goddamn waitress would venture over. *No luck.* He stewed at the growing silence. I enjoyed his pain. I really did. I rode it out, twirling the fork in my hands like I had all the time in the world. I ignored the rock in the bottom of my stomach. It weighed my attitude down, but I wasn't about to let this guy ruin my mood.

"Frankie, right?" he said some time later. I winced.

"Fiona," I replied through gritted teeth. The bastard knew my name. "My name is Fiona. You know, like the famous Cincinnati Hippo that the Reds just wished Happy Birthday to?"

"Fiona," he mocked, but his eyes widened for a brief second. "What will it take for you to leave?"

"Nothing." Ah, the waiter had finally arrived. It was a burly man with a long beard grunted at us for drinks. I ordered my precious coffee and waited until he brought it before glancing at Gideon Titan. "Now, we were discussing a truce?"

"There's no truce. You'll quit eventually." He sat there, all smug and shit, and I wanted to toss my coffee on his skin-tight white shirt. He leaned on his elbows and narrowed his eyes. Then, he spoke in a tone so low I felt it to my toes. But it wasn't desire. No, it was aggression. "I'm going to tell you how this will go. I'm going to run the parent meeting. I'm going to coach third and make the line-ups. I'm going to do everything. You don't know the sport like I do and my guess is you sincerely lack the experience. And I will find out who you slept with or blew to get this. You won't get me, if that's what you're after."

Holy shit. Every thought and comeback blurred together in my mind. I sat there, mouth agape, and couldn't form the adequate response. *Fuck you. Fuck your face. Maybe there's a reason you're here.* But I said nothing. In fact, I blinked back tears of anger when he got up and left the diner.

That left me with the bill. Sure, it was five dollars, but the entire situation enraged me. I chugged the rest of my coffee and thought of everything I wished I could say. Why couldn't I be that person? The one who said the right thing at the right time? *Ugh.*

"Asshole, asshole, fucking asshole." I hit the steering wheel three times on the way to the school where the meeting would take place. At least the fucker had told me the name of it. I thought about calling Jade, but chose not to. She'd had a hand in this and didn't deserve to hear me bitch. She'd told me about him. I'd ignored her. Admitting she was right was not an option. She would keep score on the bulletin board and I couldn't live with seeing her beat me. *Nope.*

The bastard leaned against the hood of his sleek, just-rode-off-the-lot black Mustang, aviator glasses perched on his nose, and if a guy could exude an asshole vibe, he did. In bundles. I parked my beat-up car next to his and watched him take in the appearance of my clunker. *Let him judge.* I gave zero fucks.

My door let out a long, agonizing squeak and I barely avoided hitting him. It was a cryin' shame I didn't ding his car. I bet he'd have hated that. I slammed the door, crossed my arms and glared at him with all my fury. "You are an entitled fuck. Don't assume you know *anything* about me."

"Calm down." He removed the glasses and bore his gaze into me.

"Calm down? Me? I'm having a hard time *calming down* when someone I respected, admired and rooted for turns out to be the biggest prick I've ever met. I'm disappointed, offended and sad for this team. These boys look up to you. And you're...you're a goddamn entitled jock. And you left me with the bill — they aren't just going to comp you for playing a sport. So, thanks for that, asshole." I took a breath and pointed my shaking finger at him. "I'm *going* to help. And I'm *going* to have a say." I didn't wait for a response. He didn't deserve one. I plastered on a smile and marched my ass into the school cafeteria with the goal to not break a sweat. I wanted a challenge — well, Gideon Titan would be the biggest challenge of my life.

Chapter Four

Gideon

I had to admire the sway of her hips. The feisty, not-too-bad-looking Barbie was a firecracker. Her words stung, but I rarely let people affect me. She would be gone after a week. I'd bet a lot of money on it. And I had a lot of money, despite what the tabloids liked to say about me. *Fuck those leeches.*

The meeting began like I'd imagined. Parents fawned all over me, bringing their kids up to shake my hand with stars in their eyes. I ate it up and made sure Prissy Fiona watched it all. She could try coaching, but I actually knew what I was doing. I enjoyed the extra attention and made sure to give my *co-coach* pointed looks each time. Yeah, I was being a dick, but what did she expect after her little rant?

And maybe, just maybe, I could run her out. "Mr. Titan. I can't tell you how excited we are to work with you this season."

I smiled at the MILF. Shit, she was hot as fuck. Long red hair and perky tits. "Likewise, Ms.?"

"Loretta. My son is Garth. He's ecstatic he shares your initials. GT. Thinks he deserves a Mustang because of it." She laughed and I thought of ten ways I would take off her dress. I would start with the silky strap. Shit. She'd said something else.

"What?"

"Is that *the* Fiona Davis?" Her eyes widened as she took in my fireball of a co-coach. I nodded. *How the hell does this woman know her? What the ever-loving fuck?*

"That's her name."

"Oh my. Excuse me." She left me. Just up and walked away from me. *What the fuck?*

I shook another couple of hands but my attention kept going back to Fiona and her long blonde hair. She'd braided it, a personal favorite of mine, but the damn fanny pack got to me. She looked so nerdy. It also annoyed me to no end that she didn't look back at me once. Not fucking once. Shit — maybe I had pissed her off. A miniscule part of me thought about caring, but then I didn't. Caring led nowhere.

"Can't believe the two of you got paired together. Who would've thought?" A father maybe ten years older than me stood to my right. His nametag read *Jack*. "My name is Jack. My son will learn so much from the two of you. Can't wait to see how the season goes, man."

He patted my shoulder and went to Fiona. *Seriously...who the hell is this chick? Why do the parents know about her?* Resentment at her persistence and jealousy of the way parents flocked to her combined and I snapped. "Fiona. Let's start."

Her dark blue eyes dimmed, enough for me to see, before she smiled at Jack. Fucking Jack was a traitor. But as soon as she met my eyes, she looked away. She motioned her hand for me to go, whispering *dick face* under her breath. *The nerve of this girl.* "Hey, everyone. I'm Gideon Titan. I'll be coaching your kids for this four-month season. I'm looking forward to working with them."

The MILF winked at me again and I hid my reaction when another mom gave me the up and down. Hell, even the dads present looked excited to meet me. I gave them my *smile*. The one I knew got reactions. "I plan—"

"We. We plan," Fiona interrupted me. She continued to talk, too. But I didn't hear her. No one interrupted me. No one insulted me. No one hung up the phone on me. Yet this *woman* had done all three. "We plan on teaching your children the basics of the game but also how to be a member of a team, a community and how to compete at competitive levels."

"Yeah, as I was saying—"

"I set up a Remind account and I'll write it on the board. If you could all sign up, it'll be the easiest way to get a hold of you in case of a game change, emergency, or questions. You just text this number—"

"What? We don't need a Remind anything," I interjected and a hushed silence fell over the parents. *Great. This bitch made me look like the asshole.* "Fiona. Can I speak with you in private?"

"After the meeting," she replied through clenched teeth. The vision made her a little scary. But I had seen worse. "Now, *Gideon*, please let me continue providing the contact information. Okay?"

Her smile didn't mean shit, but I nodded anyway. I swore, if she gave them my number, I would cut off her hair or something. I would get revenge.

"Sorry about that. We didn't practice beforehand." She laughed and the parents and players followed her lead and laughed along. I found it annoying. "So, the app prevents two things. First, you all can text us through it without actually having our number because one of us is famously famous."

Laughter ensued and I imagined her getting hit with a foul ball. Not enough to injure her, but enough to rattle her. *Yeah. That'll be funny when it happens.* She kept talking but I didn't listen. I studied the good-looking moms and their kids. We had some height on the team, which was good. Seemed like a couple of them had strong arms. If I was forced to coach, then I wanted to win.

Hell, if you ain't first, you're last. Thanks, Ricky Bobby.

"The second is a mass text format. I've already scheduled texts to be sent out two hours before every practice and game, and I've set it up so you can text back questions, but it only comes to me."

What is this nonsense? I rolled my eyes as she continued to explain the app. *If she wants to run it, be my goddamn guest.*

"Now, I know the season is packed, so I encourage a carpool tree. Our first practice is tomorrow, six to nine. We'll practice every day next week to prepare for our first tournament in two weeks." Fiona held up her fist and did a little jig. She looked downright ridiculous. I doubted she knew shit about baseball. "Does anyone have any questions?"

"What about uniforms?"

"How will playing time be disbursed?"

"Do you need extra help? I played for years."

"We have a vacation this week — will it affect my son's playing time?"

Fiona nodded, taking each question in stride, but the tiniest bead of sweat formed on her forehead. *Ha! Good.* I wanted to see her fall on her ass. I crossed my arms and smiled real wide. She still hadn't looked at me.

"We are pretty stacked for coaches, but if we need any I'll be sure to reach out. We might encourage parents to be fans and support the team. As far as vacations, the season is very short and any missed opportunity can prevent time on the field."

Shit. She had a good answer. But the parent was insistent.

"Coach Titan, you were telling me about all the uniforms and starting line-ups at breakfast this morning — care to share with the parents and players?" Fiona threw the attention my way.

That. Little. Sneak. I glanced at her and the smug grin was enough to have me almost snarl at her. "Of course."

I walked up to stand next to her. The parents and their kids looked up at me with awe and a bubble of pride formed in my chest. I still had their respect. And that was enough for me. "Okay. Uniforms are determined by the league. We'll be one of the national league teams. Fiona here can write down sizes for you before you leave. Playing time will be determined on strengths. This is not a rec league. It is competitive and if you want to make it big time, then you play your heart out until you earn a spot. Everything is earned."

I paused and met all the players' eyes before continuing. "Not one of you deserves a single playing spot. You hear? It all depends on grit. Who's there early, who hustles the most, who stays late and who is a good teammate. There are no egos in baseball."

Fiona snorted. "If you miss a practice, you can consider yourself out of the next game. That's fair. And the team should be a priority. The decision about who we put on the starting line-up will be made after practices. Any more questions?"

"No, sir." The smallest, skinniest boy stood and held out his hand. "I am excited to learn from you, Coach Titan."

"Thanks, kid. What's your name?"

"Allen." He beamed. The gesture reminded me so much of Quinn I had to shake the image out of my head. This kid had guts and I appreciated it.

"Nice to meet you, Allen. Can I call you Big Al?"

"Yes, sir."

I snuck a glance at Fiona. Her lips curved into a small smile and when her eyes met mine, there wasn't a war brewing. No. We shared a brief moment admiring Big Al. "Are we good here?"

No one else answered and I wanted to leave, but Fiona made a noise in the back of her throat. It resembled a snort, or a cough, but then again it could've been a growl. It was enough to have me stopping in my tracks. "Yes?"

"There are more questions. Sometimes people like to come up individually, rather than talk in front of a group. Stay another thirty minutes." Her dark blue eyes flashed at me and I didn't like it one bit. Who did she think she was, bossing me around? *Check again, sweetheart.*

"Fiona. You have—"

"Mr. Coach Titan. I have a question." A small, maybe six-year-old girl tugged at my shorts and I glared at Fiona before putting on a smile.

"Yes?"

"My name is Opal and I love you."

"Yeah? That's awful nice of you, Opal." I bent low to be eye level with her. "Does your brother play on the team?"

"Yes. I'm watching all the games. Look for me."

"Of course, sweetheart." I grinned. Now she reminded me of Quinn. And, soon enough, parents and kids came up with questions.

What kind of glove should we get?

What's the best bat?

Are batting gloves necessary or just to look cool?

Do athletes drink water or Powerade?

I answered every question and sure enough, thirty minutes went by. There was the MILF from earlier left and she was talking with Fiona. I had zero idea what those two could talk about. They came from different worlds, but the MILF reached out and pulled Fiona into a hug.

The firecracker's gaze met mine and she narrowed her eyes. And I flipped her off. My work here was done and, without saying bye, I marched out of the worn-down cafeteria to my precious car, Margo, named after a wild girl I'd known in high school. Nice to look at, easy to drive and roared like a machine when I put her in gear. Yeah, Margo was the perfect name.

It hadn't been an entirely shit day. The kids had surprised me with their respect and eagerness to get started. The thorn in my side was Prissy Fiona.

"Hey, asshole."

Ah, there she is again. I let out a long, dramatic sigh and faced her. "Yes?"

"You do admit you are one, then. Good. Admittance is often the first step to recovery." She laughed at her own joke, like an idiot. "Should we go over practice plans?"

"Nope." I crossed my arms. "I got them up here."

"Oh, in that big thing you call a head?"

I closed my eyes before replying. "You're annoying."

"I've been called worse." She mirrored my stance, but her tiny frame had nothing on mine. I outweighed her twice. "Are you going to fight me every step of the way?"

"Yup. I see no other option until you quit." *Please quit. Just say yes.*

"Ain't happening." She shook her head and pursed her red lips. She did have nice lips, but they made too much noise and lost their appeal. "Should I bring anything to practice?"

"For someone desperate to succeed at this, you aren't prepared." I slipped on my glasses and didn't wait for a reply. "Oh. Did I tell you I changed the location of the first practice?"

Her mouth fell. *Score.* She didn't have to know I was lying. "No, you didn't. I'll contact the organization and double-check because they have to reserve the fields. They can't just move the entire location based on your whim."

"Yeah. Ain't telling you shit, Hermione. If you're a goddamn know-it-all, you'll figure it out just fine." I left her there in the parking lot, fuming mad and shooting daggers at me with her scary blue eyes. I wondered why I suddenly was in a better mood.

Chapter Five

Fiona

I stormed into practice on a mission — ruin Gideon's life. *I changed the practice location.* God. I hated how I let one total bullshit comment fluster me. *He didn't have the app to text the parents.* I did. He'd lied. He'd gotten under my skin and tricked me. And I'd let him.

That was why I was at the field an hour early despite the fact I had the homework from hell to do. I had at least two hours before my class at nine the next morning. Financial modeling, AKA, the death of Fiona Davis.

I hated Excel. I would die happy if I never saw it again. *But my major is finance. I'm screwed.* The daunting decision to work for TTL hit me again, but the perfect distraction approached. It came on long, strong legs and wearing a black wind-breaker jacket that fit him like the leather glove he held. Wind-blown hair, the aviators and the scowl topped off the look.

"I see you found the field."

"I see you're still an asshole."

"Good one." He gave me a quick smile before tossing a bag down next to mine. He snorted and pointed to the book in my hands. "Did you make a practice plan? Oh god."

"Yes." I yanked the plans out of view. "I figured you didn't plan a damn thing."

"Of course I didn't. Baseball is my life. I don't need to make a plan."

"We have fifteen teenage boys. We need a plan." Anger formed in my chest. "They can't just run around for three hours."

He gave me a long stare, putting the glasses onto the top of his head. "What does your precious plan have them do?"

"Going over the team norms and expectations first, then warmup. After a warmup, I figured we could divide them into infield and outfield to get a notion of who goes where. We could create a line-up to work with from defense today." I puffed out my chest, or what people would call a chest, because I was not gifted in that department. Pride blossomed. I'd worked hard researching practice plans. But I should've known better. Gideon Titan raised one eyebrow and scoffed.

The throaty sound made me want to fight him. It was smug, condescending and rude. I stood taller and matched his stare. "What is the damn problem?"

"Nothing. We'll run it your way. *Coach*." He gave me a withering stare and sauntered off toward his car. A brief thought had me chuckling. His longest relationship had to be with that damn car.

Oh, good one. The longest one I've had was two days since Justin.

I told myself to shut the fuck up. The treats I'd splurged on were in the car and it was the perfect time to get them. The two dozen cupcakes had been pricey, but worth it. The tray wobbled in my arms when I bent to set it down on the dugout bench. "There."

"What the hell are those?" His gruff voice came from the other end. I'd somehow missed him.

"I brought the team cupcakes. What is the damn problem?" I got into my battle stance—hands on my hips, sneer on my face and boobs puffed out. Gideon's frown deepened into a scowl and the urge to kick him in the shins crossed my mind. "They are kids, Gideon. Children. Youths. Teenagers. Sugar is their bread and butter."

His jaw tightened and he took two large steps toward me. Without a word, he tossed the entire tray into the trash. He met my eyes. "Sugar is unhealthy."

My eyes stung. I'd spent a lot of money on those, and I budgeted precisely each month. And he'd just tossed them without asking. *Asshole. Fucking asshole. I hate him.*

I rubbed my temples—it was the first practice and I was already plotting ways to murder the guy. Michelle had said she knew a guy and I wasn't beyond hitting him up. Gideon sucked that much. The bastard in question stared at me with a comment ready to fire at me, but I held up my hand. "No. Just...no."

"What's the big fucking deal? Coaches shouldn't promote sugar." He scoffed and waved to the parents dropping off the first player. "It's not too late to run. Scoot along now, Barbie."

No. I will not run. I will not let this chauvinistic guy win. My dad ran, Justin died... I will not run from my problems. I was a badass. I could do it. "Fuck yourself. Then, do it again."

I plastered on a huge smile and shouldered his side when I walked out onto the field. Big Al was the first to arrive. I wasn't surprised at all. "Hey, Big Al!"

"Coach Fiona!" He held up a small hand for a high-five and I wanted to squeeze the punk. He was that cute—his small frame had me thinking of him as ten, not fifteen. "I'm early. Mom says the early bird gets the worms."

"Your mom is a smart lady. Early is good." It was all I could do to not give him a noogie. He was so stinkin' adorable.

"Is anyone else here?"

"No, sir. Just you." I smiled at him and heard shuffled steps behind me. *Fucking Gideon.* "And Coach Titan."

"They can call me GT."

"Like your car?" I snapped back, but said it with a smile. Big Al didn't sense the tension.

"Yeah. Just like my car. Hey. Garth is here now. He goes by GT, too. Kid has great taste."

Gideon waved at the kid, but I think we all knew it was Garth's mom. The woman had been a little too nice to me at the meeting. She had gone on and on about the Texting PSAs I had done and how awesome it had been for her kid's school. I felt mollified, but it was a little overkill wearing a tight dress to a baseball practice in sixty degrees. Anything below eighty was cold in good ole Arizona, but hey, I wasn't one to judge. Whatever tooted her horn.

"I wouldn't mind showing her how to hit a homerun. You get what I mean?" Gideon had the gall to say to me as he nudged my shoulder. I recoiled at the contact. His hand probably had an STD.

"I think everyone in the county knows what you mean. I hope you wear batting gloves, if you know what I mean," I fired back. *Boom.*

"Don't be jealous, Barbie. It doesn't look good on you." He ran his tongue over his bottom lip and I wanted to rip it off. He was infuriating.

"Trust me. Jealousy is nowhere near what I'm feeling. Murderous, aggressive, physical are more like it."

"I bet you're aggressive." He lowered his voice and I swore the asshole enjoyed being a dick to me. He got off on it. And I made the decision not to react. He had to have a real shit life for him to be this miserable.

"I'd love to see your claws come out, especially in the bedroom." He wiggled his eyebrows at me in all his cocky, obnoxious glory.

Don't react. Deep breath. Jail colors won't suit me.

I released a long breath and decided to join the kids. They were the whole point. Almost all of them had arrived in that short timeframe—Gideon's speech about being early had worked. Soon after, the first practice had begun and my heart swelled with pride.

Justin would be proud. The thought had me stumbling It came from nowhere and I wasn't prepared. My breath hitched, my palms sweating. "I need a drink. I'll, uh, be right back."

"Doesn't matter to me. Come back, don't. Life goes on."

The unfriendly, unhappy man helped with the distraction, but thinking of Justin hurt. These kids, they were fourteen and fifteen. They all had their phones and weren't old enough to drive yet. There was still time to teach them the dangers. That way, they didn't have to leave the earth at eighteen, with one last message sent before crashing into the median. My eyes stung—*fuck. Fuck! Not today.*

I didn't want to show emotion, let alone to Gideon Titan. I found my water and chugged about half of it. *Calm down. Suck it up. Move on.*

Yeah—I had some major issues with *feelings.* As in, I had about two and all the others I shut down. I preferred being happy or not happy. There was no in between and yet, little bits of emotions snuck through and when they did, they hit me hard. Thinking of that final text was enough to send me into a spiral. "Coach Fiona? Are you okay?"

Al stopped at the edge of the dugout with a concerned look on his face. "You look like you just seen a ghost."

"Nah, I'm good. Thanks for asking. How's practice going so far?"

"Pretty good." He grinned and the brief attack of sadness evaporated just like that. *Thank you, Al.*

"Yeah? Let's see what you got, man," I challenged him and soon after, I had fifteen teenagers ready for drills. We did countless grounders and pop-flys then relay drills. I knew within minutes who should be in the outfield by their running speed and arm strength, but infield was trickier. Agility was important but knowing the game mattered more. Baseball was more mental than skill. And no one could convince me differently.

Three hours later, I hadn't smiled so much since Jade and her sister took me out country line dancing. Laughter echoed off the field and I had given more high-fives in those three hours than in my entire life. "Today rocked, guys. Do you have any questions before tomorrow?"

"Why do you know so much about baseball if you're a girl?" Felix asked, but he had such a friendly face I didn't think it was sarcastic at all. I grinned at him.

"An excellent question, Felix. This might shock you guys, but I was a tomboy in school. I preferred baseball over softball. I played it for eight years and wanted to give coaching a try. So, be nice to me, okay?"

"Of course, CFD."

"CFD?"

"Coach Fiona Davis. I like CFD better. Plus, you gotta have a nickname."

"I dig it." I adjusted my hat and stuck my hand out in the middle. "Big Al. You arrived first. You pick the cheer today."

"Me?"

"Yes! Now, let's hear it."

"All right. Uh, get tough on three. One, two, three, *get tough*!"

I waved and grinned as they all left. *Holy shit.* I hadn't had that much fun in months. How sad. But my joy was short-lived. My co-coach decided to make an appearance and ruin my little bubble of happy. He didn't even have to talk for my mood to sour. I held up my hand. "Don't even bother. Don't ruin this for me."

"Just going to ask about a line-up." He plopped down on the bench and crossed his ankles in that *bro* sort of way. It reminded me of a former hookup who liked himself more than humanity. *Huh.* The comparison wasn't far off.

"We have three kids who can pitch."

"Yeah. I know. Who's your pick for first?"

"First? I didn't think about it. I think Garth would be the perfect shortstop. He has the personality to lead and has the arm."

"Garth should catch. Now, who would you pick for first?" He crossed his massive arms and my gaze didn't divert to them once. Not once.

"We need a kid who can catch. Bottom line. Garth can, yeah. But I think he should be in the field. He's quick."

"We need a leader behind the plate or we'll lose by passed balls. I think Timothy should be at first."

"Timothy?" I paused. "I saw him more outfield."

"You're wrong. He's tall, can catch and he's smart. He adjusted his position every time we did a drill. We need smart ones at first."

Shit. Good point. Really good point. But I wouldn't admit that to him in a million years. "I think Jason should catch. He did last year on the summer team and has a strong arm."

"Agree to disagree, but I am the professional. Let's not forget that, shall we?"

I stomped my foot. I wasn't proud of it—but I did it anyway. His response was just a lazy smile. My hand twitched.

"So, are we going to talk about your freak-out in the beginning? I thought for a second you were being a girl and couldn't handle the pressure."

Rage burst through me. How dare he? He didn't know shit. I made sure no one was around before exploding. "You don't *fucking* know me. You don't know *anything.* You are just a sad, unhappy, miserable guy that I want nothing to do with. I'm staying because these kids mean something to me. You wouldn't understand and I don't expect you to. Fuck. You."

Chapter Six

Gideon

Well, shit. Barbie made me feel bad. Not bad enough to apologize or not find ways to get her to quit, but an inkling of remorse hit me. I considered that a major breakthrough. Cheryl would be ecstatic. Barbie stormed out of there like a cat out of hell with her wild hair and pink cheeks.

If she wasn't such a hothead, determined to piss me off, prissy and annoying, I'd think she was cute. No, more than cute. But when there were MILFs out there, my thoughts shouldn't be with my co-coach. *Nope.*

I drove home without any hope for the rest of my evening. Cheryl and Quinn were already in for the night and I could've crashed there, but I was in a shit mood. My leg was killing me. I didn't want to show weakness to the kids, or to Fiona, but even the small number of grounders had hurt.

I sent a quick email to my physical therapist for an appointment the next morning—and replied to my agent. Did I want to do another endorsement for some watch? No. But did it pay? Yes.

And my nightly routine began. I answered emails from people who really didn't like me. I was a product that made them money. It didn't bother me on most days, but today it felt cheap. What did I have in my life besides baseball?

Cheryl and Quinn.

But that was it. I'd had a handful of friends throughout the years but no one that had stuck. I had no pets. No relationships that had lasted longer than a night together. And it pissed me off. I needed to get back into shape. I craved to get healthy, and I said fuck it. I went into my personal gym and did the reps the therapist suggested. The hardest part was getting my knee to straighten—I had to try to get it entirely straight and compare it to my other leg. I groaned in pain and frustration when I set up two even chairs and got my leg stretched out. I had to put weights over my knee for a half an hour, the gravity of them pushing down to straighten it. Pain shot up my entire body and a brief wave of nausea hit me. But I powered through minute by minute. I survived and went to stage two—icing.

And by the time I was done, I passed out from exhaustion.

I had no dreams of gabby blondes.

But by the next afternoon, the annoying nuisance named Fiona had me anxious to head to practice. Was it interest? *No.* Was it for the pure entertainment of bantering with someone? *Maybe.* Either way, I had a semi-smile on my face when I pulled into the parking lot. Fiona's piece-of-shit car was already there and I wondered how long she'd driven it. It had to be at least fifteen years old. Maybe more.

I got out of the car with a hiss. God, my leg didn't feel better even after stretching and icing it yet again after physical therapy that morning. We did TENS therapy — transcutaneous electrical nerve stimulation — which could've been a synonym for hell. I not only felt jumpy and unstable, I chose not to wear the brace because I didn't want Fiona to see any weakness. God, I was messed up.

Today had to be a situation day for practice. I couldn't hit or throw — but I refused to tell Fiona that. She would gloat and I couldn't deal with her if she had any upper hand. Despite being injured, I preferred winning in all areas of my life.

Her last words to me had been *fuck you* and while I didn't expect a nice greeting, I also didn't expect her to completely ignore me. I couldn't think of the last time someone had ignored me. *Years?*

"Fiona?"

Nothing. She stared at something in her notebook and I wanted to rip it out of her hands. And I did just that. I snatched it — unleashing the beast.

"Asshole! Give that back!" Her eyes fumed at me.

"No. I want to see what had you so focused you couldn't even reply to my greeting."

"Give it back. Now," she seethed. And I swore her eyes glistened. I snuck a glance at the page and saw lines of writing. I held it high over her head and she jumped to get it, but I stood a foot taller. I smiled.

"Why did you ignore me? Not very friendly or cooperative coming from the person spouting the importance of teamwork."

"I was wearing headphones, you douche nozzle." She picked up the white wire and made a face at me. "Give me back my stuff."

"Are you writing about me? Dirty thoughts, I hope."

"No." She reached up for it again and started blinking too fast. She sniffed and I swore I saw an entire shift in her expression. "Please? I... That... Don't read it."

And I felt like a tool. What was I doing? She looked desperate but I was at a loss. Feisty Fiona, the obnoxious ballbuster, looked like she was going to cry. *Oh fuck. Tears.*

"Fine. You win. Okay? Please. Just, give that back. I'll quit." She collapsed into a defeated heap on the bench and I deflated. I handed her the book and took two steps back.

She'll quit? What the hell was in that book to provoke that reaction? An irrational thought took over—the sight of tears shocked me. I wanted to prevent her from crying ever again, and the numbing realization that I'd caused it hurt me.

"Thank you." She clutched it to her chest and her entire face turned pink. "I'll head out."

"You aren't quitting." *What did I just say? What am I doing? This is what I want, right?* But I kept talking. "Stay."

Her lips parted. Her eyes widened and she didn't say a word for a brutal thirty seconds. "I don't... What?"

"I don't know what was in that book, but I shouldn't have done that. I was pissed you didn't acknowledge my greeting. Pissed you were assigned to coach with me. Pissed at the world for a lot of things, but taking your item was childish and unnecessary."

Her bottom lip trembled and her arms tightened around the weathered book.

And, once again, I felt smaller than dirt. My stomach hurt, and it was a new feeling. *Regret.* It sucked. I had no way to save myself in the situation. *None.* "It won't happen again."

"You being an asshole? Yeah, it will." She picked up her things and shoved them into a dark green backpack. "I should quit. I really should. There's tons of other things to do."

"I won't be as much of an asshole." *There.* That was truce. I held out my hand, a huge gesture on my part, but she stared at it. She made no move to meet my hand and worry bubbled up. "I was out of line."

"I'll say." She sucked in her cheek and finally met my hand. "I don't respect you or like you. At all. And if I could quit and live with myself, I would. But I don't want to let the kids down."

"You'll stay?" Something resembling hope went through me, but that would have been stupid. Why did I care?

"Yes." She released my hand and pulled out her forsaken folder. She wore her fanny pack, this time with black and purple leggings that gave a great view from behind. Fiona had a fine ass. "I made a practice plan again."

Thank god. "Naturally."

She narrowed her eyes before shoving it at me. "*You* can run practice today, then. I'll watch and be as unhelpful as possible."

No. Shit. No. "Wait. We can do your plan today. You already made it."

"I don't need you to mock me. You know my weakness." She paused and her gaze went to whatever was in the backpack. "So, we'll do it your way."

54

"Fiona," I raised my voice. "I'm not mocking you. You ran practice decently yesterday."

"Decently? Wow. That must've hurt coming off your mouth." She laughed and took the clipboard out of my hands. "Fine. I'll run it even though I know you're laughing behind your glasses. Assholes like you don't scare me."

No, but whatever is in that journal does. I didn't say it, though. I buried my asshole comments and attempted to not piss her off. It was easier to busy myself with prepping the field. That way, I didn't have to watch my tongue and comment on her asinine ideas. She wanted to do a team bonding? We were together almost every day for four months. We had no time for bonding. *Psh.*

Women—well, besides Cheryl and Quinn—were nuts.

I raked the mound and home plate while Fiona talked to herself in the dugout. Despite her toned body, she was an odd duck. Was she singing to herself, too? *Jesus.* Garth arrived first, running toward Fiona with a grin. "Hey, CFD! I get to say the cheer today, right?"

"You betcha, kid. Got any ideas?"

"No. Do you?" He plopped on the bench next to her.

"Boys drool, girls rule?"

"Ha. Nice try. Boys are from Mars, girls are from Jupiter."

"Hey, hey now. Girls are *not* stupider. That is not the way to get ladies," she scolded him in a way that wasn't insulting. No. The kid grinned and nodded. *Great.* I'd thought GT and I would be buds. Now he preferred Fiona. Kid didn't know shit.

"Hey, GT. How do you get ladies?"

I about choked on my own spit. This fourteen-year-old kid should not have been worried about ladies but, then again, I remembered what I had been doing at that age — maybe the kid wasn't half-bad. "Well, Garth, compliments help."

"Like telling them they smell nice?"

I laughed. "That's a start, yeah."

"Are you going to listen to this clown, or take it from a woman?" Fiona butted in. I glared at her. What would she know about what women want? She was crazy. She waited for the kid to respond and I prayed he gave her shit. But he didn't.

"Yeah! Help me, CFD. I have this girl in my class and, well, she doesn't know I exist." He closed his eyes, rivaling a middle-aged man going through a crisis. Damn. I liked the kid, even if he preferred her company over mine.

I paid them no attention when more kids arrived. Half the kids thought Fiona walked on water, where the other half were too shy to talk to her. Damn kids had a crush or something. I didn't see it — she wore a bulky sweatshirt and an old baseball cap that had seen better days. But I preferred a different type of woman. Like the MILF.

"Gideon. Did you hear that?"

Shit. Fiona had asked me something. "Hear what?"

"When can the kids see you throw?"

"Soon. Not today," I said with clenched teeth. The mention of throwing had my body tighten in anticipation of pain. People didn't realize that throwing used all parts of the body when done correctly. I could lob the ball without putting pressure on my leg, but it wouldn't impress the kids. "You ready to get started, Coach?"

Her eyes warmed at the term I used. Without the fire in them, they quite were unique. They were blue but had different shades of brown in them. *Why the fuck am I analyzing her damn eyes?* "Let's go, kids. Three laps around the field. Brad—you lead the stretches."

"Yes, sir!"

And they took off. Fiona joined me on the field with her clipboard and moved close, too close. Her floral scent surrounded me. "I did a mock line-up this morning, rather than do my homework. Not that you care. But, what do you think?"

I took the paper from her hands. Her perfume clouded my thoughts. The mere thought of her smelling good also annoyed me. *Focus.* I scanned the position chart and made a clicking noise with my tongue. "Almost."

"What? What's not right?" She moved close to me again. *Does the woman have no sense of personal space?* "I moved Thomas to first, like you said, but I refused to move Garth to catcher. Tayler should be there. He has the best reflexes."

"Tayler should be at third—Garth catches and Max will be at short." I handed the paper back to her. My muscles did an odd clenching thing when she neared me again. She huffed. "What?"

"I disagree with Max. He should be in center. He has the best arm."

"These kids are fourteen and fifteen. They aren't in the majors, honey. Trust me." I scolded myself for saying *honey* but it got the job done. She sneered at me and left me alone. Her and her little fanny pack joined the team stretching and her laugh echoed across the field. I needed a drink.

"Grounders, next. Lots of grounders. We need you to get lots of reps with the right fundamentals. Gideon, can you hit grounders and I'll watch them?"

"You hit. I'll coach them. I *do* play shortstop for Los Soles." The boys all cheered and a flash of embarrassment crossed her face. I would've felt bad if it weren't for my leg killing me. But this got me out of hitting. "I'll grab a bucket—hold on."

The idea was brilliant. I got to show off and not have to hurt myself. An empty white bucket sat at second base and I modeled how to cleanly scoop up a ball. "Leather to the belly. One motion. Don't get fancy. A lot of professionals do, but errors happen that way."

"Yeah. My dad said you got a golden glove because your stats are great," Big Al said with awe. It mollified the crap out of me. Fiona scoffed and tapped her nails against the metal bat. *Metal bat? Why is she using a metal bat?*

"Sure did, kid. Thanks. Now, let's take some grounders. Stay low and focused. Let's go, CFD. Hit 'em hard."

She smirked at me and the fire came back into her eyes. *Shit.* She tossed the ball into the air and used her entire body to hit a hell of a grounder at me. But I lived for this shit. I scooped it up cleanly and placed it in the bucket. Pain shot down my leg but adrenaline won. "That the best you got, girl?"

And hell ensued. She hit me ten, maybe twenty of the hardest grounders I had taken in a while. Whatever the hell was in that bat, I was damn glad the guys didn't use it. My hand stung. "All right. Show's over. Your turn, boys."

She continued hitting, but not nearly as hard. I chose to stay with the kids and critique their fundamentals — backs straight, legs low, loose on their feet. Most of them weren't bad. They impressed me, and I told them so. "Water break."

The minions charged into the dugout and I snuck at glance at Fiona. She stretched her arms over her head, bending low to the ground. My stomach tingled. *Tingled?* What the hell?

"Coach Titan. I have a question." Big Al pressed his face into the fence. "Are you and CFD together, together?"

"Ha, no. No way, kid." *Together? Ha. Ha. Ha.*

"Oh. Well. Okay." He frowned and went back to his water bottle. So much disappointment came from that little body I had to shake my head to get rid of the weird emotion.

"Are we having a sleepover at your house this weekend, Coach?" Garth asked and his place as the natural leader on the team didn't surprise me. He should be the catcher. I was more certain than before. "CFD said something about it during warmups. My mom told me lots of the other parents are willing to chaperone. I wish they wouldn't, because my mom is annoying."

"Did she now?" I searched for her, but she remained out of sight. Smart girl. "I don't know. Do we have a game this weekend?" *Nosy parents in my house? Will the hot one be there?*

"No. Just practice. I figured Saturday night. Bonding and stuff." He smiled and I found myself nodding. Sleepovers were a fond memory from when I'd played travel ball. I'd been thrown into camp after camp at their age, but the nostalgia hit me harder than I would've guessed. "Hell, yeah! Sorry. Heck, yeah!"

I laughed. The team cheered and I went to find the little sneak. She stood behind the dugout, pretending to search for something. "Fiona."

"Oh, hey." She blushed. "What do you want?"

"Make sure you pack a bag when you stay the night with me." I bent to the ground so we were face-to-face. I enjoyed flustering her. The pulse at her neck raced and I didn't have to fake my smile. "I always knew we would spend the night together."

"Wh-what are you talking about?"

"The team sleepover you planned. You're spending the night, too. Make sure to pack something silky. I sure as hell ain't being left alone with all the moms who sacrificed their night to *volunteer*."

She mumbled a response, but all I heard was *asshole*. And suddenly, Saturday didn't seem like a bad idea.

Chapter Seven

Fiona

To take the job, or not to take the job. That is the question. It is the thing that keeps me up at night. Well, thoughts of torturing Gideon Titan were there, too. I pressed my palms to my eyes and rubbed them. Maybe that would relieve some stress. No such luck. Now I had raccoon eyes and a headache.

"You look like you need some good whiskey, or some good dick." Michelle walked out of her small room and joined me at our quirky kitchen table. I'd found it at a garage sale and it was the perfect fit for us. Each chair was a different vibrant color. We had almost every color of the rainbow except for yellow. It was on my list, though.

"Don't brag because you've been with Mr. Magic Penis the past week." I eyed her and ended up smiling. She didn't even deny it. She had a small smile toying at her lips, her sex-hair going in all sorts of directions. *Lucky her.*

"Mr. Magic Penis. God. I love it."

"Is he going to visit our humble abode anytime? Or will he remain mysterious a little longer?"

"Definitely mysterious a little bit more. I'm not sure if I like him or just his magic stick. It's hard to say."

"I bet it's real *hard.*"

She burst out laughing. "Thank you for putting it into perspective. You're such a hoot."

"I'll add that to my Tinder. *I am a hoot.* I'll get all sorts of invitations." I had no qualms about my dating life — I had no time. But self-deprecating humor was good for the soul. If I couldn't laugh at myself, then I would be miserable. *Like Mom. Like Amanda. Like Bea.* Yeah — my mom and sisters were one bad story away from being a Lifetime movie. They preferred dating awful men and loved talking about their misery. I shook off the thought and met Michelle's gaze. "Anyway, I'm going to be spending the weekend with sixteen immature boys."

"And Gideon Titan." She grinned so hard it made her look creepy. "Think about him."

"He was included in that. And, best part. We're doing a team sleepover at his house. And I have to go." I shook my head and took a long sip of coffee. "I meant it as a ploy to piss him off. Invite the boys to his house and I would get out of it. But he conned me right into it."

"Holy shit. You're going to be in Gideon Titan's house."

"Yeah, a week or two ago I might've lost my shit. Now, the magic is gone."

"Hey, he could have a magic dick. Don't assume." She pursed her lips at me and I snorted. She technically was right. He could.

"He is a dick. His penis is irrelevant." Even if he was sex on a stick.

"Fair enough." She eyed the papers on the table. "What you working on?"

"Ah, well." I flushed. We didn't talk about the personal shit often, but I trusted her. I liked her. I could do it. "I'm making a pros and cons list of accepting a job offer for TTL."

"Yeah? What position?" She leaned forward and paused. "Mind if I look?"

"Go ahead. I could use some advice outside my sisters and mother." I bit the nail on my thumb. She didn't make a sound or any facial expression. *I am an idiot.*

"Interesting." She plopped back down in the chair and grabbed my pen. "What do you want out of your career?"

"Uh, stability." *That's what Mom beat into my head.* "Wait — no. I want to love what I do. I want a passion."

"What do you like to do? Finance? Money? Coaching?"

"I like math. The whole numbers of things. I like how it fits." *Unlike our life growing up.* "But I've had more fun working with these kids this week than I have in years of schooling for my major."

"Would accepting the job with Texting Too Late provide you with the coaching aspect? From what I know about the organization, you'll get to work with kids to help spread awareness about texting and driving, right? I picked up pieces here and there from you talking about it and the news but I never felt comfortable asking you about it. It sounds pretty amazing. I, uh, watched some of the videos of your speeches."

"Yeah. I spoke at some schools last year." I bit the hell out of my cuticle now. I tasted blood. "But it's with family. It's given to me. Does that make sense? I want to make it on my own."

"Hm. I get it. But, girl, you are making it on your own." She eyed our apartment, with its shitty decorations we'd found at flea markets. My mom gave me no money and I was proud as hell about it. "When do you have to let them know?"

"After the holidays." *Six weeks. Six weeks to decide my future.* "I like to write things down. I know, I'm a weenie."

"Nothing wrong with a pros and cons list. How do you think I agreed to the rendezvous with Mr. Magic Penis?"

"You made a list?" I about threw my pen at her. "That's hilarious. What were the cons?"

"Who he is. That was it. So, I said fuck it." She gave me a devilish grin and I envied her. She had to be getting it real good to smile like that. "Anyway, I have to head to work. I'll be there all night. I'm covering for one of the girls. I'll bring you breakfast in the morning."

"This friendship is really working out."

"Yeah. Yeah it is."

"I want to know who this mystery man is, by the way. But I won't push it...yet."

She left me with my thoughts and an hour until I had to leave for practice. I randomly searched online, reading articles about local charity events. One picture caught my eye. Gideon Titan. The guy wore a suit and hot damn. The suit looked thankful to be on his body —

that was how good he looked in it. I wiped my forehead. "Okay. Gid. Why are you dressed to the nines?"

Scrolling through more pictures, I gasped when I came across one from a charity for the baseball organization—Feeding Starving Children. Damn it. I didn't want to have anything but disdain for the guy, but that little fact warmed my cold black heart. He was featured at the event for donating a million dollars. *Fuck me.*

One million dollars. *Jesus.* I spilled coffee on my shirt and didn't even realize it. That was more money that I could imagine donating. Fifty bucks to a local girl scout troop was about all I was good for. Shame crept up my chest. He was a major-league player. I knew they got paid crazy amounts of money, but damn. My apartment felt cheap. My clothes, my practice plans, my car. I was a pathetic little dot in his world.

The thought angered me more. And with a new fire, I went to practice fifteen minutes before it started with my laminated practice plan. Thankfully, he hadn't arrived and I calmed my nerves. Was I nervous? *Shit.* I owed the guy nothing.

He stole your journal—he almost read what you write to Justin.

Yeah. He was still an asshole. Just a rich one.

"Ah, Barbie arrived early. Just my luck." The bastard walked into the dugout and appeared at home. I guess he was. "Why the sour face, kid?"

"Kid?" My pulse raced.

"You're, what…twenty?"

"I'm going to be twenty-two in a couple months." I seethed. *Kid.* I detested that word being used on me.

And honey. And doll. Just use my goddamn name. "Grandpa."

"Excuse me. What did you just mumble over there?"

"I'm glad your hearing hasn't gone out. Yet," I baited him. It might not have been fair, but when had he been? "I said *Grandpa*. Because you're old."

He didn't reply. He just stared at me with those intense dark eyes. I squirmed on the bench because the full heat of his gaze, well, it was worrying. He always had a comeback. A retort. And an insult. But silence? *Did I unleash a monster?*

"I guess I deserved that."

Wait – what? Did he... Did he just admit he was wrong? My mouth dropped open and he pointed to it.

"Close that sucker up. You look ridiculous."

And he left me to get the field ready. I felt slapped in the face. He didn't try to offend me? Hurt me? Make me cry? I brought my hand to my forehead. Was I sick?

He turned back around and shouted at me, getting my attention. "Stop being dramatic. Help me rake the field. I want to scrimmage today."

Scrimmage? Hell yes. I bounced toward the field and went for the other rake, but he shook his head. "I want to teach you how to chalk a field."

"The white powder stuff. Yeah." I had no idea where it was, or the machine that set it down. But Gideon laughed. Oh, the sound was painfully beautiful. "What's funny?"

"White powder stuff is cocaine. Chalk is behind the visitors' dugout. Get it loaded."

I nodded, ignoring his comment entirely, and found the bag. I used my keys to rip it open and heaved the bag to dump the contents into the silver wheelbarrow.

Only, I didn't have a good grip and an explosion of sorts happened. "SHIT!"

"You good over there, Barbie?"

"Fine. Just fine." I couldn't see anything outside the puff of white cloud. It covered my entire outfit. I looked like a powered donut. My black dry-fit shirt now appeared gray and I did my best to wipe off the chalk, but it didn't budge. Fine. I'd succumb to looking like an idiot. I put what I could into the wheelbarrow and took off toward the foul line. I knew how to set that up. I needed to place the measuring wire to set the straight line.

"Holy shit." He dragged out the words, making them each four syllables long. "Holy shit."

"Take a picture. It'll last longer," I replied, bringing back our first meeting. I kept my head held high—if I were to make a fool of myself, no one could say I did it without flair.

Flair was my middle name.

"Fiona. I can't... I can't breathe." The bastard leaned over and made awful, wheezing sounds that rivaled a hyena. I went about setting the line and paid no attention when he got on the ground and slammed his fist, his laughter growing louder by the second.

I couldn't really blame him, though—I was a hot mess.

"Coach Fiona, why are you all white?"

"Well, Big Al, I dropped the chalk."

"You look ridiculous. Can I pick some up, too?"

"Yes." An idea struck. It was brilliant. Genius, even. "Go ahead and take a handful and take it over to Coach Titan. He just asked me for some."

"Okay!" I felt a miniscule amount of shame for using the young kid to punk Gideon, but it was worth it when the kid threw an entire handful onto his pullover. He swung his head over toward me and I shrugged.

"*You're dead,*" he mouthed and a thrill went through me. *Wait, what? A thrill? Why? Why am I excited?*

I avoided him for a good half an hour. It wasn't until all the kids showed up, Big Al beating Garth for the cheer, and they were started on their warmup when I faced the barbarian. "King Titan."

"Ah, I do love that nickname." He smoldered. Like a damn cartoon character. Those eyes *smoldered* at me and I put up all my blockers. *No, sir. He is not going to get in my head or my pants.* "You're going to regret your little act earlier."

"I doubt it." I pointed to home plate. "Can you show me how to line home?"

"Can I trust you around chalk?" He leaned against the wooden post and looked like a model. His hair reflected the sun perfectly, and a small part of me wished I didn't hate him. "Hello? Are you having a blonde moment?"

There. He's back. Phew. "Don't be an asshole."

"Takes one to know one."

"Wow — that was a snarky teenager reply if I ever heard one." I chuckled and was tempted to hit him in the shoulder. But that would have been friendly. "But yes. You can trust me. I won't throw chalk at you, your *highness.*"

He didn't react besides a slight flair of his nostrils. "Let's keep it at four inches. Easier for them to see. Did you set the chalker at it?"

"This thing has a name?" I eyed the chalker. "I didn't set it at anything."

"Here." He bent down, low enough for me to take a long glance at his ass. Damn, it was toned. "This switch down here moves to four or two inches. You're lucky it was already set at four. Now, you need to make a rectangle on either side of the plate. Size doesn't matter at this point for practice."

"I thought we had a liner or a stencil to do that?"

"A stencil? Jesus. No. You make two rectangles for each side. That's it. And technically, you do this first and line the corners up to the foul lines. But hey…we can't all know everything."

The smug bastard winked at me and took the chalker right out of my hands. I could either watch him with chagrin or check on the kids. I preferred the kids. They were easier. But Gideon couldn't let me have control.

"Okay, guys, get into two lines. I'm going to hit fly balls in the middle. You have to communicate and catch the ball. If you both miss it, you do a lap. If one of you misses it, you do a lap. Got it?" They took off from his directions and he pointed to the chalker. "I'll get it later."

Gideon snatched a bat from the fence and hollered for them to hustle. The drill seemed rough. *Running if you miss it? Shit.* "Are you sure this is the best drill?"

"Most errors in the outfield are because of communication. They need to learn how to call the ball. Trust me. After they're gassed from running, they'll learn."

I didn't believe him, but it didn't matter. Ten minutes into the drill, two kids asked to sit out a round and two others had their hands on their knees. But I chose to not say anything, although that was hard.

"You need a drink break?"

"Yes, Coach. Please." Garth panted.

"Three minutes then hustle back out here." Gideon set the bat against the fence and met my gaze. "Any comments, Fiona?"

"Nope. Not one."

He nodded and began to stretch his leg. He winced — then tried to play it off. But I'd witnessed it. *He is injured.* My guilty conscience smiled for his pain, but it was brief. The bastard didn't like showing weakness. I couldn't fault him for that. "Your highness, can I hit the next round?"

"Why?" His dark gaze narrowed suspiciously at me. "Thought you disliked this drill."

"I do. But it's working. They're all talking and cheering each other on."

"Fine. Hit, then."

But I didn't miss the relief on his face. His smile relaxed and he favored his left leg as he walked toward the bench. *The bastard is in pain.* I took the bat and went up to pat his shoulder. I had never been called sweet in my life, and this was no different. "Your old joints hurting you? Don't worry. This *kid* can swing for you."

He growled and stormed off. My mood brightened and I couldn't keep the smile off my face.

Chapter Eight

Gideon

Cheryl: How was the first week of practice? Quinn wants you to come over.

Gideon: Why isn't that monkey in bed? I eyed my watch. It was late for her, even for a Friday night.

Cheryl: Fucking Sour Patch Kids.

Gideon: Uh, is that code for something?

Cheryl: Candy. She had too much candy. Stop by if you want.

Seeing my favorite ladies sounded better than going back to my empty fortress. I never should've listened to that realtor, but he'd been convincing. It could be a place for great parties and lots of kids. Maybe Quinn could host them here since I'd lost some friends and kids were out of the question. *Because feelings suck ass and happiness is a myth.*

God, I had issues.

I made the short drive to their cozy two-bedroom house in the east valley. My thoughts drifted from Fiona and her insistence about Garth still playing short. Damn woman wasn't a baseball player. But she wasn't wrong. No. The first week of practice had gone better than I could've imagined. The only issues were that my leg killing me and Fiona was driving me up a fucking wall by entering my thoughts way too damn much.

The kids respected her. I hadn't expected that. It definitely made getting her to quit out of the question. *Damn it.* I pinched the bridge of my nose. Maybe I was stuck with her. The thought didn't repulse me as much as the first day I'd found out about her. Actually, thinking about her scrunched-up face after the chalk incident had me laughing on the drive to my sister's house.

"You look…not happy, but not mad. This is weird." Cheryl answered the door with a typically sarcastic comment. "Are you okay?"

"Don't be a bitch. Where's my little human?"

"I'm here, Uncle Gid!" The excited voice carried from the kitchen and I ignored Cheryl to pick her up. She squealed and I held on to her like a sack of potatoes as I walked into their small and cozy home. Her laughter was like an ax to my heart. It didn't make sense, but I would go to the ends of the earth for this kid.

The same went for my sister, but I expressed that in different ways. I glanced at her and caught a soft smile. Sometimes, she did this thing where she wiped her eyes when she watched me and Quinn together. I used to make fun of her for it, but after the hell this family had gone through, I got it.

'Work on finding the little joys,' the therapist had said. Well, fuck that big-glasses-wearing guy.

"How was your day, Quinn?" I tickled her. Then tickled her some more.

"The best. We watched little ponies and I painted at school and Mommy let me not eat the broccoli."

"Wait. Your mother didn't make you eat all your vegetables?" I held her upside down. "Cheryl. What did I say about the veggies?"

"You were raving like some lunatic so I tuned you out. Sue me."

I hoisted Quinn up higher until our eyes met. "Quinn. You promised me you'd eat them. They make you healthy and I need you to be healthy."

"I'm healthy!"

"Promise me." I narrowed my eyes at her, but she just laughed. I fought a smile and, in the end, let her win. *Damn it. This girl.*

"Ah, the manipulative little queen got ya." Cheryl patted my shoulder. "She's sneaky. I have no idea where she gets it from."

"Obviously, her favorite uncle." I scoffed and moved Quinn to sit on my lap. Her eyes were already showing signs of sleep. It wouldn't be long before she conked out. "Today oddly rocked, Cher. My co-coach annoys me to no end, but the kids had fun. And she ran the practice well."

"She?" Cheryl's eyebrows disappeared into her hairline. Her face was so expressive she had wrinkles on her forehead at a young age.

"Yeah. She. They paired me with this young blonde thing. Drives me fucking nuts."

"Gid!"

"Sorry. She's practically asleep." I checked on her, and, sure enough, the hellion was passed out in my arms. "See?"

"God. I could try that for hours and nothing. But you come in. Ugh. It takes a lot to not hit you." She rolled her eyes and handed me a beer. Her face paled and a ball of nerves formed in my stomach. "*He* contacted me again."

I tensed up. *Fucking Vic.* "And?"

"Wants to meet for coffee to *talk*. He hasn't been around in seven years and now he wants to talk? I could kill him." She picked up a fluffy pillow from the couch and gripped it so hard I was surprised it didn't burst. "I can't say no, because he could use that as ammunition in the trial. If there is a trial. But I don't want to say yes."

"I'll go with you. Get Jenny to watch Quinn." I ran my hand down Quinn's dark hair and fought the urge to take both of them and run. Vic would *not* get custody. "Jenny would do it in a heartbeat."

"Yeah. But she watches her so much during the season, I try not to abuse our friendship too much." Her eyes watered again and guilt about the season hit me. "Sometimes it sneaks up on me pretty hard. Not having them. Like now. Dad would know what to do."

And my gut turned into a hard pit, like a solid batch of concrete. Bile threatened to come up, but I swallowed it down. It had been years but I'd never gotten over it. I couldn't. "We'll get through this, Cheryl. Just like everything else we've had thrown at us. Trust me."

"I do, Gid." She gripped my hand and shook her head. "If I meet with him, I do want you there. I just don't know yet."

"Tell me the time and place. I'll be there."

"Give me the princess. I'll put her to bed. You sticking around for a bit?"

"Yeah. I'll finish this beer. Go tuck her in. I'll plot my scavenger hunt for Thanksgiving."

"Asshole," she fired back, but it was playful. Our annual Titan Thanksgiving scavenger hunts were the best. Ten clues, each sibling timed and one winner. I'd beaten her the last two years and thoroughly enjoyed the ridiculous clay trophy that sat on my desk. Soon enough, Quinn would be in on it.

I used the free time to finally research Fiona Davis, because the girl intrigued me and she kept popping up in my thoughts. I didn't like that. I needed to know her story. And as soon as I typed in her name, multiple links popped up. *What the fuck?*

Fiona Davis speaks at local high school – don't text and drive, it kills.

Fiona Davis speaks about losing a loved one to texting and driving.

Fiona Davis gets personal. Texting Too Late Saves Lives.

Personal? *What does that mean?* I clicked on the link and a video popped up. It was dated a year ago, but she looked the same. This time, she wore a tight form-fitting dress that showed off curves I hadn't seen. *Hmm. Interesting.*

But her voice captured me.

"My name is Fiona Davis and Justin had been my best friend for most of my life. At five, we bonded over Power Rangers. We cemented our friendship during the Pokémon

craze, the Razor Scooter phase, and when life didn't have cell phones. But then cell phones became everything. We began dating my senior year. We had plans, but all that stopped when he texted while driving. He veered off the road and...he was killed on impact.

I asked myself every day what I could've done differently. Could I have yelled at him to not do that? Have I ever done it? Yes. I have. But It's more than that, and I'm going to tell you what you can do to make a difference. Because you never know how much you can affect one person's life. Justin changed mine and I want to help anyone who will listen. You are not alone."

My muscles tightened and a small part of my heart shattered. *That* was why she wanted to coach. *That* was why parents knew her—she spoke at high schools in the valley about it. TTL had gained popularity in the Phoenix area and even the baseball organization had done an event with them last year.

Fiona Davis was not who I'd thought. *Nope. Not at all.* I was an asshole. I closed my eyes as shame rolled off me in waves. It wasn't pleasant, no. It was fucking miserable knowing I was the bad guy.

But I was a glutton for punishment. I kept researching her and stumbled across her social media. She would graduate in the spring. She'd volunteered at TTL for the past three years and, from her posts, she waited tables to save money. Everything about her seemed happy and normal, except for the fact that her boyfriend had died almost four years ago.

It was stupid to think we had something in common. But it was there. And I felt an inkling of admiration for her. Cheryl came back and, in her typical fashion, pestered me. "Gid, why do you look constipated?"

"Have you heard of Texting Too Late?"

"The charity to help spread texting and driving awareness?" She frowned and took a long swig of her beer.

"Yes." I couldn't take my gaze from the photo. It was Fiona, but years ago, with a tall lanky kid. Fiona looked so innocent that my chest tightened.

"Yeah. Of course. We adore Fiona, Jade, their whole crew at TTL. They come into the hospital sometimes and talk to some of the patients who are sick, needing company. They never allow cameras in there and, hell, I admire that. Why do you ask?"

"Fiona Davis is my co-coach."

"No fucking way!" Her eyes bugged out of her head. "Fiona is awesome. Jade is kind, but Fiona... She brings such a joy to the place. She cracks jokes with the staff, the sick kids and makes people laugh. I can't believe it."

"Yeah." I grunted. My co-coach had a better reputation than I did. And I played in the majors. Okay, I had an ego problem. *Bite me.*

"I thought you said she was annoying, Gid. Fiona wouldn't hurt a fly."

"Well, we didn't get off to the best start." Shame filled me again. "It might be my fault."

"Of course it is. Jackass," she scolded me in her Cheryl way and shook her head. She had done that look a million times, from the fallout from my injury to leaving the toilet seat up. "What did you do?"

"I tried to get her to quit by doing everything in the book. I offended her. Baited her. Insulted her. Ignored her. I thought she was just some chick wanting to score with me. Shit, you know how crazy fans can get, Cheryl."

"I know. I really do. But, Gideon, Fiona Davis is a force of good in the world. It isn't good karma that you tarnished that."

"Shit. You don't think I realize that now?" I rubbed my forehead. A light ache began there. "To be fair, she gives me just as much shit. She called me old."

"You are old. Older than her at least." She snickered and a glint came into her eyes. I didn't trust her when she wore *that* look. "This is perfect for you. Name someone besides me that gives you shit? Insults you? Keeps you grounded?"

"Calm down. I don't need an ego check constantly. I'm fine." I pouted. I was a grown man and I was pouting because my older sister was picking on me. *I need a handle of whiskey.*

"No one. That's who. Damn, this'll work out good for you. I know it." She flipped on the TV and I went back to researching my co-coach.

Yeah—I wouldn't call it stalking, but I wanted to know more about her for whatever reason. By the time I crashed on Cheryl's couch, I was ready for tomorrow.

* * * *

I scanned my call history to get to the day Fiona had called me. I found it and pressed Call. The ringing left me time to wonder.

Why the fuck did I agree to a sleepover?
Why did I insist on having her there?
Why do I care?

"Hello?" Her singsong voice irritated me. Why was she so happy?

"Fiona. It's Gideon."

"Ah, yes. Your majesty. How is it going in your world?"

I ignored her. "What time are you showing up tonight?"

"I was going to blow it off. I could think of about a million other things I'd rather do than go to your place."

I tightened my grip on the phone. This woman was infuriating. "Fiona. You insisted on being a part of this team. You aren't fucking leaving me with—"

"I'm kidding. Undo the knot in your panties, Gid. I need your address. That is if you trust me with it. I could sell it to all your fangirls you insist are obsessed with you."

"I'll text it to you. Can you use that Remind thing you mentioned to let the kids know to come at six? Text them the address?"

"Let me enjoy this moment. You need me." She fucking giggled. "This is great. But yes, I'll make sure the kids know what's going on because I rock."

"You're annoying."

"See you later, Gid." She hung up. I couldn't explain the odd sensation in my chest or my gut, but it wasn't unpleasant. The thought of having my place filled with people cheered me up. It would be the first time in years the house would have life.

And that was fucking sad.

Chapter Nine

Fiona

"I'm heading over there now. And I brought all the essentials." I pulled onto the huge driveway moments later. "Jade. You should see this guy's house. It's...wow. I feel inferior breathing near it. It looks like it could be on *Million Dollar Listing* — blah."

"Yeah? How many windows does it have? Is there a maid? Oh, I bet he has a butler."

"You are no help," I scoffed at her and parked by the sidewalk. The property had red brick all the way to the door and a perfectly manicured lawn. I eyed the stain on my shirt. *Fuck.* I'd spilled coffee on it and hadn't thought it mattered, but now embarrassment and unease took root in my chest. "But really, if I don't call you tomorrow come search for my body."

"Ha ha. You'll be just fine. Have fun. Maybe we'll get brunch tomorrow?"

"Sure. I'll tell you all about tonight. Shit. He sees me awkwardly standing outside. I gotta go. Bye."

Her laughed echoed when I hung up and I shouldered my backpack. I'd made the choice to not tell my sisters I was staying at his house. They would've concocted some asinine plan to seduce him. They were crazy that way. Telling Jade was the smart decision. Backpack on, attitude in place, I marched up to the door. It was all I needed for the night. "Your eminence. Your place doesn't look too shabby. Hope you got a good deal for it."

"I did. Why do you call me that shit? Explain." Arms crossed, signature frown, deliciously tight shirt. He leaned against the huge wooden front door and made no moves to help me with my stuff. Not that I expected it. He was *not* a gentleman.

I ran my tongue over my bottom lip, a grin bursting to get out. But I remained stoic. "Nah, I'm good."

"Because I look like a king?" One eyebrow rose and it would've been endearing if I didn't despise the guy.

"I'm not sharing my secrets with you." I laughed to myself and picked up the large sack of snacks. "Don't worry about helping. I got it, big guy."

Annoyance flickered over his face and he stormed into the house. *Cool. Glad we're off to a good start.* I entered the foyer and stopped. It was marble. Sky-high windows. It was gorgeous, yet there was almost no furniture. "Git, you have a fucking nice house."

"That's it. What did you call me?"

Oh shit. I'd thought he was in the kitchen, but nope. He appeared right in front of me. Maybe a foot away. His aftershave or cologne smelled like heaven and my mouth watered. I jutted out my chin, setting my stuff on the ground. The sound echoed in the empty room, but I was ready to battle. "I said Git because you're acting like one."

"My name is Gideon. I thought we were past this." He sighed, his lips forming the perfect unhappy scowl. His minty breath hit me in the face and I briefly thought about what he tasted like. *But I hate this guy.*

"We're *way* past it. I know your name. I prefer your highness, git or douche-canoe, though." *Why am I baiting him? Why do I enjoy it? Am I sick, getting off from annoying him? Yes. Yes, I am.*

"Explain." He reached out to do something, but he pulled his hand back, the muscles in his arm teasing me. His dark eyebrows came together, creating the cutest dimple between his eyes. *Damn his face.* "I don't get it."

"Look, I'd rather not. You hate me. I really don't like you. Let's not complicate it for the next eleven weeks." I went to move past his arm, but it remained in all its muscly glory. He stopped me with his strong hand. He brought his digits around my arm and the stark contrast of his tan fingers and my pale skin made my belly swoop.

"I don't hate you."

I burst out laughing. Like, belly-laughing. "Wow. Thank you. I feel so blessed. Yes. Thank you for not hating me." I picked up my stuff and wiped tears from under my eyes. "Now, be helpful and show me where the kitchen is before the vultures arrive."

He didn't respond. Instead, he picked up the bag of treats and scoffed. "What did I tell you about sweets?"

"They are teenagers. We will have fifteen in your house. What do you suppose we entertain them with? Books? Fruit? Hm?" I cocked a hip and waited, but he just stared at me. He eyed me from my feet to my face and I blushed. *Shit.* "Don't make fun of me. I wanted to be comfortable and not attractive. Not with sixteen teenage boys here."

There. That'll explain why I chose to wear old sweatpants that said WINNER on the ass with a baseball tee with a stain. But Gideon frowned. "There are fifteen on the team."

"Yeah. I consider you another kid." I crossed my eyes at him and sorted the treats and movies I'd brought. I didn't miss the slight, barely noticeable lift of his lip. *Interesting.* "Tell me you have videogames in this mansion."

"I do. I have four TVs downstairs. My bedroom is down there too, if you're wondering."

"Why in the ever-loving hell do you have *four* TVs?" *Our piece of shit hardly works.* A shot of jealousy went through me. I couldn't imagine having that much wealth. *He donated a million dollars. Go easier on him.* "And I wasn't. But thanks for divulging that info. I can text it out to the moms if you want."

His nostrils flared twice before he answered. "When I had surgery earlier this year, I couldn't do anything. I needed to entertain myself. Two are for watching games, the other two, playing videogames. It's a nice setup. Plus, my therapy room is down there." He picked up the box of popcorn and I jerked it out of his hands.

"*Don't* throw my food away, please. If you refuse to let them eat it, I'll just take it back."

He nodded, releasing his grasp on it. He hoisted himself up onto the counter and continued to stare at me. A hundred retorts went through my head but I chose the mature route. "I got RSVPs from every kid. They'll be here at six. I figured we could order pizza. I'm having them all bring five bucks."

"I can order pizza for them."

"So, pizza is okay?"

"Yes. Pizza is always okay." He leaned forward, his knee almost hitting my side. God. He was huge. Deliciously muscly and assholey. *What a combo.* "Did you make a precious plan for the night?"

"Hey!" I smacked his chest. Mistake. Such a mistake. It was firm. And strong. And perfect. "Practice went well this week with my plans. Don't you agree?"

He sighed and shrugged. "I guess."

"God, would it kill you to give me a damn compliment? Would it? I thought this week was great." I took the bag of candy and threw it at him. He caught it, of course, and grinned at me.

Holy wet my panties shit. That smile. "Fiona. The coffee stain on your shirt looks nice."

"You're such an asshole! Ugh!"

I left the kitchen to the sound of laughter and gave myself a tour. Fuck that guy. Fuck him and his gorgeous face and dick personality. I needed space — especially if I would be there all damn night. I snuck a text to Jade.

Fiona: Don't worry about finding me dead. Worry about bailing me out of jail.

Jade: I can't wait to hear about this. Diane can't wait. I may have told everyone.

Fiona: Give me a camera and I'll livestream it.

I entered the living room, if this mansion had just one. It held two black couches, one small white table and a stereo. What captured my attention the most was the sleek bookcase. It had to contain at least three hundred books and it covered an entire wall. "My god. A shelf has never been so sexy before."

"Interesting," he replied, standing a foot behind me.

I jumped. "Do you tend to slink around your own house without making a goddamn sound?" I put my hand over my heart and got closer to the beauty. Classics, mysteries, biographies — he had them all. "I'm impressed. I didn't realize you could read."

He gasped for a second before letting out a snort. Like, an unattractive, embarrassing sound that combined a laugh and a cough. "Shit. You really are good for my ego."

"Excuse me — can we talk about the sound you just made?" I smiled. I couldn't help it. Gideon Titan, baseball legend with billboards everywhere, had just snorted. And he looked damn adorable standing there. "Sexy fantasy dreams would be destroyed across the nation if women knew about *that* sound."

"Are yours destroyed?" Those eyes smoldered at me again and *Christ*. My breath hitched. *How amazing would he be in bed... No. Stop it. STOP IT.*

"Nah. I think about your body, not your mouth. Whenever you make sound, it pisses me off."

"Right back at ya, Barbie." He grinned, wickedly. We stood there, feet apart with our breaths coming out a little faster. Okay, I was breathing weirdly, but I couldn't help it. He had an aura about him that told me he was an animal in bed. I mean, shit, all that aggression and anger needed a release. "Let me show you the basement. I figured all the guys could stay down there tonight."

"It's not a dungeon, is it?"

"God. Do you think before you speak?"

"Not really. Life's more fun that way." I laughed and he led me toward another long hallway. It stretched toward the south of the house. The sun began setting and the view struck me. "Wow. This is beautiful."

"Yeah?" He didn't stop walking until he realized I'd remained in front of the window. "The AC bill is huge in the summer. The sun heats this place up."

"I'm sure it is, but with a view like this, it has to be worth it. Damn. You can see the mountains in the background. Can I take a picture of this?"

"I guess."

I took my phone from my pocket and found the perfect angle. The palm trees and the mountains clashed against the setting sun. It rivaled a painting. I snapped a couple of shots and froze when Gideon bent low. Like, his cheek was inches from mine. "Uh, whatcha doing?"

"I wanna see the shot. Damn. Will you send that to me? That's a good one."

"Sure." I cleared my throat. Whatever was happening, I didn't like it. "So, the dungeon?"

"Right this way."

I followed him, checking off all the reasons I hated this guy. It didn't matter how he looked. Distraction. I needed a distraction. "How many rooms does this place have?"

"Eight."

"Why?" He disappeared down a deep stairwell and I caught up to him. It was easy because he took his time, and at each step his grimace thickened. "Why buy a house this big?"

"I wanted the space. Here. This is the game room." He flicked on the lights and words left me.

It was the coolest room I had ever seen. Sleek black tile covered the entire floor, except for a plush green rug that actually looked comfy. Arcade games lined the wall on one side, a ping-pong table next to them and a pool table to the left. I had to use my hand to close my mouth. It was *that* nice. "Jesus."

"Wait until you see the other room." He grinned, two small dimples coming out on each side of his face. "It's over here."

"Another room? Good lord." I dropped the bag of stuff and took in everything else I'd missed. The stereo speakers all in the ceiling, a fridge, bar and table off to the back. But when I entered the back room, I almost moaned. It wasn't carpet that covered the large room. It was soft, almost like fake plastic, and rustled when I pressed down on it, which was when it hit me. *Oh my god.* "Is this... Is this a bean bag floor?"

"Yup."

"My god." I didn't ask. I didn't wait for permission before throwing myself onto it. It defined amazing. I stretched out as far as I could and rolled around like a damn dog. The TVs sat off to the side and I never wanted to leave. I might've even groaned a little. "Can I live here?"

"Ah, no." He smiled again. That made three times in one afternoon. "But I'm glad you're enjoying yourself."

"All my problems are melting away in here." I closed my eyes and relaxed further into the bean bag. "I don't care why a grown man like yourself has this. I really don't. Because I love it and will use all my life savings to buy one. You went up one notch on my scale."

"Where does that put me?"

The plush floor shifted next to me and I cracked open one eye. He'd joined me on the floor, his arm supporting his hand while he stared at me. I stumbled for one second on my words. "Um. It puts you right above Hitler."

"Thank god for that."

Oh my god. "Are we joking now?"

"Looks like it, Barbie." He faced the other way and flipped on two of the TVs. A zing of pleasure went through me. I liked friendly Gideon. Well, more like not-asshole Gideon. The two closest TVs powered on. One was a hockey game, the other some action movie. The surround sound blasted throughout the basement and the bass shook in my core. "This is how I recovered from my surgery."

"I want to recover from my daily struggles in here." I kept it simple. I wanted to ask about the injury but I didn't. I was proud of myself. "The boys will be just fine tonight. Keep them in here."

"It's the plan."

And we lay there without talking until the doorbell went off a short time later. I joined him, greeting the parents and kids, but as soon as the rascals found the basement, it was game over. I ordered the pizza, hoping the kids had remembered the money because I couldn't afford two hundred dollars of pizza. *Nope. No way.*

But when I asked the kids, half of them had forgotten. And I started sweating. I could use two credit cards to cover it, rather than ask Gideon for help. He'd mentioned he would buy it, but I'd brought it up twice and he hadn't said a word. *Shit.*

It would be there in forty minutes. That was all the time I had to figure out how to pay the difference. I paced the kitchen, no solution coming to me. I could ask Gideon, but I hated showing weakness. I bit the tip of my knuckle, hoping it would give me an answer. It didn't.

Twenty minutes left. I gulped. I hated having money issues. "Fiona?"

"Yes, Gideon?" I snapped at him. He frowned and glanced out of the front window.

"Is the pizza here yet?"

"Twenty minutes." I bit harder on the skin.

"Here." He handed me a wad of cash—a wad I assumed drug dealers used. "Pay with this."

I couldn't hide my sigh of relief. "*Thank* you. Yes. I will."

His eyes narrowed and he brought his fingers to his jaw. "Can you afford the pizza?"

I didn't answer and shrugged. But he was persistent.

"Fiona. Were you going to pay for it without asking for help?"

"I was in the midst of figuring it out. It wasn't going well." *There.* I'd admitted it. He knew I was poor. But how could he not with *this* house? *God.* Shame took over my chest, but he didn't look at me with pity. Not once.

"You're a stubborn little thing."

"When you say it, it doesn't sound like a compliment." Awareness grew between us and his nostrils flared.

"Wasn't meant to be one. Go downstairs and make sure no one sits on Big Al. They were trying to fart on him before I came up."

"Boys. Such idiots." I chuckled and moved toward the hallway, but he stopped me for the second time. "Yeah?"

"You can ask me for help." His eyes burned into me, daring me to argue. "I'll help you."

"Thank you?" I gulped. The lump in my throat increased at least three times.

"And I owe you an apology." His jaw tensed and I froze. Had this man ever said those words to another human before? "I'm sorry I threw away the cupcakes. I shouldn't have done that."

I didn't get a chance to respond when he reached out and squeezed my shoulder. Then he walked away. *Hot damn.* The asshole had a different side to his personality and I didn't hate this one.

Chapter Ten

Gideon

I will never have kids. Not after surviving that all-nighter. I waved as the last parent picked up Brad. Fucking Brad had kept forgetting to call his parents for a ride until I got firm with him. They'd had a blast — video games, movies, snacks and aggressive card games had kept them entertained the entire time. Even I'd enjoyed myself at some moments when the volunteers weren't acting like my shadow, following me around every second. Fiona enjoyed my misery and did nothing to swoop in and help. *I wasn't the only asshole.*

I cringed at the disaster in the basement.

Crumbs. Trash. Wrappers. And a lingering stench that was hard to describe. But my head pounded from lack of sleep and the bean bag floor was calling my name. I washed my face, brushed my teeth and made the trek to the basement. Fiona said she had to grab some stuff before heading out and I didn't wait to say goodbye.

Because the blonde got under my skin. Her refusal to ask for help, her easy way with the kids, her incessant jokes, loud laugh and obnoxious smile. Yeah. I wanted her out of my house.

But no such luck. She lay on the floor, sound asleep with half her shirt pulled up. Her lower back was exposed and dear god, why was that hot? The curve of her spine, the low-riding sweatpants were not sexy. Yet my cock woke up.

I didn't even like her.

She definitely disliked me.

But the attraction was there. I stepped onto the floor and she turned over, letting out a small moan. *Fucking hell.* "Fiona. You need to go," I barked at her. It was more to protect myself, but her wounded expression still bothered me.

"Yeah." She rubbed her hands over her face. "Sorry. I didn't mean—" She yawned loud and hard. "I didn't mean to fall asleep. I'm so fucking tired."

Goddamn it. She shouldn't drive home. It's dangerous. She could crash. Fuck that.

"Stay. I'm sorry." I shook sleep from my head and fell onto the ground. My complete one-eighty gave me a headache, and it didn't combine well with the lack of sleep. "You shouldn't drive like this. Stay."

"You're sure?" she asked, but her eyes had already closed. "I can-I can leave."

I wasn't that much of a heartless asshole. "No. Stay. Sleep."

And she was out. I chuckled and felt the exhaustion of the night hit me. It had been ages since I'd had a sleepless night and I was conked. I barely counted to ten before blackness took over and the exhaustion from the week hit me. *Lights out, Gideon.*

* * * *

My neck ached something brutal. The angle I'd fallen asleep in had caused the entire right side to cramp up and I needed some goddamn ice. *Why did I fall asleep on the floor?*

Oh, right. The sleepover. Fiona.

Fiona. I wiped the sleep out of my eyes — I had no idea what time it was. She wasn't on the bean bag floor anymore. Good. Maybe she'd left. It was easier that way. Less messy.

My watch read eleven — and I had an entire day to do whatever the fuck I wanted. *Now what do I want to do?*

My sister and Quinn were at church. The few friends I had spent the entire off-season with their families. That left no one. *God. This sucks.* Sure, I could head to a bar and take up with some random woman who recognized me. It would satisfy my temporary sadness but that was just it — temporary. The sadness would come when I crept away after spending hours with her. And avoiding it altogether sounded better. That left me with what? Working out with a leg that hurt like a bitch?

No wonder I was a miserable sack of shit. I succumbed to the fact that I would spend my Sunday afternoon alone, doing something worthless. But before I could decide what that worthless activity would be, my stomach let out a growl. *When did I eat last? Oh yeah, the fucking shit pizza.*

I hated cooking — especially for myself. It was tedious and boring to cook healthy meals filled with vegetables and protein. I much preferred to order out, but then Agnes would find out. Agnes, the agony-inducing nutritionist. Food was a beautiful thing, but she wanted me to suffer.

I made the slow trip to the kitchen and scanned the fridge. The lack of variety annoyed me. I guess eight eggs it was. I was about to crack them into the bowl when I heard a loud grunt. Setting the carton down, I scanned the foyer. *What the hell?*

It came from the front room, or maybe outside. I didn't have neighbors so maybe a kid had forgotten something. I peeked through the little window on the side of the front door and suddenly, my mood lifted.

Fiona kicked the side of her car, hair flying everywhere and nothing but swear words escaping her large mouth. I fought a snort — who kicked their car? *Oh shit.* She did it again, pointing and yelling at the hood of the car. She then threw her bag on the ground and kicked the beat-up piece of metal again Good lord. She was a train wreck. I continued to watch her — she had someone on the phone and was pacing around the vehicle. I guessed she hadn't received good news when she hung up and narrowed her eyes at my house. *Shit.*

She saw me and curled up one side of her lip. *Busted.* I flung open the door and prepared myself for a verbal attack. But it didn't come. I could be a gentleman when I chose to and I considered being one. "Issue with the car?"

"Nope. I'm boycotting American-made cars. I heard about a protest people are doing all over today. Just today. And you pretend to kick your car...to raise awareness."

Jesus, she couldn't lie. I grinned. "Raise awareness about what?"

"People who need cars." She crossed her arms and her gaze darted in every direction. Her voice even went an octave too high. My little co-coach was amusing as shit. I remained silent, waiting her out. She sucked in one side of her cheeks and the gesture sent a burst of desire to my groin. *How would her mouth feel on my cock? Woah. Don't go there.*

I cleared my throat and leaned against the doorframe. "Well, good luck with your *protest.*"

"Wait—" She cringed and mumbled something to herself. "Do you... Do you have jumper cables?"

"Is this part of the protest?" I couldn't help myself. I wanted to fluster the hell out of her. Maybe it was how cute her blush was, or how her words slurred when she spoke faster.

"Goddamn it." She licked her lips and ran her fingers through her hair. It gave her a wild, free look. "My car won't start. I've been trying for twenty minutes. Do you have cables?"

"Well, it'll cost you." *What am I saying? Am I fucking flirting with her?*

"I have twenty bucks." She reached into her bag before I stopped her.

"It was a joke. Jesus. Come on." I shut the door and opened the first part of my four-car garage. I had three cars and a motorcycle. Cheryl's words haunted me. *No one needs this many fancy cars. You look like an idiot. A rich idiot.*

But Fiona whistled and ran her finger over the hood of my Corvette. I know I got shit for it, but I had a Mustang *and* a Corvette. I could afford it. "Hot damn, a 1968 Stingray?"

I stopped. "You know the date? The model?"

"I dated a petrolhead. Spent a lot of time in that model. I'm surprised I remembered the details, actually." She bent down without shame and pointed at the handle. "Did you know this is the only year they had the release button like this? It forces you to open the driver's side with your left, the passenger side with your right."

I blinked at her. She left me speechless. *She spent time in this model naked?* "Uh, I think— I think my cables are in the Blazer."

"Cool."

I took three long strides to the back of the SUV and spied them in the corner. "I'll bring it out closer to yours." She didn't respond and I stuck my head out. Her ridiculous outfit seemed out of place next to my Harley-Davidson. "Fiona?"

"What?" she snapped. *Woah.*

"You ready?"

"Yeah, sorry." She faced me and a slow blush crept up her neck. Her eyes heated over...or I thought they did, for a second. *Does Fiona have a thing for motorcycles?* "I'll go wait out there."

But I didn't move a muscle. Neither did she. She brought her fingers down to the sleek black of the Lowrider S, her breath hitching enough for me to hear. *Holy shit. The motorcycle turns her on.* Anticipation flamed in my stomach. "Do you want to go for a ride?"

"Fuck. Yes."

And she grinned so widely that both her eyes turned to squints. My joy matched hers and for the first time, we were on the same page. "Let me grab the keys."

She nodded and ran her hands over her neck—a telltale sign I knew well. I clapped my hands with glee and snatched the keys off the rack. I kept them in the garage, a notion my sister bitched about, but I had three layers of security. If someone got past that, they deserved a joyride. "I need to get an extra helmet."

"Okay." Her singsong voice had me do a double-take, but she stared at the bike, then me, then back at the bike. Her tongue traced her bottom lip over and over, and fuck me. I wanted her. It made no sense. She annoyed me. But her mouth... I wanted to claim it.

My dick jumped to life and I forced myself to think of something else. Riding around with a major wood was not a great idea. *Practice. Mowing the lawn. Cleaning. I wonder if Fiona gets waxed? Is she bare or does she leave a little landing strip?* Fuck. It didn't work.

"Honestly, I don't need a helmet."

"Yes, you do." I snapped into gear. The extra one remained in the locker when it wasn't used, which was most of the time. "Safety is a must. Have you ridden before?"

"A bike? Sure. A Harley like *this*?" An unreadable glint entered her pale blue eyes. "No."

"Get ready. It'll change your life." I grinned at her and passed her the helmet. Her petite frame clashed with the manly beast of a machine. I helped her fit the helmet on just right and walked her to the bike. I knew exactly where to go. She slid on right behind me. *Big fucking mistake.*

Her small arms clung to my abs and I was as hard as a goddamn rock. I gripped the handles and sprang the bike into action. The engine roared, the penetrating sound ricocheting around in my chest. I loved this bike. I loved the freedom, the possibilities it brought and Fiona's body pressed against mine.

I headed down the long path and went toward the North Mountains. The valley had no traffic on Sundays.

It was my favorite day to drive. And drive we did. We cruised through the scenic route, the fresh cool air blasting us both. I remembered why I'd bought this thing. It was moments like this. I didn't think about the horrific way we'd lost our parents, or my injury and setback in my career, or Vic taking Cheryl to court. I didn't think.

I admired the southwestern colors that meant home. The browns, reds, pale dull greens of the saguaro cacti all blended together into the perfect landscape. We saw a lone coyote and a javelina. She squeezed my arm and I slowed on the dirt path to the right of the highway. I came to a stop and she jumped off the bike.

"Oh my god. I've never… All my life I wanted to see a wild javelina. Can you believe it? I need a picture." She bent over the railing and snapped about ten pictures of the wild pig. I didn't get the craze about it, but Quinn did have a pig obsession before it turned to glitter and princesses. I sighed, following Fiona's foolish antics, and snapped a picture to show her later. "You know, I thought javelinas would be a bigger problem in my life. Kind of like quicksand. They talked about it when we were kids a lot, well, when I was a kid. When did you graduate elementary school, 1990?"

I let out an obnoxious snort. "I'm not *that* old."

"You act like it." She sent me a wicked smile and went back to looking over the rail. "What are you, twenty-nine?"

"I'm twenty-six." *God. I do act older than that.* "I'm not even five years older than you."

"Been doing some research on me, bud?" She turned around with her lips pursed. She didn't appear offended. No. She smirked, like she knew where my thoughts had been recently.

"Sure did." I scanned her body, sweatpants and all. I tried intimidating her but it was an empty threat. She didn't give a shit about me and it turned me on to no end. "Know quite a bit about you from the internet."

"Good. Most of it is probably lies anyway." She dragged her teeth over her bottom lip before taking a step toward me. Desire and heat shot right through me. "I didn't look up anything about you."

"No? Not even remotely curious about me?" I stepped closer. Her nose almost touched my chest. "Because I'm *quite* curious about you."

"I'm an interesting person. You are not." And she twisted my nipple like a goddamn teenager and snapped her fingers. "Let's get back. My car won't tow itself."

I was flabbergasted. *She gave me a titty twister. A legit twist of the nipple to the point of pain.* And I wanted to return the favor. I lowered my voice so she wouldn't have any illusions about what I meant. "Careful what you start, Fiona."

She grinned and patted the black leather seat. I had no choice but to get back on. I'd just started the bike when her fingers grazed my pecs again, this time carefully tracing them. *Naughty.* This girl awoke the beast and he couldn't be put away. I raced down the narrow roads, damn well knowing where the nearest secluded area was. It was a lake that stood about thirty minutes away from the city. And it had privacy. Especially in the winter.

I arrived there with the worst case of blue balls I'd ever had. I threw off my helmet and slid off the bike. Fiona's eyes widened to small saucers. I caged her in, her little body having nowhere to go.

"Where are we?"

"Do you care?" I gripped her hip, tight enough to hurt. She squirmed, letting out the smallest moan. *Fuck yes.* "I'm going to fuck you senseless on this bike regardless of where we are."

Chapter Eleven

Fiona

My cunt throbbed against the seat of the bike. It begged and screamed to be pounded and, for whatever fucking reason, I wanted *him*. "Is that so? You're gunna strip me down and spread me wide out here? You're gunna fuck me in the middle of the desert?"

"Hell yeah, I am." His slack jaw sent shivers down my body. "You're gunna scream my name so fucking loud, it'll echo off the lake."

"I don't even like you." I moaned when his hands dug deeper into my hips. He pushed me farther onto the seat, his weight coming down on me.

"You don't have to." He ran his tongue across my jaw, biting my neck in a torturously perfect way. I closed my eyes and leaned farther into him. No. I shouldn't, but *fuck* I wanted to. "But I know you want me."

"Yeah?" I pulled at his hair, dragging his face to mine. "What gives you that impression?"

"Am I wrong?" He froze millimeters away from my mouth. "Tell me I'm wrong, Fiona."

I snapped. The way he said my name... It was a challenge and a caress at the same time. I grabbed his face and crashed our mouths together. It was rough. His mouth captured mine, our teeth clashing as he sucked on my tongue. This wasn't some romantic gesture. It was a goddamn claim. I arched on the seat of the bike and he held on to me. His stubble scratched at my face with each demand his lips made.

It wasn't a tender kiss.

It was an inhibition-forgetting, panty-wetting, set-my-blood-on-fire kind of kiss. Oh, baby, I wanted more. I sucked his tongue, hard. A slight burn of peppermint mouthwash rolled off him and it tingled all the way down my throat. He took my lips between his teeth and sucked so hard I squirmed. Then he stopped.

His chest heaved, his eyes almost feral. "Take off your clothes."

I hesitated for a second. And he shook his head. "All of them, Fiona. I told you what I'm going to do to you."

A fiery desperation formed in my chest. I sucked my bottom lip into my mouth, tasting him again. And I removed my sweatshirt in a second. He helped with my pants, but I wouldn't call it helping. It was more of removing a barrier, and I lay there, bare for the world to see and not one fuck was given.

"God. I wondered how you kept your pussy. Perfect." He growled and bent low, running his nose all the way down my body. Goosebumps broke out all over me. He bit down on the tender patch of skin below my belly button. It hurt—and would leave a mark. *Let him mark me.* "I smell how turned on you are. It's hot."

"What you gunna do about it? I'm dripping wet after that ride."

"I'll show you a ride." He gave me a smug smile, pulling out his wallet before he dropped his pants. I wanted to explore his chest, but he stood there in tight black boxers, his Adonis body messing with my head. I sucked in a breath, desperate to touch him. I trailed my gaze down his core, past his snug boxers, and almost winced when I spied the three-inch scar around his knee. *Jesus.* I wanted to ask about it, but he pulled down the black shorts and his massive cock sprang out, and I forgot words.

I wanted to get dicked up by him, repeatedly. "Please. I need that inside me."

"First time I have to agree with you."

He sheathed himself with a condom and he pounded into me without waiting a second. I didn't need any foreplay—the ride had been enough. My walls stretched to the point of a sweet pain. I gripped the edge of the bike while he lifted my legs high into the air. He rested them on his shoulders and held onto my legs so hard I knew there would be bruises.

But I focused on the movement of his cock. His amazing, large, perfectly girthed cock that thrust inside me with so much aggression I screamed out in ecstasy. *God, I like it rough.* "Yes, Gideon. Destroy me."

He obeyed. He brought his fingers around my shoulder and held on. I saw stars. Beautiful, gasping stars as he stretched me further. I had never been fucked like this and I relished it. He dug his grip deeper, the pleasure rippling through my core. I clutched to hold on to something since the pressure began to form in my clit at an overwhelming rate. The bubble of pleasure grew rapidly and, suddenly, I needed more. He grunted and held on to my ass. I moaned. "Squeeze my ass harder," I begged. "Do it!"

And he dug his nails into my bare skin, the pain counteracting the roaring pleasure and I screamed his name. My feet flung in the air and I swore I heard a hitch in his breath, but I couldn't analyze it. I barely had time to catch my breath before he flipped me over. "Arch your back."

I did, my chest pressing onto the seat as he slid into my throbbing pussy from behind. I had a beautiful view of the lake, but I paid it no attention. A loud smack followed by a stinging broke out on my ass. Gideon had spanked me. "W-what was that for?"

"Your mouth. God." He slipped back inside me and smacked my ass again. "Do you like that, huh?"

"God. Yes." I did. I did so much. "Go harder. Pound me so I can't walk tomorrow."

"That what you like?" His breath came out gruffer. "You want it rough?"

"Yes," I said with clenched teeth. My tits bounced everywhere, the pressure of him fucking me giving me a burn on my skin. He brought his hand down on my ass again and I let out a high-pitched moan. "Touch my clit. Touch it now."

He followed directions, brought one hand to my desperate clit and flicked it with a fierce determination. It gave me the needed push and the coil loosened – an orgasm was close. I rocked against the bike and stuck my ass out toward him. He grunted my name and let out the sexiest fucking moan I had ever heard. He spilled into me and kept working my clit.

I would never call him an underachiever in my life. "God...almost. Yes. *Yes.*"

And I exploded. It was unlike any orgasm I'd had before. It was raw. Dirty. Quick, to the point and thigh-shaking. I rode it out, Gideon adding the right finger strokes by aggressively rubbing my clit. When I could breathe again, my ears rang, my pussy hurt and my legs wobbled. "Damn."

"About sums it up." He slipped out of me, the wet sound drawing attention to what we'd just done. I was thankful I didn't face him, even for a couple of seconds. *What have I done?* "You're going to have handprints on your ass."

"Yeah? I consider those fuck trophies." I found my pants and slipped them on quickly, my sweatshirt right after. I loved going bra-less in the baggy material. I waited to be clothed again before meeting his gaze. His dark eyes swirled, the glint in them easing my tension. "I'm not sure I'll enjoy the ride back. You tore me up."

"You wanted it." His eyebrows furrowed, barely. "You surprised me."

"Because I fucked you? Liked it rough?" I chuckled and found my bearings. I was not shy in the bedroom or inexperienced. I knew what I liked and what I didn't and life was too damn short for mediocre sex. His mouth hung open and he hadn't responded. "You have a stupid look on your face. Why did I surprise you?"

"You were bossy." He ran his hand over the back of his neck and gave me a small grin. It was almost cute. "I mean, you *are* bossy, but I'm not used to a woman telling me what to do. I'm normally in charge."

"This is good for your enormously large *ego*." I grinned at him and patted his cheek. His startled expression would be etched in my mind. I mean, so would his delicious cock, but for other reasons. "If it helps, I'm surprised too."

"It better not be about my performance." He lowered his voice and moved an inch toward me. "I know what I'm good at."

"Calm down. No." I shook my head and moved to sit on the back of the bike. I winced. My entire pussy was sore in the best fucking way. I felt like I'd ridden a goddamn horse for four hours. Then I laughed to myself. *He kind of is a horse.* "I still don't like you. Even with your magic dick and aggressive skills."

He bit down on his lower lip with a knowing smirk. "All I heard was magic dick."

"Such a boy. Now, be a gentleman and take me back, would you? I need to get a jump for my car." *Shit.* Reality crashed around the fragile pleasure I had. It would be at least a hundred dollars and I didn't have that. I could use the credit card, but I would have to see if the restaurant would take me back on part-time. *Shit, shit.* "Let's go, Gid."

"I'm Gid, now?" One lip quirked up.

"What would you prefer? God? King?" His lack of hustle annoyed me. I had places to be. Okay I didn't. But his sexual abilities did not match his personality. "Sir?"

His entire mouth curved up and he let out a low chuckle. "Yeah. I would answer to sir. I wouldn't mind putting a gag in your mouth."

"And it's time to go." If there had been a moment, however brief, it was gone. "I'm into wild sex—not gagging."

"I'll remember that next time."

My entire body tensed up. *Next time?* My inner slut jumped around in a circle, cheering her face off. But my rational personality did not. "What does that mean?"

"Don't look shocked, Barbie." He jutted his head to the bike. "Ready to go?"

"How can you switch gears like that?" I scoffed and slipped on the helmet. It was better not to overanalyze his words. He was Gideon Titan. Superficial, narcissistic, rude...yet aggressive and amazing while fucking on a motorcycle. Jade would slap me silly if she knew what I'd done.

But I would do it again.

The loud roar of the engine drowned out all my thoughts and I relaxed into him. The Sonoran Desert was and always would be my home. Justin had known all sorts of random facts about the cacti and plants. My heart clenched. *Does Justin know what I do? Does he know about my one-night stands, crazy hookups and inability to express true emotion?*

Great. I loved my moments of self-doubt. They tended to hit me after a night of drinking, or after a real sad movie. But after a great bout of getting fucked by an equally emotionally challenged man? I should be high as a kite.

What does this mean?

I didn't feel any better when we pulled back into the mansion Gideon called home. I hung up the helmet back in the locker, shouldered my bag and walked to my piece-of-shit car. I sensed Gideon following me, but the big guy made no sound. I pulled up the number of a tow service and meant to hit Send but Gideon's commanding tone stopped me.

"I know a guy who can help."

"You sound like a mobster." I leaned against the car and raised my eyebrows at him. "Can this *guy* tow my car?"

"Yeah. He owes me a favor." He made no moves, just kept his hands in his pockets of his form-fitting jeans. I should've felt self-conscious in my raggedy outfit, but I didn't care what he thought about me. It was a gift.

"I won't say no to help. But what do I owe you?" My heart picked up at the double meaning to my words. I knew he heard it, but he didn't say anything. He shook his head.

"Nothing. Hang tight for a second, I'll give him a ring."

And he left me standing there. I heard tones of laughter but couldn't decipher what he said. My emotional range was the size of a carrot, and this act of genuine kindness didn't sit well with me. He was an asshole. He didn't do kind things and this would be considered kind. Unless...

Unless he thinks it's payment for the fuck. Anger seeped its way into my chest and when he came back with a small smile, I prodded him in his hard pecs. "Tell me you didn't do this because we fucked."

"What? No." He dismissed me with an expression I hadn't seen on him before. "He'll be by in an hour with the tow."

"What'll it cost me?"

"I told you. He owes me. Won't cost you a thing." His gaze assessed me and I fidgeted. I didn't like how his stare seemed to go through me, somehow. "Come on. I'll make you some lunch while we wait."

I wanted to question him—I really did. But he seemed sincere. I followed him into the kitchen and watched one of the most sought-after men in the country make me a meat sandwich. Just meat. No fun stuff. It sucked. He used the same hands that had had me walking funny, and I knew it had to happen again.

No one had made me come like that and I wanted more.

Chapter Twelve

Gideon

"Garth—block the ball. That's your job. Block it."

"But it came in fast," the kid whined. I pinched the bridge of my nose and annoyance took over. It was our first game of the season and the kids felt brave enough to talk back. I clearly hadn't imposed my alpha-ness on them. "Coach Titan, I'm *not* a good catcher."

"Yes, you are. You have the skills necessary to succeed. Use them." I placed two hands on each shoulder and held his gaze. "Confidence, kid. Confidence is what you need. Now, forget about the passed balls and get ready to bat. We need runs."

"Yes, sir."

He nodded at me and went to stand in the on-deck circle. Fiona brushed by me in her ridiculous getup. She wore tight black pants, a large zip-up jacket and her damn fanny pack. God. I wanted to strip that fanny pack off her and spend an hour between her thighs.

Focus. The game. "Team! Listen up. The pitcher's arm isn't strong. Take one step towards the mound when you're in the box. Wait an entire second before swinging."

"He's throwing fast," one of the taller kids in the back replied. I eyed him, but he shrugged. "Faster than we practiced. My dad said to choke up on the bat."

"Mine too. He said —"

"Fake bunt the first pitch." Fiona leaned against the dugout. All their eyes shifted and she had their attention. "Stick the back out, like this, and watch it."

"There's no bunting in baseball," I scoffed but her frightening blue eyes narrowed at me. "We talked about this about ten times, *Fiona*. That's small ball. We don't need to do that."

"Ignore Coach Titan. Trust me. When you do the fake bunt, three things happen. One, you time the pitch. You say it's too fast, then time it. Two, it makes their defense antsy. And three, you get a better view of the strike zone. Tayler, fake bunt until you get a strike and see how you feel."

"Okay, CFD. I'll try." He put on his helmet and smacked his hands together. "I don't want to lose to this team, I really don't."

"Rivals?"

"No. My stepbrother plays for them and I hate him."

Fiona and I shared a look and hers had nothing but sympathy. Then she jogged over to the first base side. I took my position at third and clapped at Tayler. "You got it."

He gave a brisk nod and scooted up in the box. Fiona's idea wasn't bad. But it was more a softball move than baseball. Tayler showed the fake bunt, pure determination on his face, and the pitcher threw him a drop ball. Tayler pulled back, the umpire screaming loudly for all of us to hear. "Ball!"

"Do it again, Tayler." I snuck at glance at Fiona, but she ignored me. Fair enough. "Let's go, kid — we need runners."

I became an observer of the game after that. He faked a bunt twice more, the count still not having any strikes. *Maybe Fiona is right. Damn it.* I clapped as Tayler watched a strike go by and gave a big nod to Fiona. She gave him a measly thumbs-up and the next pitch, he crushed it to right field. I waved him on, swinging my arm around as pride burst through me. "*Keep going!*"

The kid hustled, using every part of his body to make the double into a triple. And it worked. He slid head first, every member of our team on their feet. I jumped up and down, ignoring the sharp pain shooting up my thigh. The momentum was set and adrenaline could hold off the throbbing for a bit.

Brad followed Fiona's advice and got a single, giving us our first lead. The next four guys all got on base and the other team switched pitchers. It was the third inning and we all knew we'd gotten into their heads. Most pitchers lasted until the sixth at least.

We scored five runs that inning. The kids ran out onto the field and Garth gave me a wounded look before putting on the gear. He was made to catch — I would bet money on it. He needed encouragement and I would make it a personal goal to help him. It was purely for his sake and not at all to tell Fiona she was right.

I'd rather eat knives.

The smugness rolled off her when she perched up next to me on the fence. She cleared her throat at least twice before staring at me. Her knowing gaze hit me. I gave in. "Yes?"

"Interesting how we scored five runs, yeah?"

"If I agree with you, you'll walk around thinking you're six feet tall. But if I disagree, you'll throw it in my face until I agree. I can't win."

"Yeah. Your life is so *hard*." She smacked the back of my head before walking to stand on the south end of the dugout. It wasn't hard. It didn't hurt. But it insulted me. The nerve of this girl. I thought of a million things I could do to tie up those hands. And that mouth.

Because her mouth got her in trouble. *I know what I want to stick in there.*

"Coach?"

A small voice distracted me. Big Al frowned at me and puffed out his chest. *Aw, hell. Kid wants to play.* "Yeah, Big Al?"

"I know we aren't supposed to talk about playing time. But I want to work on my weak areas. My mom said I can stay after, if you can. If you can't, I understand. You're busy." He kicked dirt around and a sour taste entered my throat. I couldn't describe why I had a tug at my heart, but I did. *Weak areas?* God.

"Sure. We can work on some grounders. Your speed is something we can fix."

"Okay." He grinned and ran over to Fiona. She was about the same height as the kid and they shared a co-conspirator smile. *What are they up to?*

The rest of the game remained uneventful, which was good for our first game. We won by a margin of two runs and our pitcher, Kit, earned a win. It was all cheering and smiles after we shook hands with the opposing team. "Sprint to left field. Now. Last one there picks up trash!"

All fifteen kids took off and I fought a grin. I missed when guys had that zest for the game. Like it was the best part of their day and their entire decisions were based on the sport. A wave of nostalgia hit me. I used to be like that. My dad and I would pack a cooler with food for days at a time, and drive hours to different fields. We rocked out to Van Halen and talked strategy. My stomach lurched at the fond memory.

"Guess who's picking up trash?" Fiona hollered at me, pulling me from my momentary trip down Memory Lane. I didn't have time to react before she took off sprinting faster than I would've imagined to left field. She rolled onto the grass, the guys all cheering "CFD!"

I got to the grass and every single one of their hands pointed at me. "What?"

"You're last to the field. You have to pick up trash." Tayler stood and nodded at the rest of his teammates. "It's only fair."

I narrowed my eyes. I gave them my scariest look I saved for game time, but they didn't flinch. *God, teenagers are weird.* "Fair enough. I will today. But next time, we'll see who's last."

They snickered and Fiona joined me at the front. I wanted to flip her off, but the damn kids would see. I filed away the memory to seek revenge on her. Soon. "CFD. What are the positives from today's game?"

"Well, Coach Titan, let's give it up for the bats coming alive!" She clapped so loud, the ring echoed. The kids ate it up and whooped and howled.

"Yeah!

"Heck yeah!"

"One and zero! One and zero!"

"Okay. Yes. Offense was fantastic. What else?" I pointed to Jared, the left fielder. He shrugged and nodded toward Kit.

"Kit threw a hell of a game. Shout out to him."

The team all hit him on the back and he beamed. Fiona ran through a list of cons and what we could work on in pregame the next day and everyone agreed we had to focus on not throwing the ball around when the play was dead.

If we didn't get the original out, there was no sense tossing it around like a tee ball team. Tayler got to call out the end of the game cheer and belted out an "Undefeated" before dismissing for the night. I succumbed to the fact that I had to pick up the trash. It irked me. The players should do it—but I would set an example.

"Excuse me, gentlemen. Rule number one of not being a crappy person. Listen up." Fiona's tone was unlike one I had heard. It had a zap to it and I tensed in response. "All of you are going to pick up trash today. I am not your mother and Titan is certainly not your father. You will pick up and every piece that is left over is one gasser after the game tomorrow. Do you understand?"

Some mumbled, others gave a mere nod. It was the first sign of disrespect and I fumed. "Excuse me? Answer your coach. Do you understand?"

"Yes, sir." More of them mumbled and hustled over to the dugout. I caught up to Fiona in two strides and tried to give her a reassuring look. But she didn't appear to be upset.

"You okay?"

"Yeah. Why wouldn't I be? We won." She quirked her lips and I wanted to bite the hell out of them. *Bruise them. Mark them as mine.* But I did none of those things. "Don't let the kids get you all worked up. They're teenagers."

"They didn't respond to you."

"That's fine. I'll count the pieces of trash and they'll run. The first time is the worst. After that it won't happen again." She bent down and crumbled up an old sunflower seed wrapper. "Trust me. I'm right about some things, you know."

I scoffed and found trash to busy myself with. There were water bottles, protein wrappers and leftover tape from the bat all over the dirt. I couldn't imagine what a mess we made at the stadium. I'd always assumed there was a cleaning crew. But coaching? I hadn't seen this side of it in a good while. My conscience wasn't happy with itself. Each piece of trash felt like a regret I had.

Why did I blow up at a teammate over an error?
Why did I dive for a ball and fuck up my career?
Why do I have to be an asshole all the time?

"Coach. I'm ready for some grounders and it seems like everyone is almost gone." Big Al joined me by the pitcher's mound and, like a snake I couldn't control, I unleashed my self-pity on him.

"Maybe not tonight." I dug my fingernails into my palm. *God. I sucked.*

"Oh." His voice broke and his muffled steps carried farther away from the mound. I counted the ways I was going to hell but stopped. Fiona let out a cackle that no woman should have. I spun around and met Fiona's fiery stare. *She'll kick me in the balls.*

"Why the laughter?"

"Big Al has a great joke. It killed me." She hit her knee and put her hand on Big Al's shoulder. "Tell him. It'll lighten him up."

"Uh, okay. Have you read the book on how to be a great baseball player? It's written by Ben Schwarmer."

Oh. My. God. No. The burn of laugher crept up my throat. I tried to fight it. I did. But it burst out. The joke was so dumb. So bad. But Big Al grinned at me and Fiona gave me a small nod. "Good lord, that was awful."

"But you laughed, Coach."

"You have me there." I met Fiona's eyes and understood the meaning behind them. I rarely communicated with people from just a look—Cheryl being the other person. Her eyes read *work with Big Al or I'll kill you.* "Al, go grab your glove and head to shortstop."

"Yeah?"

"Don't stand there. Hustle out. We'll work on your crouch to throwing position." He didn't wait a second more before sprinting toward the dugout. Fiona let out a slow whistle and I gave her a pointed look. "Where do you think you're going?"

"Home. I have homework."

"Nice try. You're helping, too." I picked up a bat and handed it to her. "You're hitting the grounders. I'll help him with the motions."

"Feeling old today, gramps?" She pointed to my injured leg and my first reaction was to bite her head off. But she just grinned at me and all my fire left.

What was easier—having her joke about my injury or getting sympathy? I despised sympathy. It boiled my blood when people gave me *that* look. So. Her jabs were better. I grinned like a fool at her. "I might need you to carry me home. I'll let you touch my muscles."

"You really are a man for the people." She patted my chest, her fingers remaining a little longer than necessary. It sent a spark down me. "Al. Hustle, little man. I have homework to do."

"Yes, ma'am!"

And we spent twenty minutes working with the kid. He made error after error, but his confidence grew. And confidence was half the battle. "Al, what are you going to work on tomorrow?"

"Not shuffling my feet. It's a jump to pivot. Not two steps."

"Good. I'll make sure we look for it tomorrow. Nice work." I clapped his back and caught Fiona staring at me. I smirked at her. "Yes?"

"You're not a total asshole."

"Why, thanks." I laughed and went to pick up my duffel bag. I thought about asking Fiona for a drink, or coffee or something. But fate had other plans. MILF approached me wearing a sinfully tight dress. *Good lord.* "Hi. Good to see you again."

"You as well," she purred and darted her gaze to Fiona before meeting my eyes. She lowered her voice. "Do you give *private* lessons?"

I chuckled and flicked my gaze to Fiona, but she was gone. No goodbye. Nothing. *Hm.* "Are you wanting lessons for Garth?"

She pursed her lips and giggled. "I was thinking for myself."

Say yes. Say yes. Do it. "My line-up is pretty stacked. Maybe another time, though."

I kicked myself the whole walk to my car. *Why did I turn her offer down?* What the fuck was wrong with me?

Fiona. Fiona is the problem.

Chapter Thirteen

Fiona

"You realize a mimosa can't be considered healthy, right?" I quipped at my sister Bea, who was on her third drink. Amanda — the oldest and most judgmental of us three — turned up her nose and gave me an annoyed look.

"There's orange juice. Orange is a fruit. I'm on my third fruit serving of the day." She sucked the straw into her mouth and flipped off Amanda. I snorted, but let the matter go. Amanda did not.

"It's eleven on a weekday, Bea. When are you going to get a job?"

"I have a job. It's not my fault you don't consider bartending a job," she fired back, but her tone changed to an icier one. It had been a hot topic the past year. She'd started working at a semi-controversial bar where bartenders danced on a stage and hung from rafters. Amanda hated it, our mom despised it, but I thought it was cool as hell.

"Anyway, sister dearest, thanks for inviting us to our bi-yearly sister brunch." I held up my coffee mug to cheer them, but they ignored me and continued their stare-down. I was used to it, being the youngest. They'd had a rough time growing up together and, while I would always love my family, I didn't particularly like them too often.

"You're a shade away from being a stripper. Aren't you embarrassed?"

Great. I love when this conversation happens again. "Amanda—"

She cut me off with a withering stare. "No, this doesn't concern you, Fi. You basically show off your body to get tips, Bea. That's not respectable. You hang from the ceiling. Is that the life you envisioned for yourself?"

"I envisioned a life with Landon, with kids and a house, but that all changed when he had a baby with someone else. So fuck you, Amanda. I make better money than you, can afford a nice studio with it and am just trying to get by. You think you're so perfect with your cute little office job and your cute cheap work outfits—"

"Jade! Hey, girl, come join us!" I shouted at my friend and potential colleague the second she walked into the small café. *Thank god.* I couldn't take my sisters' bickering anymore. Her face lit up when she saw us and she made her way over to our small brunch table, her positive energy desperately needed. "Hey, Fiona, Amanda, Bea. Good to see you all."

My sisters smiled and said the right things, but then they went right back into their stare-down. Jade gave me a questioning look, but I shook it off. "How've you been?"

"I'm about to meet my mom to begin planning the big event this spring, but more importantly, how is he?" She plopped down and grabbed my unused water. "Dish it all."

"How is who?" Bea asked, curiosity replacing anger in her eyes. I had a soft spot for my messy middle sister — we had the same wild soul.

Jade paled and made a face at me. "You didn't tell them, did you?"

"Nope. Thanks for that." I took my time, getting one more drink of coffee before facing my sisters. "I'm coaching with Gideon Titan." I enjoyed the look of shock on their nosey faces. Too often, they gossiped about my life, so it felt great to be the one holding all the secrets.

"What. The. Fuck," Bea said, her voice rising way too loudly. "Holy shit. How? Why? How is he?"

"It's all my doing, I won't lie." Jade popped her red lips and raised an eyebrow. "I heard whispers about his blow-up at a teammate. One of my brothers works for Los Soles and we have the connection. Gideon got in trouble last season and was forced to coach. My brother knows Fiona well and thought they would be evenly matched."

"Wasn't he one of the best players ever?" Bea widened her eyes and a blush crept up her neck. We had the same coloring and ability to blush instantly. It sucked. "Wow."

"Uh, duh," Jade scoffed and shared a look with me. I fought the urge to roll my eyes. Jade knew my relationship with my sisters was rocky, but she sure liked the dramatic flair.

"He is the face of Los Soles. Or he was until he tore his ACL back in June. His recovery has been rough, I've heard. He's an asshole now, but sometimes a rough guy can be great in bed." Jade gave me a pointed look.

The hot tingles started in my cheeks and crept down my neck. Bea continued talking and ignored me, but Jade gasped. "Holy shit."

"What?"

"You-you slept with him." She pointed at me. "You did. I can tell."

"Jade." I shook my head, but now Bea and Amanda had all their attention on me. "Why do you think I slept with him?"

"You're blushing. You've been awful quiet this whole time." She chewed on her nail, the confident expression slipping into uncertainty. *Thank god.* I didn't want to tell them. And I had no idea why.

I had kept two secrets from Jade the entire time I'd known her.

I had many more from my sisters, but the two biggest regrets of my life choked me.

The day Dad had left, he'd accused Mom of stealing money from his wallet. *I did it.*

The second, Justin had died minutes after I'd kicked him out after a fight. His last text to me had been an apology, him stating he loved me no matter what. But I'd responded for him to get the hell out of my life and to leave me alone.

He'd been texting me when he died.

Not a soul knew those two secrets that I had shouldered for most of my life. Sleeping with Gideon Titan would be the third. Was I ashamed? No. Embarrassed? No. Did I regret it? Also no. But something held me back.

"Jade. I would tell you if I did. I don't keep things from you." My words mollified her, but Bea continued to eye me. "Bea. If I slept with him, I would want the world to know. Do you know how good-looking he is, despite the fact he's a raging dickweed?"

"How's working with him going? I can't believe you didn't tell us! I want to meet him," Amanda finally spoke.

"This is why I didn't tell you. He likes his privacy and I'm going to respect that. But he's hot and cold. I'm torn between wanting to jump his bones and strangle him most days." I laughed and froze when the dark eyes I thought about in my dreams appeared just beyond our table. *Oh hell no.* "He's a pain in the ass."

"Why are you shouting—oh!" Jade spun around at my evil grin. "Gideon Titan!"

The devil sauntered over to our table with a deliciously mischievous grin. God. It had been over a week since our fuck, and my body knew he was close. I clenched my legs together and gave a fake-ass smile. "I was *just* talking about you, your eminence."

Jade raised an eyebrow at my nickname, but I ignored her. He ran a hand over his strong jaw and glanced at my lunch mates. "I wondered why you yelled pain in the ass across the room. I assumed you were talking about yourself."

"Nope. That phrase is reserved for you."

"Pity. I prefer it when you call me a hot piece of ass. Not a pain in the ass."

God — is it getting hotter in here?

"Who are these beautiful women?" He put his hand on the back of the empty chair and amped up the charm. *Asshole.* "My, you two have to be Fiona's older, better-looking sisters."

"H-hi. I'm Bea." She held out her hand, her lips too pursed for my liking. Her pink cheeks were a dead giveaway. She had the hots for him. "Nice to meet you."

"And who are you two?" He smiled at Amanda, who blushed beet-red in return. "I'm Gideon."

"Amanda. Nice to m-meet you. Big fan." My older, snobbish sister lost her cool entirely. Bea and I shared an amused look. We would talk about that later.

"Wonderful to meet you," he cooed at her and turned his attention to Jade. His gaze flicked to her nametag. "Jade, a pleasure."

"Stop hitting on them, horn dog," I scoffed.

"Aw. Are you jealous, Barbie?"

"I don't get jealous. I get even," I fired back and humor danced in his eyes. He enjoyed the hell out of this — and I did, too. "Jade is the amazing person to thank for us working together."

"Is that so?" He dragged his heated stare from me to her. Bea had to be the most ball-busting woman I knew, and she remained silent. His looks really were a problem for the female population. *Hell, for the entire population.* "Jade. Pretty name."

"Th-thank you." She held out her hand and he took his time shaking it. "Are you enjoying coaching so far?"

"There have been some challenges." He narrowed his eyes at me before continuing, "But yes. I really enjoy the laminated practice plans."

"Oh, fuck off." I picked up my apple and threw it at him. He caught it with a loud chuckle. "Go look at yourself in a mirror or something."

"Why do that when you're far more entertaining?"

I glanced at my friends. "See what I mean? Pain. In. My. Ass."

"I need to be off. But this was a pleasant surprise. Make sure you bring your precious plans tonight. It's a double header."

"Shit." My stomach dropped. I hadn't realized it was two games and my project loomed over me. "Okay."

"If you want to skip, I wouldn't mind. Send one of them to fill in for you. Maybe they won't wear the goddamn fanny pack." He didn't wait for a reply before walking away.

"Holy shit." Jade fanned herself and shared a look with Bea. "How can you... How does he... Wow."

"I'm so turned on right now," Bea moaned and we all burst into laughter. "Fiona. He has the hots for you. All that sexual tension. *Jesus.*"

"I felt it, too."

"No, he doesn't. That's what we do. We bitch back and forth. When he acts like his injury doesn't hurt, I'll take over. And he'll do little things to help me. Nine times out of ten, I hate the guy."

"But that one time. You guys will totally get it on before this is over. And I want every detail." Jade glanced back at the direction he'd left in and I picked up my tray.

"I need to head out to get a start on my homework. But I'll see you ladies later."

"Say hello to the Greek god for me," Bea purred again and I left the three psychos there. They couldn't know we already had gotten it on and it had been unlike any experience I'd ever had. And now, all that verbal foreplay had me hot for more.

* * * *

They lost. The double header ended badly for our team and the guys sulked. They hung their heads, dragged their feet and didn't handle it well. I wanted to give them time to react. They were teenage boys and they needed to learn how to lose, because losing gracefully is a part of life. But Gideon had his own plan. He ripped them to pieces.

He went over everything they did wrong.

He yelled at them for their attitudes, their giving up.

He made them run foul poles for every error.

Two kids threw up and wanted to quit, but he didn't let them. I fumed. His eyes had a wild look in them and I knew any words would be lost on him. I comforted the kids with the promise of a fun day the next game, but they looked crestfallen.

It wasn't until the last kid had left and we were alone in the park that I turned to Gideon. He paced the dugout with a nervous energy and I'd had enough.

"Hey, asshole. What the fuck were you thinking tonight?"

He shook his head and froze. "What the hell do you mean?"

"You were an asshole to them. I don't want to be one of *those* coaches."

"Then, by all means, don't coach." He snapped his fingers and pointed to the exit. *Cool. We're back at that act, asking me to quit.*

"What the hell is up your ass? They didn't play that bad tonight. The other team was just better." I put my hands on my hips and readied for battle. "I don't appreciate your attitude toward them."

"You don't *appreciate* my attitude? You an expert? Huh? You have years and years' experience dealing with losing in baseball? Please enlighten me, then, *Fiona*."

"I'm not saying I have more experience than you. That would be stupid. But you were a jerk to them. They don't deserve it."

"If they think they can act how they were, they have another think coming. They threw the ball around eight times. They struck out without even swinging, nine times. We had six errors in the infield alone. If they want to be prepared for the harsh reality of baseball, then they need to deal with it. If not, they, along with you, can join another league. I don't play half-assed."

"God," I muttered under my breath and stormed to my car. I was so mad. So damn mad. No one should talk to kids like that. I fisted my hand and threw my bag into the back seat. His heavy steps followed me toward our cars. An ache began in my chest and traveled to the rest of me, as though I wanted to pick a fight. I spun around with fire in my eyes and pointed my finger at him. "What was in their attitudes that was so bad? Explain it to me."

"You wouldn't understand. It's a man's sport." He dismissed me with a flick of his wrist and it set me off. I smacked his hand. I swung my arm back and collided our hands to create a loud smack. The sound echoed off the empty gravel in the parking lot, the darkness of the night surrounding us.

He gasped when my hand hit him. He clasped his fingers around mine, aggressively. He shoved me against the side of my car. My back hit the cool metal as he closed me in. Anger rolled off him in waves and he growled my name. "Fiona."

The way he said my name, everything stopped. It wasn't an invitation, but its meaning was clear. My chest heaved, my pulse raging in my ear. He stepped closer so our hips touched and I felt his hardness. His taut muscles. His temper flared and he slammed his mouth against mine.

I couldn't taste him enough. He tasted too good, too rough. I clawed at his chest, desperate to get him as close as possible. Because I wanted him despite how much I hated him. I wanted his firm body all over me. "God —"

"Shut up," he barked into my ear and brought one of his hands to my neck. He gently clasped around my air pipe, and by god, it turned me the hell on. He slid his large hand down the side of my body, heating me up even more. I nipped at his bottom lip and sucked it into my mouth as hard as I could. He retaliated and I moaned. The mixture of pain and pleasure was too much. "I shouldn't do this."

"I shouldn't want it," I replied, dragging my fingers down his abs and fisting his enormous erection outside his tight pants. "Your magic dick is the only reason."

He stuck his tongue into my mouth again and prevented me from talking. He used his free arm to pick me up. I stopped trying to talk and relished the pleasure coursing through me. He smelled like a perfect mixture of leather and sweat — and I wanted to lick it up. He unlocked the hatch of his Blazer and threw me in, in one swift motion. My back hit the hard surface, but I didn't have time to react. He followed me in and shut the trunk door behind him.

I was about to fuck Gideon Titan in a parking lot. And I was okay with it. "You piss me off so damn much."

"Right back at ya, babe." He slid his hands down my hips and removed my yoga pants within seconds. "God. How soaked is your sweet pussy for me?"

"Take a feel." I readied myself for his fingers to enter me, but he lowered his head instead. I jumped when he brought his tongue down on me, the pleasure almost too much. He licked, sucking all the way from the back to the front. He took my clit between his teeth and bit down. I screamed and he chuckled against me. "Jesus."

"That was for pissing me off."

Deep down, anger flowed through me, but I was too damn turned on to put up much of a fight. I tugged at his shirt and didn't wait before yanking it off. His bare chest glistened in the little light we had. "You're hot as fuck."

"Mm," he replied before running nose between my thighs. He prodded my clit with tongue, teasing and firing me up even more. He rushed, then slowed. Bit then sucked. My core was on fucking fire, and I squirmed for release. But he stopped, licking me from my clit all the way to my mouth. "Suck my tongue. Taste yourself."

And I did. It fueled my fire and I ravaged his mouth. I tasted blood but didn't give a fuck. I needed him inside me five minutes ago. "Get your cock out."

He didn't obey and took his time exploring my mouth. I pushed him off me and tugged his pants. "Please tell me you have a condom. *Please.*"

"Pocket."

"You carry it with you to a baseball game?"

"Are you complaining?" He grinned and ripped it open. "Flip over. I like looking at your ass."

I'd barely made a move before he flipped me. It was such a turn-on. I liked control, but his dominance made me wetter, needier. He took his sweatband from his wrist and wrapped it around my hands. Then, he placed them on the passenger headrest. It left me in a perfectly vulnerable position, and I trembled with need. "Hold on. I'm fucking the shit out of you."

"*Yes*," I moaned and gripped the cool metal bars under the headrest. He spread open my legs, slowly dragging his tongue down to the deepest part of me. I jerked against the restraint and whimpered in anticipation. Then he slammed into me. His cock hit my G-spot within seconds and I rode each wave of pure ecstasy. "Gideon. God."

"Fuck yeah, scream louder," he commanded and gripped my hips like his life depended on it. His balls slapped against my ass, each sound sending me into a tizzy. I needed more pressure on my clit and he wasn't providing it. I tried to move, but I couldn't reach it. "What do you need?"

"My clit. Touch it. Pinch it." I let out a piercing cry when he brought two fingers to the swollen, pounding nub. He flicked and pinched it as he continued to thrust into me and I exploded. I cried out, his cock growing bigger inside me. I arched my back and he groaned the sexiest growl while his entire body tightened with his release. I gripped the metal bars harder and rode him out. The orgasm seemed to echo and bounce around my body, fulfilling every need.

It wasn't a love fuck. It wasn't a pity or a fun fuck. It was pure anger and it was mutual. He slid out of me and the ringing in my ears drowned out the awkwardness of the situation. My entire body hummed with the release, but I wanted to leave. "Gideon. Please undo the band."

"Sure." He reached over me, our bodies touching without the heat of the moment. I tensed and blew out a long breath of relief when I could use my hands. I found my clothes within seconds and avoided his stare. I opened the door and walked to my piece-of-shit car.

Gideon was a beautiful, troubled guy and I'd used him for sex. Again. Something formed in my chest. It wasn't shame, or regret. I couldn't recognize it, but when he stuck his head out of his window and made a douchebag comment, the feeling went away.

"We might've lost the games, but you sure hit a homerun. See you tomorrow, Barbie."

I flipped him the bird and smiled the whole way home.

Chapter Fourteen

Gideon

I hate jazz music. It's supposed to be calming in the doctor's office but it's annoying me. The saxophone didn't ease the discomfort when the doctor made me wait thirty minutes for a checkup. I shouldn't complain entirely — they let me wait in a private room where no one could approach me. I tapped my fingers against my chest and tried to close my eyes. It could be good news. Maybe my knee was healing well. I had followed all the directions and gone to all the physical therapy sessions. But it still hurt and I could barely coach without having constant pain.

Picking up Fiona in the parking lot didn't help. But my cock felt real good about it. Yeah. That *might* have been worth it.

"Gideon Titan?" the nurse called out from the ugly green door. "Come on back."

"Thanks." I nodded to her and tensed when we went to the familiar back room. "How've you been?"

"Fine. Just fine. Doc will be here soon. Have a seat."

I followed directions and prayed it would be a good diagnosis. The surgery had been months ago and I should be fine. But I needed a professional's opinion. Five minutes later, he walked in. "Gideon Titan. How are you, my man?"

"Doing okay. I'm desperate for your insight." I leaned forward in my seat. "Please tell me this'll be good news."

"Let's have a look."

He ran various tests and tested the ligament's ability to stabilize my knee. Putting weight on it, flexibility, balancing, then pressure on the muscle itself. I winced and fought a cry. "You seem to be healing well. No setbacks. Are you doing the recommended exercises and icing?"

"Yes, sir."

"Good. I don't see any issues — are you having a lot of pain?"

"I am. I'm —" I paused, trying to find the right word. "I'm afraid to use it. Put pressure on it. The season doesn't start for a while yet but I'm afraid. I'm worried I won't be ready."

"Gideon. ACL replacement surgery can take up to a year for rehab, or longer for competitive sports." His eyebrows came together and I wanted to smack them off his face. I didn't need his condescending bullshit.

He doesn't get it. I'll be a free agent after this year. I need to play well. Start to finish. "I'll be ready."

He gave a tight grin and bent my leg up and down, applying pressure on the tendon. I cringed. I'd overdone the physical therapy that morning. "How active are you?"

"I'm coaching. Light workouts in the gym."

"Hm. I suggest going back to wearing the Defiance brace, every day. It'll support you if you're on your feet for long periods of time. How long would you say you're on the leg a day?"

"Six hours, give or take."

"Hm. Yeah. Wear a brace and ice in the morning and night. You have pain. I can see your face. Pain is part of the healing process. You're, what…five months from the surgery? You should be able to jog by now if you can handle it. Forward motion only. No pivots or quirk turns just yet. Try to avoid downhill motions to avoid lateral pressure on the joint. Why don't you try a ten-minute jog on a flat surface tomorrow?"

"Sure. I can try." I grunted. I bade him farewell, feeling a little better. I'd been terrified I would have bad news, but instead it wasn't awful. I needed to push myself more. My jaw ached with tension and each time I ground my teeth, a shock of pain went to my forehead. I drove to our game, thinking about every other place I wanted to be. It was just one game against a small team. We should win — and I wanted the guys to have their confidence back.

Fiona's words had ingrained themselves in my mind and replayed all night. Baseball was a game. It would have ups and downs. *Did I react poorly?* No. *Trust yourself.*

I parked in the same spot I always did and looked around for Fiona's car. Despite my sour temper at her annoying positive attitude, her comebacks always made me laugh. Her piece-of-shit car was nowhere to be found. A small twinge of disappointment hit me. I wanted to see her, pester her, annoy her…but no luck. I went through a rotation of stretches to pass the time. I'd barely gotten through ten reps before the obnoxious ringtone Cheryl had set for herself went off. It was an old girl band song and I was grateful no one heard. I would *not* live that down.

"What's up, Cheryl? Everything okay?"

"Yes, worrywart. We are coming by to see the game!" she replied and Quinn's loud squeal carried over the phone. Her high-pitched cry made me wince.

"Hell, yeah." I clapped my hands together and part of the weight on my chest left. "That would be great. You can see the team. We're really something."

"*And* see Fiona."

Cheryl ruined the moment. She didn't know, but was smart enough to pick up that something was there. I remained silent and she spoke over her own question, as she often did. "I want to see my little brother coaching a bunch of teenagers. Of course, Quinn wants to be on the field and scream her little head off."

"This'll be great." I meant it, too. It brought back a wave of memories. *Mom and Dad bringing lunches to games, all four of us spending the day at the ball park, Dad overanalyzing the game with me.* I coughed. "I'll see you when you get here. I need to get ready."

"Sure thing."

She hung up and I kicked the ground for a second. The nostalgia had taken over my mood and the sight of Fiona's car cheered me up. Thoughts of our parents had the power to slay me and right now was not the time.

I studied her as she slammed the bent door shut. Her makeup-free face stood out with her long hair pulled into a ponytail. *God – has she always been this pretty?*

She struggled with her bag from the truck. I moved toward her, planning to help her. *Help her? Why?*

"What's up, Gid?"

"Gid?" I paused and met her eyes. Humor danced in them. "Or did you say Git?"

"Wouldn't you like to know?" She yanked the bag out of my hand and shouldered it. "You're feeling *gentlemanly* today. Did last night mess with you? We can still dislike each other and have a good fuck. Don't feel the need to be nice."

My back went rigid. Surely she didn't mean it? I searched her face for any indication she was trying to guilt me, but I came up empty. "You okay?"

"Yeah. I'm great." She smiled, but it didn't reach her eyes. Something went off in my chest—something resembling concern. I frowned, but fought the urge to ask her a million questions because I had a feeling it wouldn't go well.

"Good."

I followed her toward the dugout and thought about her words again. *Do I really dislike her? No — but she does not like me.* My chest felt heavy and I didn't like it one bit. "How's your day going?"

"Chatty Gid is here. Great."

I might not be the brightest bulb, but I had no idea what I'd done to piss her off. She brushed past me and threw her stuff onto the bench. The same book I'd taken from her weeks ago fell to the side of the bag. The desperate need to find out what was in there took over. It felt like a sneeze—a tickle in the core of my chest. It spread and I cracked my knuckles. I gazed around. She wasn't in sight and I took two steps. I could reach out and see what the—

"What the *hell* are you doing?"

Shit. Shit. I spun around and plastered a smile on my face. It didn't work. If she could shoot fire out of her eyes, I'd be dead. No question. Those frightening eyes bored into me. I wracked my brain for something...anything to get out of trouble. "Uh, well, see...I—"

"You what? You wanted to look to see what's in my stuff? Huh?"

Uh-oh. Her voice cracked. She was either furious or about to cry. I braced myself for both scenarios. But she did neither. I stumbled back two steps and flinched when she threw the book at me.

"Take a look. Laugh your ass off at me. I don't give a shit. I write to my dead best friend. My first and last boyfriend. I'm crazy, right? God." She ran her fingers through her ponytail and pulled on the end. The wild look, I recognized it. Something flipped inside me. "I don't need this shit. Not from *you*."

"Fiona. Please, sit." My calm tone shocked us both. Her lips parted. *To hell with our little game.* I handed her the book and thought about touching her, but pulled back. She sat on the bench and brought her knees to her chest. There was so much fire and passion on her face, but the turmoil hurt to see. "Are you okay?"

"Peachy. Can't you tell?"

"Knock it off. I'm asking as someone who cares." Fuck it—I placed my hand on her knee and took the spot next to her. I left no room between us. She tried to pull away, but I didn't let her. "You want to fight with me? I can take it. You want me to ignore you? Let me know. But something's wrong."

"Why do you care?" Her goddamn lip trembled. It wasn't much, but the small gesture hit me right in the chest.

"Honestly? I normally don't give a shit about others. But with you, I recognize it. The pain, that is." I released a long, pent-up sigh and patted her. "I'm sorry I thought about snooping. I won't cross the line again."

She nodded, ran her hands over her face a couple of times and sat up taller. I admired her strength. Not many women I knew could piece themselves together like that. Hell, even my teammates couldn't. "Thank you for apologizing."

"It won't happen again."

"You said that." She sniffed and I grinned.

"I meant the apologizing. I won't apologize again. That's my apology for the month."

"Oh god. You're serious." She smacked my chest and let out a small chuckle. The rope around my chest loosened. "Gideon, about what I said…"

"Stop." I closed my fingers around her hand. I waited until she met my gaze. "We all have our demons. You don't have to explain anything to me. I shouldn't have pried."

"You don't think that I'm crazy?" She lowered her voice, barely above a whisper. Her left eye twitched a bit and for the life of me, I couldn't figure out why it was so damn cute. I shook my head.

"Nope."

"I don't believe you, but fine. I think I hear the kids anyway." She stood, dusted off her tight black pants and gave me a long look. "Thank you. You could've been a real asshole about it. But you weren't. Let's get a beer after the game. Maybe we can talk about it."

"Sure. We'll take *my* car."

My words were not lost on her and she winked at me. Suddenly, I couldn't wait for the game to be over.

* * * *

"I can't believe you won the game. It was a nail-biter! That play at the end…well done!" Cheryl cheered and patted me on the back. Quinn gazed at the baseball players with an evil grin, the she-devil already planning to charm them for candy, I was sure. I hoisted her up onto my shoulders and faced my sister. Little did she know that *Fiona* had called the play to win the game.

I would rather take ballet lessons with Quinn than admit it. "Thanks, sis."

"Excuse me, did you just take credit for the sacrifice bunt?" Fiona jogged over with fire burning in her eyes. Shocking. She could hear anything from anywhere. "Hi, Cheryl. You must be Quinn!"

"That's me! I'm Quinn." The rascal held out her hand from atop my shoulders, and Fiona took it with a huge smile. "You're pretty. I like your hair."

"Thanks, girlie, I like yours too. It's pretty, like your mom's." Fiona's genuine smile annoyed me—I so rarely saw it pointed in my direction.

Quinn giggled and I rolled my eyes. If the three of them got to gabbing, I would be done for. *Shit.* I needed to get Cheryl on her way out. "Thanks for coming, ladies. I'll walk you to the car."

"No, you don't." Fiona reached out and put her small fingers around my arm. "Explain why you were taking credit for my idea. Sorry, Cheryl. This jerk likes to stir the pot, you know? Takes credit for stuff he doesn't do."

"Ha. Don't I know it. Carry on. I'm curious." Cheryl stopped walking and gave all her attention to Fiona.

Her mouth curved up. *I might as well surrender.* It would be minutes before they would all turn on me.

"Okay. Stop. Fiona had the dumb idea to do a squeeze bunt. It's a girl move in softball. It worked this *one time*. It's not going to win games every time and I would've let Garth hit the winning RBI in."

"He still gets the RBI. He also gets the confidence and they understand how the little plays can make a big difference."

"That's not baseball, Barbie," I scoffed and caught Cheryl eyeing the two of us with a knowing grin. "No one does that in the majors."

"Yeah, well, hate to break it to you, but the chances of them making it that far are slim. It's more about life skills. They're learning how to work together, take chances and how putting pressure on the other team is just as effective as your *holy* homeruns."

"Holy homeruns," I cackled and Quinn joined me with her giggles. "That shit is hilarious."

"Shit!" Quinn yelled and I got the eye from Cheryl. I took her off my shoulders and held her with my non-throwing arm. I had a pretty nasty stare and zeroed in on her.

"What am I going to say, Quinn?"

"I can't use adult words." Her little mouth trembled and I handed her off to her mother. "I'm sorry, Uncle G. It won't happen again."

"Nice try, monkey." I ruffled her hair and met Cheryl's eyes again. "Sorry."

"No, it's not like you're the only one who's said a cuss word. The other day she called me a bitch. She'll learn. Maybe I'll bust out the soap like Mom and Dad used to."

I laughed. "Please film it."

Cheryl gave Fiona a nod and turned to leave. *Finally.* "Fiona, next time you're at the hospital, let me know. We can grab coffee and gossip about old Gid here."

"I'll put it first on my list. I would love to get some dirt on him."

"I'm so glad you two got paired together. I have a feeling it's entertaining."

"It's something, all right," Fiona mumbled and I nudged her with my hip. Cheryl caught on immediately and I shooed her away. I did not need my meddling sister to have any sort of thoughts about us. *Nope. Not one errant thought.* "I'll see you next week, Cheryl."

"Bye, guys. Quinn — say bye."

"Bye!" she shouted and we all laughed. She was such a damn pistol. But after they walked to her car, it left me and Fiona alone. Something buzzed between us. It wasn't pure lust, no. It was something else. An anger, an urge to push the other person further. Who would lose in this game of push and pull? I had no idea. When her clothes were off, I stopped caring.

"How about that drink you suggested?" I slung my arm around her, but she shoved me off. She had been acting weirder than normal, and my attention to it irritated me. I shouldn't have cared.

"You were a bit of an asshole today." She waved at the MILF, who'd lingered. She'd been doing that quite a bit lately and it irked me. I'd already decided not to mess with the kid's mom — I guess I did have some scruples left in me. I wanted to tell Fiona, but I didn't think it would make her proud of me.

"Barbie, stop fighting it. We both know you want to get in my car with me."

Chapter Fifteen

Fiona

How presumptuous he was…and right. I pursed my lips and made the decision to use him entirely for his body, not his personality. I craved the release, the distraction, the chemistry that was hot enough to help me forget. Yeah—I wanted all that in the shape of Gideon Titan.

A shadow of guilt stole over me. *What would Justin think about me now? Would he think I was trash?*

Did he have any idea of the daily struggles I had with emotions…he being one of the reasons? My stomach soured, but then Gideon gave me *that* look and it all went away. He provided the perfect opportunity and there was no chance I would pass him up. I was an opportunist.

"Well, am I right?"

"Goddamn it." I brushed past him toward his beautiful Corvette. It wasn't large enough for what I

141

had in mind, but it could work. "Let's go, piece of meat."

"Is that what I am to you? A piece of sex meat?" He opened the door for me and paused with his face inches away. I tightened my jaw, with my spine standing straight. I jutted my chin out.

"Is your one *feeling* hurt if I say yes? Aren't I just the same to you?"

His eyes crinkled at the sides and he nipped at my ear. "You're frustrating as fuck. Get in."

I couldn't read him at all. He tormented me but smiled at me. His smile, the real one, was dangerous. His cologne mixed with sweat didn't help either. My mouth watered, wanting to taste him. *Stop being a fucking headcase. Justin's death anniversary coming up doesn't give me the right to act psycho.*

"Any ideas where you want to have that drink? I'm assuming it's to take advantage of me and have your way with my meat."

"Don't make meat have that many syllables. It's creepy." I glanced out of the window as he pulled out of the parking lot. Garth's mom still remained — and a small part of me was pleased he'd chosen to leave with me rather than her. "I'm still annoyed at you."

"I can't recall a time when I wasn't annoyed with you. That feeling is definitely mutual." He hummed and tapped his fingers against the wheel with ease. It painted a different picture than most knew of him. And it struck me that I was one of the select few people who got to see Gideon in his private circle. *Huh.* The thought didn't sit well with me. It felt too personal, too *close.*

"You're fancy. You want beer or a cocktail?" *Change the subject. Keep it neutral.*

"Beer sounds good tonight. Especially after that win."

"That I engineered."

"Whatever you say, Barbie."

"Ugh! Give me credit. Why is that hard?" I yelled and got a smirk from him. It infuriated me, the smugness that radiated off him. "You're making me crazy."

"Nah, you're that all on your own." He patted my knee and continued with his dumbass grin. "You realize, Blake wouldn't have been on third if I hadn't called for the hit-and-run the play before, or if I hadn't told Ben to wait for a strike. One play doesn't win a game—it seems a little egocentric of you to think *you* won the game. It was a number of plays to get to the point that yes, the risky call got us the win. But it can't be used again. Teams will talk and play around our small-ball tactic."

Fuck me sideways. His response had merit. My eyes widened and it felt like a ball of cotton in my throat. I would not apologize. I would not eat crow in front of him. I crossed my arms and vowed to remain quiet until we arrived at our destination—and I had no idea where we were going.

"Cat got your tongue, Barbie? I must say, it's a first, seeing you speechless. I prefer to leave my woman speechless after a rough fuck. But this is nice, knowing I'm right."

"God, shut up." *Real mature. Awesome. I sound five.*

He let out a small chuckle and turned the music up louder. At least it was a classic, *Hurt* by Johnny Cash, and I could tune out my angry thoughts. It sort of worked, until he turned into an alley. *Are we going to do it in an alley? Do I want to? Yeah. I do.*

"I'm not taking you here to kill you, if that's what you're thinking. There's a hidden bar here. It's low-key, off the beaten path." He parked and gave me a long look. "What crossed your mind?"

Do I tell him? Yeah. I want to shock him. "I thought you brought me here to fuck me in an alley. I would've let you, too."

Then I left the car with his mouth hanging open. *Score one for me.* Feeling loads better, I waved at him and I went up to the single door with a lone light above it. "Cat got your tongue, hotshot?"

"Careful, Fiona."

I shivered at his tone. It was a threat and a promise all wrapped up in two delicious words. He snuck his hand under my shirt in the back and slipped it into the waistline of my pants. I froze. Just as the bouncer opened the door, Gideon had palmed my ass.

"Head on in. You're good. Nice to see you, GT."

"You too," he replied and pushed me ahead. His hand somehow remained on me the entire time. I was hot enough to explode. I closed my eyes in pure ecstasy when he ran his tongue over the back of my ear. "I'll take an IPA. You get drinks, I'll find us a back booth."

Then he pinched my ass and I jumped. The dirty dog. I bought us two beers and chugged about half of mine before finding him. He wasn't kidding — the semicircle booth was in the back with little light and away from everyone. It was shaped like a half-moon, leaving one small bench for us to sit. I slid in right next to him, not pretending that I didn't know what was coming. My thoughts went haywire as my pussy throbbed.

I set the beers on the table. Gideon's eyes lit up. "I have an idea. You game?"

"Depends on what it is." He pulled me closer and bit down on my lip. I winced but he just winked at me.

"That was for your mouth always getting me hard." He licked his lips and moisture pooled uncomfortably between my legs. "Are you turned on right now?"

"God, yes."

"Good. Here's what's going to happen. I'm going to ask you some questions. You answer and I'll provide you with the relief you need. If you refuse, then I can make it real hard and unpleasant for you."

I tensed in need. I nodded. "Wh-why do you want to ask me questions?"

"I want to know more about you, Barbie. That simple. Now, scoot closer to me and pull your pants down enough in the front I can slip my fingers inside you," he commanded in such a sweet, domineering tone I wouldn't dare disobey. I obliged and moaned when two large fingers slid into me. "Good god. Is that wetness all for me?"

"Yes," I groaned. He brought them in and out, not as good as his huge cock but enough for me to get the tingling need. I rocked against him, but he stopped me.

"Question first." He rubbed my clit real slow with his thumb and kept his face neutral. "What was wrong today?"

"Hangry. That's all," I lied so quickly, as though it was second nature. "Finger-fuck me, Gid."

"Nice try." He slid his fingers out and brought them to his mouth. I gasped and a strong lust took over. I lunged for him, but he held me back. "You taste like heaven. But you lied to me. Not part of the game."

"Your game sucks," I whined and squirmed in my seat. I couldn't recall a single time I'd been this fucking horny. "I'm dying inside. Let's leave."

"Good. It'll be that much sweeter when you come all over my fingers. If you answer me. Are you ready to try again?" He hummed and leaned over. He pressed an aggressive kiss on me, my salty taste turning me on. "Answer me."

He stroked the insides of my walls and my eyes began to roll back. He said my name, stronger this time, and I stopped caring. "Tomorrow is Justin's death anniversary. I-I have a hard time with it."

"Good girl," he said in a gruff tone. He quickened his pressure on my clit and lifted me so the pressure was just right. My core tightened at the closeness of the explosion and he brought his other hand behind my neck. Everything combined into one — the questions, the public finger-fuck I was getting and his mouth coming down hard on me. I burst like a fucking firework in the middle of a speakeasy bar. He swallowed my cries with a rough kiss. My lips would be bruised, but I relished the invasion of my mouth. For a brief second, nothing else mattered except how we were connected. I rode out each wave of pleasure and when I landed back on earth, his grin was the size of a damn dinner plate.

"Holy shit." I panted and leaned back in the seat. "Did — did anyone see us?"

"Don't know, don't care." He hadn't removed his fingers from inside me and he massaged me in the gentlest way. "Thank you for answering."

"You left me no choice." I laughed, my eyes watering from the strength of the orgasm. "I'm pretty sure I left the earth for a second."

"Good. I have more of that." He used his free hand to take a long sip of beer. "I'll wait until the next one. But I'm not removing my fingers."

"Oh, okay." I mirrored him and took a huge swig of the amber ale. I was about to say something when a waiter appeared right in front of us. He smiled at us, but with no hidden meaning. *Thank you, baby Jesus.*

"Hi, folks. Want any food tonight?"

"I think I'm good. You, Fiona? You need something to *fill* your appetite?" His wild eyes danced at me and my face turned ten degrees darker red.

"I'm g-good." I tried to clench my legs together, but he didn't let me. He kept his strong hand right there. He even began to swirl his fingers inside me while the waiter continued talking about something. I couldn't concentrate. *Fuck.* I couldn't do much besides focus on not making noises.

Gideon said something to get him to leave, then scooted closer again. "How did that feel, Barbie? Knowing I was finger-fucking you when he stood right there watching?"

"*Ohmigod.*" I moaned as the sensation in my lower stomach began building again. "Fuck."

"I have another question for you." He kept moving and pinched down on my swollen, painful clit. "Why do you use sex as an escape?"

"Why does anyone? To avoid feelings and for pleasure," I moaned and tried to keep my eyes open. He didn't accept my answer and pulled out. I wanted to hit him for the loss of contact. "Why do you? Same reason."

"I doubt that." He lowered his hooded gaze and a warning bell went off. But my hormones took precedence and I didn't dig further. "Have you had a relationship since...you know?"

"Have *you*?" I fired back. The game had changed and become real. The moment of ecstasy evaporated and anger replaced it.

"Yes, but this isn't about me. It's about your throbbing cunt." His hooded eyes assessed me with a little too much understanding. My entire body clenched and I made a move to go, but he pulled me back with no effort. "Are you running away from me when you're shaking with need?"

"I-I'm not running," I seethed. I needed to find balance. He had too much control and I wouldn't stand for that. *Make him thirsty for me. Make him lose control. Yes!* "I am shaking with need. You're right. Care to visit the ladies' room with me?"

His eyes twinkled with malice. He didn't wait two seconds before sliding out of the booth. He reeked of cockiness and determination. But I didn't miss his pupils dilating. Someone was horny. I took his hand and dragged him to the individual bathroom I'd passed earlier—yeah, this wasn't my first time in a public bathroom. I liked my sex dirty and quick. *Sue me.* "Lock the door."

"I think I'll keep it unlocked," he growled and slammed it behind him. I spun around and stripped off my shirt within seconds. "Unless you're too chicken?"

I laughed, the throaty sound a little sexy. *Note to self— my horny laugh sounds awesome.* "Suit yourself, Gideon. I'm not the one who's worried about my photograph being leaked."

"A challenge?" His eyebrows rose and he stalked me like prey. "Let's see what you got, Fiona. I'm all yours to play with."

I took in my surroundings—toilet, sink, counter. None were ideal for what I wanted to do and I sucked in my lip. "Hmm."

"I knew it. You're all talk," he scoffed and took a step toward the door. I gasped and threw myself at him.

Hell to the no—I would not let Gideon get the last word.

"Don't you fucking leave." I slid my hands down his body and lifted the ends of his tight Under Armour shirt. It had to go. It got caught on his broad shoulders so I added extra effort. I admired his sculpted back muscles. They were glorious—tan, defined and moving in all sorts of ways as I ran my nail down his spine. "One thing you should know about me, Gideon. I never go back on my word."

"Yeah?"

He tried to turn around, but I stopped him. Sure, he outweighed me, but he respected my move. "Oh yeah. Now, are you sure you want the door unlocked when I do this?"

I reached around his waist and straight into his tight waistband. The athletic shorts looked so good on him, but with his growing erection, they became too tight. His gigantic cock burst out of the waistband like a free man and I gripped it. I pumped it a couple of times, his wetness almost enough. "God, I want to taste your cock so bad."

"Do it," he grunted. One hand held him up on the wall, the other reaching for me. "Put that filthy mouth on my dick and suck me off. It'd put your mouth to good use."

Yes, it would. I moved him and pushed his back against the brick wall. I had never felt so free in my life. The unlocked door, the pure, animalistic look in his eyes. Fuck feelings. This was sexual. I ran my tongue up and down his length and enjoyed the way he bucked under me. My Adonis co-coach fisted my hair, pulling it to the point my eyes stung. But I savored it. I hummed against his shaft and closed my lips around the bulging head. I gently brought my teeth to his sensitive skin and he jumped, his cock touching the back of my throat at the motion.

"Christ—Christ almighty. You deep-throated me." His strangled voice was music to my ears. Yup. He was thirsty for me all right.

"No gag reflex," I managed between breaths. I did it again, the tip going deeper into my me and his salty, musky scent driving me wild. A cold sweat broke out on his thighs and I knew he was close. I took him harder and as something like a growl came from him, I slowed down.

"Wh-what?"

"Now, Gideon, I'm going to ask you some questions. Answer honestly to get the release you so desperately need." I giggled and took a step back. His mouth hung open, his wild eyes blinking rapidly. "Why do you use sex as an escape?"

"Feels good. Now suck." He reached for me, but I dodged.

"Wrong answer." I ran my finger down his chest and took a couple of steps back. "Do you want to put your raging cock inside me right now? Do you want to pound me into this wall so hard I get bruises on my back?"

"*Fuck.* Yes. Come here." He picked me up, using one hand to remove my yoga pants and panties in one swift motion. He shoved me against the wall, supporting all my weight, but I held up a finger.

"Give me the answer I want."

His gaze met mine. His hard, ice-cold gaze devoured me and he didn't wait before slipping inside me. I arched my back and screamed in pleasure. "Gid!"

"I'm answering you. This. This fucking." He grunted and plunged into me harder than before. He held my entire weight and the pressure built around my G-spot within seconds. My silken walls had him going deeper and farther—tears burst down my cheeks and I swore he would split me in two. I forgot about our game. I forgot about Justin and crumbled around him as he spilled into me. He held me up, both of our heartbeats racing. I refused to look at him. This was raw. But he gently set me back on the ground and lifted my chin toward him.

"This is worth escaping reality for. It helps with the guilt, doesn't it?" His voice was low and soft. He pressed the lightest of kisses on my forehead before putting his clothes back on. I blinked a couple of times and cleared my throat. Gideon Titan had me all sorts of messed up.

Chapter Sixteen

Gideon

Meet me tomorrow, nine sharp.

I reread the text from my coach and my lungs constricted. This couldn't be good. My neck stiffened and I rubbed my face. I wouldn't be able to eat anything before then. I settled for chugging a large glass of water and watching the clock. *What does he want? Am I off the roster? Fuck. Fuck. I deserve to be.*

I'd yelled at a veteran for making a mistake.

I'd cussed out anyone who helped me.

I'd almost thrown away my career out of pain and desperation — if he wanted to chat, it couldn't be good. *Is this when he releases me? Tells me I'm traded or moving down to the minors?*

I was a goddamn asshole. I pinched the bridge of my nose and stared at the calendar, my lack of life exhibited on the bright white square. Cheryl had bought it for me to keep my life organized. It was a fucking joke. The blank date stared back at me — an off-day. No practice, no games, no Fiona. There was a list of about twenty things I needed to do. But I did nothing. My chest lurched at the thought of calling my parents and realizing I couldn't. Cheryl had work, Quinn had school… I had no one.

I checked the time again and felt stir-crazy. It was worse than before, only I knew someone who shared that feeling. I texted her instantly. Fuck if I came off needy — she was needy when she was naked. I grinned, my mood suddenly lifted.

Gideon: Want to bike for a while? Feeling crazy today.

Fiona: Not today.

I tensed. She didn't insult me or make a sexual innuendo. *Uh-oh.*

Gideon: Everything good?

Fiona: Yeah. I'll see you tomorrow.

I frowned. Something didn't sit right. I couldn't place it. I stared at the calendar and racked my brain for what was bothering me. What was off? I couldn't figure it out and spent the next two hours answering emails. My agent's message caught my attention. I called him.

"Billy, how's it going?"

"Good, my guy. How's the leg?" His cheery tone pleased me. He at least still liked me. *God, get a grip. He makes bank from me.*

"Better. I jogged for thirty minutes this morning. I feel like an old fuck, but I can use it. Resistance bands start next week," I replied with dread. I did not want the bands. "I saw your email—"

"Good. I'm assuming you're willing to get involved more? Christmas shopping for some kids, a food drive for some shelters, and...well, would you allow cameras at your practice? I would hate to miss an opportunity to get you doing something good on camera."

"No." I snapped the pen into two pieces in my hand. "No. Not that."

"Alrighty then. No to that." He let out a nervous chuckle and continued, "The media didn't paint a pretty picture of you and I'm trying to clean it up."

"I didn't cuss out an old lady or anything. Nor did I do drugs or get caught in a sex scandal."

But I did fuck Fiona without locking the door last night. Last night, our torturous game of give and take...the questions. My brain hurt piecing it together and Billy interrupted my thoughts.

"I know, man. It's not fair. Listen, have you reached out to the guys?"

My stomach sank. "No."

"Give them a call. Go somewhere public. Hell, go to a bar down by the stadium. It couldn't hurt. Post a picture or something."

Great advice, Billy. Why do I pay you again? I held my comments in and coughed. "Sure. I'll reach out even though no one on the team reached out to me."

And that was the final piece. The straw that broke the camel's back. They didn't have my back, and I didn't reciprocate.

"I get it, man. But I think we'd both agree if you reached out and hooked up with a charity it would improve your image. Small steps, then the season will be here again."

"Charity!" I shouted and tuned out his ramblings. "*Yes*. That's it," I cheered as it came back. *Today is the anniversary of Justin's death. That's why she's upset.* "Look, I gotta run. Sign me up for whatever you think, but no fucking cameras on the field. Deal?"

"Sure, man."

I hung up and hopped into the shower. Fiona acted tough but the small pieces I'd learned about her told me the truth. Justin had meant a lot to her—more than people had realized. Her tortured expression when I found out about the journal…the sadness that radiated off her. Yeah. She was probably a mess.

Just like when Cheryl and I get together on the anniversary of the accident. I sighed. I wanted to do something to help her, but I had no idea what.

Gideon: I know what today is. Dinner?

Fiona: Nah.

Gideon: Can I help in any way?

Fiona: No. Even your body can't distract me today.

She always made it about sex. For once, it was the furthest thing from my mind.

Gideon: Well, if you need me, let me know. I'm sorry.

Fiona: Thanks.

Well, there went my attempt. *Reach out to the guys…* *Who even lives in town?* Most of the team lived elsewhere and came back once spring training started. I didn't do this friendship-bonding stuff. My profile wasn't that complicated — sometimes I was a dick, sometimes I wasn't. I guess this was one of the *not* times.

I focused on baseball and my sister. That was it. I didn't need the extra bullshit of relationships. They added stress and drama. *Look how far that got me.* "Shit."

I scrolled through my phone and found Tate's number. Tate Monaghan, MVP in the National League a decade ago. Great clubhouse guy yet a real pain in the ass who was losing speed on the field. Did I want to reach out? No. But I had nothing to fucking do for twenty-four hours and I didn't know how to occupy my time. Yeah — I was bored. That was why I asked him to meet at a swanky bar downtown. It had nothing to do with guilt that *maybe* I'd acted out, yelling at him all those weeks ago.

* * * *

I watched the front door for Tate to enter and my palms moistened. I wasn't fucking fourteen and asking a girl out, yet I sweated like an idiot. There was a shift in my self-confidence and it didn't sit well with me. Cheryl would be proud I was having a *moment* but I began counting down the seconds until it was over. Hell, if he didn't arrive in ten minutes, I was gone.

Shit. He strode in and found me immediately. *Here goes nothing.* "Tate. What can I buy ya?"

"Guinness." He waved at the bartender and took the bench across from me. "I gotta say, you surprised me."

"Shit, I surprised myself." I laughed and he joined in. I relaxed into the booth when he shook his head at me. "Not quite sure what got into me."

"Probably pulled your head out of your ass. It was shoved in there pretty far. Might've taken a couple of people to get it out." His eyebrow rose, daring me to argue. But I didn't.

"It was about time." I held up my beer to him. "It's long overdue. I'm sorry."

"Accepted. All you had to do was buy me a beer." He clicked his tongue. "This game is fickle. The cameras catch the wrong facial expression, wrong string of cuss words—there's a world of trouble. It was the wrong place, wrong time for you."

"I shouldn't have undermined your experience. That was foolish and inappropriate. However—"

"You were in the right to call me out. I made a bonehead play." He shrugged and took a long swig. Laugh lines crinkled on the sides of his eyes and gray peeked out of his beard. Tate had been around and knew the game more than anyone. Shame consumed me. Again. "After it, I think a couple of things happened."

"Yeah?" I leaned forward. There was no hidden anger or malice in his tone. "What's that?"

"The camera caught your insults. That spread into the social media shit-storm and when that happens, Coach had to defend me. That automatically put people against you. Some young hotshot who tore his ACL ripping into a vet? Media doesn't like that. Then the media shit-storm hit. Third, you sort of disappeared into physical therapy. We were still in season and never got to hammer it out like normal guys. I've been waiting for you to reach out and, damn, I'm glad you did."

"We good?" I held out my hand and he took it. Words couldn't describe my relief. Pounds of stress and pressure left my chest. The rock I'd carried around in there disappeared.

"Yeah. Now, tell me about this coaching gig I've heard about. You're paired up with some blonde, eh?"

"Ha — it's a goddamn story, I tell you," I let out a whistle and paused when a familiar laugh echoed across the bar. I froze. *Fiona.* "Excuse me a moment, would you?"

"Sure."

I followed her laugh and found her cuddled up next to some guy who had his arm around her. Her eyes were too bright, her cheeks too red. She snorted and my blood turned cold. Ice-cold. My pulse elevated and my face twitched. *Fiona is drunk.*

"Fiona," I yelled. She jumped, slamming her head against the back of the booth. Her wounded expression didn't fool me. I eyed the guy next to her with the meanest look I had. He cringed and began moving. "Leave."

"Giiiideon. Who are you to s'tell him what s'to do?" Her slurred words felt like knives in the chest.

"You're drunk." I couldn't sit still. My fingers twitched to hit something.

"Ten points s'to you." She held up her fingers and giggled at them. My jaw hurt and I grabbed her hand. She jerked out of reach with wide eyes.

"I'll take you home."

"No. I'm on a date." She crossed her arms and swayed in her seat. "Wait. You scared him off. Asshole."

"Did you even know that guy, Fiona? Tell me." I leaned over the table so our faces were inches apart. Her breath came out in pants. Her neck tinged red. I was beyond furious. "Were you going to let him take you home? Hm?"

"I don't know. Maybe. Maybe not." She pointed at me. "Not your business."

"Hell." Adrenaline coursed through my body and I was torn between getting the fuck out of there or claiming her. *How dare she sleep with someone after what we did the night before?*

Wait—did I care? Yeah. Yeah, I did. That was the problem. *She won't remember this anyway.* I glanced back at Tate and sighed. "Fiona, I need to say goodbye to a friend, then can I please take you home?"

"Friend? You?" She let out a sound resembling a laugh, but it was more like a snarl. "The asshole has a friend. Good."

My chest tightened. Her words hurt more than they should have. I took a long breath, found Tate and explained something had come up. He didn't mind at all and left with a promise to come watch a game. That left Fiona. The annoying, insane sex-crazed partner I'd grown attached to. Shit—I needed to pull myself together. She was drunk. It was Justin's death anniversary. And I was a piece of ass to her. I might be upset with her, but her anger toward me was misplaced. *Kind of like I did to my teammates.* I nodded to myself. I could take her anger.

"Ready to go?" I held out my hand and waited. It took a full minute before she accepted it. Seeing her in tight jeans and a low-cut shirt threw me off—she had a killer body, but I wasn't used to seeing her in regular clothes.

A stab of jealousy came and went. Her safety was my focus. "There we go. Did you drive here?"

"Nope. Rode with Seth from class." She leaned into me and her perfume sent waves of desire through me. It didn't block out the smell of alcohol, though. She was sloshed.

"Good, I can take you back without worrying about the car." I opened the door for her and helped her inside. She was so petite yet hell on wheels. If she didn't piss me off so much, I'd even say cute. But right now, I focused on getting home without her getting sick. "I'll open the windows. Tell me if you need to stop, okay?"

"Why are you being so nice to me?" Her words were small. It was the first time venom hadn't laced each syllable. They were soft and my heart broke.

"Because you're having a shit day. I get those, too. I told you—I wanted to help. Here I am." I patted her knee and asked where she lived. She didn't respond and I prompted her again.

"Uh, well. On Oakland. Number 8380. But...never mind."

"What is it, Barbie?"

"My roommate's working tonight and I don't want to be alone." Her words stuttered at the end and I reached out to hold her hand. Something pained my chest again and I embraced her.

"Want me to stay over? I can sleep on the couch."

"My place is so small. We're different worlds. You're you...and I'm me."

I had no fucking idea what she was implying. "Come again?"

"You have a palace." She hiccupped. "I have a shack. I don't want you to make fun of me."

"Why the hell would I?" Her question baffled me. She didn't answer and I made my way to her place. I'd have been lying if I said her words didn't hurt. I wouldn't judge a person's wealth by items. Shit—she worked hard as hell. "Fiona. Can I stay at your place?"

"Sure. I don't know why you'd want to. I'm not good. I'm not a good person to be around." She hiccupped again. "I'm a black widow."

"The hot superhero lady?"

"*No.* Gid," she scoffed like I was dumb. "I was mean to you."

"You're always mean to me." I added a wink but she didn't react. She simply stared at me with big baby-blue eyes. "It's part of the fun."

"I'll never have what I *used* to have. It's why I drank so much with Seth." She leaned against the door and I couldn't follow her thoughts to save my life. "You make my life a little less lonely. You know?"

"I do."

"It doesn't matter, though. They all leave. They always do. I deserve it." Then she passed out.

'You make my life a little less lonely.' God—they weren't a declaration of love, but her words resonated with me. *Shit.* I glanced at her and approached her place. She made my life a hell of a lot less lonely. She took up most of my thoughts. *'They all leave.'*

Who's they?

"Fiona, we're here." I ran my fingers down her face, but she didn't budge. I chuckled. She had a little drool forming. My leg strained a bit from the night before, but I hoisted her up and carried her to the door. I had no idea where the key was. I searched her pockets, but nada. I set her down and she finally came to. "I need the key, sweetheart."

"Gideon." She wrapped her arms around me and something fluttered in my chest. She felt like home. She said my name like a poem and I wanted to keep it. I ran my hands up and down her back and held her against me. "Am I dreaming?"

"Nope. But I'm glad to know I star in your dreams." I pulled back and gazed at her. This was a new version. Vulnerable. Sweet. I couldn't help myself. I pressed a kiss against her lips. They were warm and inviting, but I stopped it. "Do you have your keys, hon?"

"Y-yeah." She fumbled in her purse and pulled out a ridiculous keychain. I recognized the TTL logo immediately. I helped her with the door and took in her home. It fit her. Chic, organized and welcoming. Okay, she wasn't welcoming, but her home was.

"Nice place." I looked at the photos and stopped at a picture of her and Justin. She had to be fourteen…such a baby. "What do you remember most about him?"

She sniffed and I found her with tears down her face. "His promises he never kept."

"Ah, Fiona." I gulped and felt sucker-punched. "Try and focus —"

"We fought the day he died. I was jealous about some girl he worked with. He told me I was crazy. I told him to leave. He fucking lied about working late with her. I screamed at him, Gid. Screamed. I threw him out in tears and he texted me to apologize and I refused. I did this. I caused him to die." She sobbed and wrapped her arms around herself. "I shouldn't have kicked him out mad. I shouldn't have texted him. It's my fault. All mine. *Jesus.*"

Words left me. I hurt for her. I would do anything to take it away. I wrapped my arms around her and comforted her the best I could. She shook against me and I cradled her head. "Shh. You're okay."

"No. I'm not. I didn't want to feel anything today because it all comes back. I caused my dad to leave us and Justin. The first man in my life who I'd loved left without a backward glance. He has a new family now, new daughters. Then, my first and last boyfriend died because of me."

She broke down again and I carried her to bed. I should've gone to the couch, but I didn't. I should've left her alone to heal, but I didn't. I pressed her body against mine and shielded her from the world, even if just for one night.

Chapter Seventeen

Fiona

I woke up too warm. My body was on fire and I was stuck. I pushed and a groan had me sitting up. Last night came back in blurs. *Bar. Justin. Seth. Gideon. Breakdown.* A tall glass of water stood on the nightstand and I chugged it. Regret and shame filled me, the familiar sense of dread pulling me under. My clock read seven on the dot—no chance to sleep through this massive headache. My throat dried up when I thought about what I'd done, what I'd said.

"Morning," Gideon grumbled and I didn't have a choice. I had to face him. I squeezed my eyes shut, but he ran his fingers gently over my neck. "How are you feeling?"

"Humiliated. Not wanting to look at you."

"Tough shit." He shuffled and twisted me around. His sleepy grin was a hell of a sight. I couldn't recall the last time I'd woken up with a guy. I *always* left and they never stayed with *me*. "You look better. Sleep well?"

"I tend to sleep off hangovers." I swallowed down the ball in my throat, but it didn't help the pain. I didn't know where to begin the conversation. It was probably best if I moved across the country and never spoke to him again.

"Lucky you. I don't often drink, but when I do, it takes me two days to recover. I'm not even that old."

I attempted to smile, but it came out too forced. I might be stubborn, but I knew when I'd fucked up. I had more fuckups than most and my tongue felt like sandpaper. "Words aren't enough, but I'll try. I'm sorry for what you saw, what I did. You didn't deserve any of that."

"You should have called me."

I froze. *Why? Why would I call him, my fuckbuddy? My co-coach?* "Uh, no offense, but why?"

He groaned and pushed himself up onto his elbows. Our bodies didn't touch, but my bed had never felt smaller. "You're not the only person who's been through some shit."

I stared at him. What did I really know about him? I knew he had a sister, a niece and he played baseball. I knew he'd gotten injured, been forced to coach with a loser like me and that he liked nice cars and fucking.

He was also stubborn, frustrating, annoying, mean and controlling.

But he was also patient and kind, especially when he promised to apologize to the team. My chest felt like a fist was squeezing it and I picked at the edge of my shirt. It had a loose string on the end and I pulled on it. Gideon shifted again and lowered his voice. "My parents died in a terrible car accident on the way to pick

Cheryl and me up from a party back when I was barely in the minors. We were drunk and didn't have money for a cab. We, uh, didn't realize my dad was stressed at work and wasn't sleeping. Or that my mom had had a glass of wine herself. It happened six years ago, but sometimes I still pick up the phone and want to call them."

His voice broke. The cracked syllable changed my entire perspective of him. It was all I could do to not stare open-mouthed at him. Pain spread through me. This time, it wasn't my own. *When Justin and I were laughing, worrying about trivial teenager shit, Gideon lost both his parents.* I clasped my fingers around his arm and he continued. "It was one of the most horrific nights of my life. I...I remember the call. The sound of Cheryl's screams. The look in the officer's eyes. The guilt is indescribable. Rationally, we didn't crash into our parents, but we're the reason they drove. So, don't apologize. I get it."

"I had no idea..." I continued to grip his arm. "I'm sorry. I would say it's not your fault, but the words are wasted. I told you something no one else knows last night."

"What's that?"

"How Justin died. Texting me." My jaw strained again and I glanced at the picture of him on the wall. "I made him leave when he was distracted and shouldn't have been driving. No one knows, Gideon. No one. Not my sisters. Not his mom."

"That's a long time to be carrying a secret around." His brought his fingers down to my face again and ran the tip of one over my cheek. "I know you don't trust me, but what happened stays here."

"Thank you." I closed my eyes. "I'm embarrassed, though. I drank too much. I rarely drink more than one or two—it was harder this year. The charity gave me purpose, but it opened up all the emotions I pushed down. I'm supposed to decide if I want to work there by the New Year. I have no idea if I want to. God. I'm rambling. Sorry."

"No, don't worry." He rubbed my shoulder and I swore he was about to kiss me. But that wouldn't have made sense. We didn't do that. We had sex or annoyed each other. The comforting was new territory and it scared the shit out of me. "*Fiona*. You have that line between your eyebrows. Spill it."

"You're being nice to me. It's weird as fuck." I stood and cringed at my reflection. Jesus, I had raccoon eyes. I wiped under them and met his gaze in the mirror. "We fuck. I prefer that."

"Okay. Blunt, but okay." He ran his tongue over his bottom lip with a half-smile. "We need to get a couple things straight. You listening?"

"Yeah? Are you going to lecture me?" I crossed my arms. The glint in his eyes was back. *Finally*. Back to normal. "If so, save it. I can take care of myself."

He rolled his eyes and ignored me. "I don't share. We're fuckbuddies but you're mine."

I shivered at the intensity of his words and the color of his eyes. They darkened and I squirmed. Maybe my clothes should come off... *Wait*. "I don't do relationships."

"Did I say I wanted one?"

My heart beat faster. "No."

"Then don't make it into a big deal. I expect you to sleep *only* with me. Can you manage that?" He raised an eyebrow with a challenge in his eyes. I couldn't resist that jawline. I nodded. "Good. No more *fucking* Seths."

I blushed again at the memory. "I had a class with him and, uh, he asked me for a drink. I wasn't in my right mind."

"Would you have slept with him?" His tone dropped low. Too low. Nerves took over. "Was the night before not enough for you?"

"No. That night, no. I wouldn't have slept with him. I enjoyed the attention, that's all," I mumbled and avoided his stare. "He was a distraction, Gid. That's all."

"I haven't slept with anyone else since that motorcycle ride. Not when I have to see your cute ass every goddamn day. Can't get your body out of my mind."

This. I could do this. *Sex. Attraction. Heat.* "Good."

"Next time you need attention, call me."

I nodded, but he deepened his voice. "Promise me."

"Sure, yeah." *No chance that's happening.*

"I have to go meet my coach, but I'll see you later, yeah?"

"Two games tonight. You going to let me make the starting line-up?"

"No chance in hell, Barbie." He stood. I didn't know how to handle this. *What is the protocol for a sleepover?* Did I offer breakfast? I sure as hell didn't want to. I needed to digest everything that had happened. Without him.

"I'll, uh, walk you out."

He stopped at the door and cupped my face. He didn't kiss me, but his tender gaze felt more intimate than one. I blinked back emotions I didn't want to have and called my sister the second the door shut.

"SOS. Brunch. Lunch. Snack. I don't care."

"Morning to you, too. Don't you have classes today?" Bea's chipper voice made me feel better.

"In two hours. I need your advice. Help. Anything." I paced my room and searched for my favorite sweatshirt. It was one of Justin's cross-country team. *God, I'm a mess. Why am I wearing this years later?*

"Fiona? Did you hear me?"

"Sorry, what?" I kicked the clothing across the room.

"There's a burrito place downtown. Join me. This is related to Justin, right? And not with the gorgeous grump you coach with?" I swore I heard her smile through the phone. The obnoxious twat.

"*Obviously*. When can you be there?"

"Fifteen minutes?"

"Good. Don't bring Amanda. This is the cool sisters' shit."

"I love our cool *sister* shit." Then she hung up.

I raced to my car and tapped my fingers against the wheel. Sure—I enjoyed sex with Gideon. He was dynamite. It was safe to say the best ever, but my small excuse of a heart had no room for emotions. It was sewn up, shut tight and locked.

Then why did my brain hurt from thinking?

Why did my chest constrict at how nice Gideon had been?

Why did I—*no*. I didn't want more. Justin took up too much room. "Gah!"

I slammed my fist against the wheel and blared the horn. I got some angry stares and sped off. Bea would understand. She would know what to do. If she didn't, she always gave solid advice.

She'd barely had a sip of her coffee before I told her everything. She nodded as I went through the past four weeks. I told her all except the secrets I'd shared with Gideon. No one would know that I'd driven my dad to leave and Justin to his death.

Then Bea smirked.

"Why the fuck are you smiling? I'm stressing out." I pulled on the end of my hair, enhancing the slight dehydration headache I had.

"I *knew* you slept with him."

"That's what you're focusing on right now? You suck." I threw a wrapper at her and she chuckled.

"How is he?" An annoying glint came into her eyes.

"Bea!"

"Fine. You better tell me later." She smoothed the napkin in front of her and gave me an inquisitive stare. "I think you need to let Justin go."

"Go?" Anger roared through me. "Why would I forget about my best friend? I can't let him go. I won't let him go," I argued, without taking a second to breathe or digest her words. I just snapped.

"Get it out. This is good." She clasped her hands and had a calm look on her face. It annoyed me. I wanted to act out, yell at her, maybe punch her. But she just waited with the patience of a saint.

I was a lucky bitch to have her as my sister. Our mom always told us having a sister was the greatest gift on earth—and it hit me square in the face. When Bea spilled coffee on her blouse and let out a cuss word, I had an epiphany. Bea had never hurt me. She had never used my feelings against me or pushed me away. Amanda was like a second mother with our age difference, but Bea was my true sister.

"I love you, Bea."

Her eyes widened to the point that white appeared all around her irises. *Have I told her that with sincerity before?* "Love you too, sis. Random, but appreciated."

"I still haven't forgiven you for wearing my one slutty dress and ruining it. But you're a damn good friend and I forgot. I've been in a weird bubble and distanced myself from…everyone during this independence kick. I realized I don't need to do that."

"That dress was the size of a scarf. No teenager should've worn that."

"False. It was perfect to bring the boys to the yard." I grinned at my reference and she narrowed her eyes. She'd listened to that song every day for a year. Even our mom had sung it. Bea had ordered milkshakes for dessert for months.

"Everyone goes through the independence thing. Yours is different. You stayed at home, I moved away. If you lived hours away, you wouldn't feel bad about ghosting us. It's okay. I'm not holding it against you that you haven't seen my new place."

"Way to bring the guilt." I hit my head with my fist. "I didn't realize I've been so self-involved."

"Yeah—I meant to bring a little guilt, not a full load. My bad. I know you're busy. The coaching and classes…are you still doing okay with money?"

"I have enough saved up to not work until the spring. I might be a hot mess with my love life, but my finances are in pretty good shape." I grinned and she whistled.

"So. Gideon Titan doesn't want to share you, hm?"

"Yeah. It sounds relationship-y, doesn't it?" I cringed. I was not a slut. I didn't lie, tease or lead guys on. But I preferred physical connections, not emotional ones. "Or am I just crazy?"

"Define crazy." She gave me a coy smile. "I get your point, and his. You've had hookups that went on for a while that weren't a relationship. But you didn't sleep with other guys, right?"

"Right. I thought it would be gross but we never talked about it. It just happened that way. Gideon saying it out loud...it made it official. More real." *I'm a chickenshit. A fucked-up chicken with issues for years.*

"Explain this Seth guy. I mean, you had hooked up with Gideon how many times at that point? Five? I know what yesterday was. Amanda wanted to bring you brownies, but I told her no."

"Thank you for that. I was not good company."

She smirked with confidence and pointed her finger at me. "Now — Seth. Spill it."

"I had class. I had a couple drinks with some classmates and I knew him from last year and he bought me a couple more drinks. He smiled and tried too hard. I've been in a low place...not dark thoughts or anything, but he provided the perfect way to forget the *guilt*."

"Fiona, it's not your fault." She grabbed my hand and squeezed. We'd been through this hundreds of times before. She would sympathize and tell me how she'd loved Justin, too. How I should talk to somebody. I could recite the script about to come from her. "Have you tried talking to a therapist about it? Seriously?"

I shook my head, remembering the school counselor. *I could reach out to her...maybe?* "It's fine. I'm fine."

"When you say it with so much confidence, I have no choice but to believe you," she quipped and rolled her eyes at my expense. "Tell you what. Sundays are your off-days, right?"

"Yeah, so?" I tilted my head. "Where are you going with this?"

"Bring Gideon over to the house."

"Hell no. That's meeting the family. No." I slammed my fists on the table, but Bea hunkered down. Her eyes turned a darker blue and I swore they sparkled with malice. "No."

"Then I'll have Jade do it."

"No, you won't. You're bluffing."

"Ask him. It'll be casual. Jade told us she wants to talk to him about speaking at the charity event, anyways. It'll be a business brunch with booze."

"Say that three times fast."

"Sunday. Be there, Fiona. Bring Gideon."

Chapter Eighteen

Gideon

I tried like hell to not overanalyze why Coach was in Phoenix during the off-season. He typically flew to the east coast and spent time with his family — this had to be serious. I cracked my neck twice, the bubble of tension in my chest beginning to hurt. If I didn't have baseball, I had no idea what to do with my life. It scared the shit out of me.

I wiped my sweaty palms on my black dress pants and straightened my posture. The drive to the stadium took about fifteen minutes and no amount of music or positive thoughts helped. My knee ached with each step and I used the player entrance on the south side of the stadium. It had more security and fewer people around it. On game days, die-hard fans would line the fence with chairs and coolers, chanting our names with the hope of a picture or wave. It was bare today, the crisp December air giving me a slight chill.

"Mr. Titan. Good to see you up and about, my man," Clint, the security guard who normally worked the players' entrance, hollered at me. He held out his hand with a large smile on his face and I mirrored the gesture.

"Thanks, Clint. Glad to be back. Sure missed this place."

"Three more months before baseball season is back. I hate pretending I like football — my heart is here. Well, good to run into ya. See you around."

I gave him a salute and continued down the tunnel to where I knew Coach spent most of his time when games weren't in session. His office was located to the right of the bottom floor. Monitors lined the walls, playing clips of previous games. I wondered, would my injury or outburst be on display?

I knocked on the black door and channeled my game-time zone. Focused. Determined. Desperate. I was here for baseball and nothing else mattered. I reined in all my other thoughts when he opened the door, his weathered face having a hint of a smile. "Coach Sanders."

"Gideon. Good to see you. Come in." He ushered me inside and I sat in an old red lounge chair that had seen better days. Its appearance had nothing on the comfort, though it felt like a cloud. "You seem to be walking fine."

I rubbed my knee, putting a little pressure on it, and didn't wince. "I'll be ready to go come spring training."

"I sure hope so. Now, we need to address a couple of things." His dark eyebrows came together and his hard eyes narrowed on me. I tensed, but he relaxed his expression and shook his head. "You look like I'm about to fire you. I'm not."

"That's good news, Coach." I gripped the armrest with my left hand. "I have some things to say, too, when you're done."

"Can't wait. Now, the injury. I've talked to our team doctor and he says you'll be fine at the end of February if you push yourself. His report states you're not trusting the healing process. Any reason why?"

Not trusting? What about the goddamn pain? "I'm not sure I follow. I've done everything he's asked and pushed myself. It hurts like a bitch." I gritted my teeth in frustration. "What else did he report?"

"Stubborn." He stopped and gave me a bemused grin. "I understand that. It's what makes you a good player. You are stubborn. In this case, you're not embracing the pain."

My mouth dropped open. "I don't understand."

"Frankly, I don't either. I don't speak physical therapist babble, but I want you taking grounders. I want you throwing. And I want you getting to the cages again and working on your swing. You haven't swung a bat in, what—six months?" He raised his eyebrows when he waited for me to answer. I gulped.

"Months. Yeah." Shame filled me and I wondered if I'd lost everything I'd built since I was a kid. *Six months off? Fuck.* "I haven't tried because the pain's been bothering me."

"Ice, medicate, rest and reps. Start going through the motions, slowly and only as much as you can handle, and repeat the process. Your ass is starting on opening day and I want you ready. If not, we're going to be having a different conversation than this one."

"Fair enough," I replied and weight lifted from my chest. *I'm not screwed yet.* "I'll get there."

"Good answer. Now...Tate." He let out a long sigh and ran his fingers over his mustache. "It wasn't fair how the entire thing was handled but you made some enemies."

"I know. I reached out to Tate yesterday, actually." I cleared my throat and told him about the brief encounter. He smiled, giving me an approving nod. *Thank the lord.* "I know I'll have to make amends with some other guys in the clubhouse, but with all of them gone traveling, it'll have to be in spring training."

"We're going to be doing some OTA in January. I expect you to be there, being a local and all. Make it a priority."

"Will do, Coach." I held out my hand and he shook it. "I wanted to tell you thanks. Coaching was a great idea and I'm realizing I'd forgotten about the little things."

"Can't tell you how happy I am to hear that," he replied with a huge smile. "I might make it out to one of your games soon. I'll be in town until after the New Year to help my mom move into a better retirement facility."

"The kids would shit themselves if you showed up, and good luck with the move."

"See you around, Titan. Now get outta here."

I gave him a curt nod and leaned against the brick wall outside his office. *Thank Christ.* I still had a shot. My career wasn't over—yet. I had to be ready by February and the thought of everything I needed to do frightened me. My knee shook with the pressure and I stilled, hoping it would pass. The pain did, but I had to get some exercises in before the games tonight.

Gideon: Weird request—can you show up early and hit me grounders?

Fiona: I think you MAY be too old to start.

Gideon: Smart ass.

Fiona: Are you sure you can handle my balls, old man?

Gideon: …

Fiona: I'll be there. Ignore my balls comment.

I smiled, joy radiating from somewhere in my gut. It was weird to look forward to something that would cause me pain.

* * * *

I chose to wear track pants rather than my sweats, since they allowed more room to bend and move. They didn't hide the brace as much, but I didn't care. It was part of the healing process and I wanted to play at the end of March. End of story. I arrived at the field an hour before the guys were scheduled and I was in high spirits. The perfect clear blue sky didn't have a single cloud and I closed my eyes. *This.* This was baseball weather. "Hey, psycho."

Ah, my nemesis. "Fiona." I turned to her and had to fight a grin at her appearance. She had her hair in two braids, an old trucker hat that said *PARTY* and another ridiculously bright outfit that did nothing for the figure I knew she had. "Jesus. Who dressed you?"

"Who shoved the stick in your ass?"

I let out a cackle and walked toward the dugout. "You look like a melted crayon box."

"Thank you."

The asshole smiled at my comment and her smile sent all sorts of feelings through me. Yeah—no. "At least you didn't wear the—"

She pulled the fanny pack from her backpack and winked at me. It wasn't cute or charming, but my chest warmed at the gesture. "Like I would forget this sucker."

"What do you keep in there?"

"Wouldn't you like to know?"

"Yes. I would. Thanks for the invitation." I didn't wait. I got in her space and tried to unzip the front. She squirmed, fruitlessly trying to swat my hands away. It was comparable to a kitten fighting a cow. "Hmm? What could be in there? I wonder…snacks? Girl stuff?"

"You're annoying," she said breathlessly. Her minty breath hit my neck and I froze. We were chest to chest, her face inches from mine. Her heat radiated to me and my entire view of her changed. She was tough, ballsy, unafraid of the world on the outside. But inside? She was vulnerable and scared. *Like me.* "Gid!"

Moment gone. I cleared my throat and took a step back. "Do you keep emergency condoms in there for when you can't resist me?"

She snarled at me before flipping me off. I laughed and continued to stare at the fanny pack. One day I would figure it out. "I came here to hit balls. I don't care if they're yours or baseballs. But I'm following through. Now, get your ass on the field."

"Yes, ma'am."

I grabbed my glove and jogged toward the area between second and third base. I did some basic stretches and jumps all afternoon, trying to get used to the new tightness and pulling with the motions I had done for twenty years. I felt more confident than I had before, but not sure I could handle it. "Ready, CFD."

She grinned at the kids' nickname for her and waltzed on up to home plate in her attire. *Jesus. If the guys on the team could see her now...* "Bend your knees."

"I can't," I fired back.

"Yes. You can or you don't play."

Her words resonated through me. She couldn't possibly know about the meeting I'd had that morning, could she? I flexed my hand in the glove and fought the resistance my knee gave me. I bent low, letting the edge of the leather hit the dirt. She tossed the ball in the air and planted her feet for her swing. The bat connected with the ball in the sweet spot, the familiar sound like music to my ears. I instinctively jerked to the right, her natural tendency to pull the ball easy for me to spot. The ball whirled toward me and without thinking, I scooped it and rolled it off to the side.

"Again," I yelled at her. She nodded and continued to hit me ball after ball. I didn't miss one, and by the thirtieth, I had to break. "Knee."

She set the bat down and jogged toward me. "Come on, big guy. Let's find you a ball bucket and have our post-practice debrief."

I wanted to laugh, but the pain was too much. My knee hadn't failed me, though. I hurt like a motherfucking bomb had gone off inside it, but it hadn't let me down. Sure, it was swollen as fuck and rubbing uncomfortably against the brace, begging for me to sit and ice it. I made it to the bench with sweat dripping down my face, and Fiona handed me a water. *Bless her.* "Thanks."

"You look rough right now. I'd say your performance wasn't the worst I've seen. I might put you in the starting line-up. You gave me a bit of attitude before the game that I didn't appreciate and I wanted to teach you a lesson."

"I'll show you a lesson," I replied. That earned me a slow blush up her neck before she punched me in the arm. The water helped refuel my energy. "You can't seem to keep your hands off me today."

"It's all violent. These aren't fun touches."

"Anything from you is a fun touch, Barbie."

We shared a look that went on a little too long for two people who disliked each other. She tried to act tough the longer I stared at her, but her façade broke and a smile took over her entire face. I scooted closer to her and gave her thigh a squeeze. It was less personal than pushing the hair that escaped behind her ear. "Are you feeling better?"

She shrugged and the moment of peace left. "Yeah, thanks. I talked with my sister and thought a bit about my decision in a few weeks."

"What decision?" *Is she moving? Quitting?*

"The position at Texting Too Late. I could get paid and have benefits — the whole shebang. I need to let them know sooner rather than later," she replied in a small voice. She might have been a petite person, but nothing about her personality or voice was small and concern took over.

"What's the hold-up?" *It's a family-run organization and all charity work. Why won't she take it?*

"You wouldn't understand."

"Try me, Barbie." I reached out and wrapped my fingers around her wrist, preventing her walking away. She tensed and clenched her teeth together before turning around. "Don't get worked up. I'm genuinely wondering. From my understanding from the little creeping on you I've done, it would be an amazing opportunity for you to help do what you're great at."

"Yeah? What's that?" she asked with a fire in her tone.

"Talking to kids. You're a natural at it. Why do you think the players respond so well to you? I know baseball, but you're their coach, mentor, the person they go to with problems. You're a leader, Fiona." I couldn't believe I'd admitted it to her. It made me look weak, but when I saw her reaction, I didn't feel weak anymore. Her surprise and happiness were better than the small satisfaction I'd get by putting her down.

"I... I didn't think... I do love working with kids." She gave me a feeble smile and hit her back against the fence a couple of times. "The job would be handed to me, though."

"Handed to you?" I asked without hiding my doubt. "Didn't you help Jade with a million things?"

"Yeah, but—"

"I know you're a little crazy, because who else would do what we did on the motorcycle ride, the car, or the bathroom? But, Fiona, think about your strengths and goals. Does this job help reach them? Yes or no. Your answer to that question should tell you."

Screw it. I cupped her chin in my hand and waited until she met my gaze, then I said, "You know the answer."

Chapter Nineteen

Fiona

Goals. I had them—everyone did. Yet why were they so goddamn hard to figure out? I groaned and rubbed my temples. I'd foolishly bought a new stack of colorful sticky notes—the bright, obnoxious ones with all sorts of colors—thinking it would help me organize my life. Instead, I'd covered the entire kitchen table in a starfish pattern that looked really cool, but wasted a lot of paper.

I'm a fucking idiot.

I twirled the pen and wrote down *GRADUATE* on a bright blue one. First goal, check. Second goal…get a job. And I was back to square one. Michelle's old Mazda pulled into our driveway and I welcomed the distraction. Hell, I'd even tried watching *Real Housewives* the day before and I *hated* that show. Gideon's words had repeated in my head over and over for two days. Two entire days of me glaring at him, at which he just winked or did something annoying but made it look good.

Does it help me reach my goal? I don't know what my fucking goal is!

"Hey, roomie. What—" She stopped when her gaze found the table. "I would ask if we were pranking someone else, but this is our place. Looks good."

"Way to roll with the punches. I swear I had a reason."

"Don't doubt it," she quipped and twisted up her long hair into a messy bun. She'd worked the midnight and morning shift last night—the worst combination of twelve hours ever—and still managed to look decent. I envied her a little bit. "Care to share? I had too much caffeine and am jittery as hell. I won't sleep for another hour at least."

"Well, I am currently enjoying life having numerous *what the fuck* moments per hour. For example, I don't have goals beyond graduating and that's making it real hard to figure out if I want the job."

"Where do you see yourself in five years?" She slid onto the purple chair and smirked at the design of sticky notes in front of her. "Here? Waitressing? Coaching? Doing the dirty with Gideon Titan?"

"What?" I gaped at her. "How do you know?"

"He spent the night here the other day. I saw his car. I might not be a city girl, but I can put that together," she replied with way too much joy in her voice. "I'm sorry to pry, but a selfish part of me wants to know all about him. In bed, of course."

"Might as well." I sighed and crossed my arms. "We haven't done it in a bed yet...*hm*." I paused, then laughed. "It's been public places at this point. *God*. I'm a mess."

She patted my hand and pursed her lips. "I knew we were friends for a reason. So, animalistic? Sweet? Wait. Scratch that. No way he's sweet."

"He's not at all." I burned all the way down my body at the thought of him. "For the record, we didn't go at it the other night. I was having a hard time with the anniversary of Justin's death." I glanced at her, not sure how much she actually knew about him. She just nodded and gave me a sympathetic smile.

"He's… There's this chemistry that is insane. You know? Like, I don't like him but I want to bang him." *Shit – is that true?* I didn't hate him…did I like him?

"Honey. Angry sex is the best. I have handprints on my thighs from MP." She wiggled her eyebrows and leaned forward on her elbows. "I don't want to be attracted to him, but the more I fight it, the worse it gets."

"Magic Penis. The reason you're all smiles and shit. It's been weeks now. Is this a thing?"

"Nah. Keeping it casual. We aren't anything alike. Plus, I don't want to be a hookup chick catching main chick feelings, you know?" She leaned back in the chair and began stacking the notes. "It's temporary."

"Yeah. I get it. Same with Gideon. You and I are just two young women who know what they like in bed. Ain't nothing wrong with that."

"Not a thing. And we're both doing it with famous people." She stood and gave me a sly look.

"Who is Magic Penis?" I shouted at her, but she darted into her room. *Damn it.* I liked the girl and wanted to delve into her life, not mine.

* * * *

"Good game tonight, CFD." Gideon held out his hand for a high-five and we shared a grin after a two-hour nail-biting game. Our kids had done good. They had run every play perfectly and hadn't left one piece of trash. That was all right in my book.

"You too, your eminence."

"I'm thirsty. Want to grab a drink? Say, a whiskey?"

"You know, that sounds good." I nodded and we fell into step as we headed toward our cars — mine the disaster, his the top model. "Where you thinking?"

"I got a gift in the mail today. Jameson Gold Reserve."

"I like a Jameson now and again."

"No, you don't understand. This is like top-notch Jameson. It's got flavors of honey in a sipping sort of drink."

"Jeez, I'm not some uncultured swine," I scoffed. My feelings were a little hurt at his insinuation. "Maybe I'll pass on that drink."

"No."

He came up behind me and brought his arm around my shoulders. It put my head perfectly in the crook of his arm and I would be lying if I said I didn't like it. Because I did. "Fiona. It's a top-of-the-line whiskey that should be drunk with someone you like. I want to open it with you."

I gulped. *Is this another hookup or a sort of date? He likes me? Woah.* "Uh, so it's at your house?"

"It's in my car. We can go to your place if you'd rather."

"Uh, yours is fine." He'd already seen how shitty it was. He didn't need another reminder. "I'll follow you."

"Okay," he replied in a warm tone. He brought his hand down my back, settling right above my ass where he gave me a light squeeze. "Drive safe."

I blasted some *It Takes Two* by Rob Base and DJ EZ rock and tried to relax. It was a futile attempt because I was wound tight. Fun. *This is fun.* The familiar winding road crept into view and his palace sat at the end, not really that inviting. I parked and took an extra minute to get out of the car.

There was a feeling of emptiness inside me before fluttering took over. *Fuck this. Why am I nervous?* I brushed my hands down my black yoga pants and straightened the hem of my retro Soles shirt. The team had been around fifty years without a World Series win, but the logo from the late seventies was cool. The entire team had commented on it and insisted on getting team shirts—I was in charge of ordering them after collecting all the money, being the most organized person there. I was half-inclined to order ones with glitter on them.

I chuckled at the thought and found Gideon. He disappeared behind the large garage doors and I wasn't sure if I should wait outside or head inside.

Screw that. I marched right on in and found him taking the bag of equipment out and setting it on an organized shelf. "Need any help, gimpy?"

"You're a dick," he replied but there was a light tone to his voice. "And no. I don't need help and I'm not a gimp."

"Whatever you say, muscles." I crossed my arms and leaned against the wall, perfectly content to watch him bend and move things around. I figured I might as well get my fill of him—why else would I be here unless to enjoy his body? "Where's this high-class whiskey?"

"Thirsty?"

Oh, damn. The way he said that word had me all kinds of thirsty for him. "You have no idea."

"Come on. We can sit outside."

We do like to do it outside. I clapped my hands, my body humming in response to his. We didn't agree on much, but we had no problems pleasuring each other. "I didn't realize the last time I was here that you have a porch."

"We weren't on polite speaking terms then." He shot me an amused look. "Times have changed."

"Slightly. You're still one asshole comment away from me hitting you."

He grinned again—the two dimples teasing me—and held open a large glass door at the back end of the kitchen. "After you."

"Good god. It's beautiful out here." I tried to take it all in at once and ended up spinning around like a fool. Camelback Mountain—famously named for its humped shape—stood in the backdrop with the evening colors mixing with the desert sky. A fire pit sat off to the right, unused, and a handful of comfortable chairs called my name. I approached the one closest to the door. "Can we start a fire?"

"Sure. Want to pour the drinks? I just like two cubes."

"Are you sure I can handle your precious liquid?" I fired back. He pulled on the end of my hair and disappeared inside without a word. *Jesus.* I blinked twice, the sweet gesture too much. *Whiskey. Fucking. Leaving.* I walked into the sleek kitchen with all sorts of modern appliances. I wouldn't be surprised if the refrigerator had a camera on it. "Gid! Do you have that thing where you can call your fridge when you're getting food?"

"That's not a thing." He snuck up behind me, his cologne making my ovaries go into overdrive. He was so big. His chest brushed up against my back and he pressed some buttons. "Fridge. Prepare drinks for us."

"What?" I gasped, but elbowed him in the ribs when I realized he was joking. "You're an asshole."

"You fell for it. That's hilarious," he said between laughs. "God, you're adorable. Glasses are over the stove, the whiskey on the table. Three fingers, please."

I let out a puff of air and thought about pinching him or something, but he was soon out of reach. I found the glasses and his precious two cubes and poured two neat whiskeys. I took a whiff, the strong, bold amber liquid burning my nostrils. I preferred it with some diet cola but it didn't seem to be that type of night. I used the time alone to collect my thoughts and snoop. He had nothing on his fridge. It was black and empty. Michelle and I had all sorts of shit — takeout menus, pictures of our families, our lame attempt at art when we'd tried to do a paint-by-numbers one night. His was…nothing.

I brought the drinks outside and he bent over, his occasional grunt amusing me. "Need help reading the directions?"

"Your smartass remarks just make it all the better when you're screaming my name later."

"Such a cheesy line."

"Yet still true. Can you shine your phone light over this for a second?"

I set the glasses down and joined him by the pit. This put us next to each other, my legs touching him. It took about ten seconds, then the fire started with small embers. He let out a small cheer and squeezed my hip. "Thanks, Fiona. Ah, let's enjoy this."

That hip grab. That was new. I cleared my throat and took the seat next to him. He held up his glass and I found the courage to meet his gaze. It seemed intense. "Cheers to reaching our goals, yeah?"

"Sure," I agreed and brought the cool liquid to my mouth. I took a small sip, the flavor bursting when it hit my tongue. I coughed at the strength and tried again, taking a smaller amount. "Wow."

"Smooth and bold. Good shit."

I chuckled. "Good shit doesn't make you sound as classy."

"I'm not a classy guy."

I nodded and leaned back into the chair. My stomach swirled and some unknown feeling took over my body. Comfort? *Am I comfortable here, sitting in silence and drinking expensive whiskey?* I took another sip and snuck a glance at him. He stared right at me. "What?"

"Do you ever wear makeup?"

Great. I tensed. I blinked before giving him my nastiest smile. "Sure. If I feel like it or want to spend extra time in front of the mirror. Most of the time I forget, but thanks for pointing it out."

"No. *No.* You're missing my point. I just wondered if your eyelashes were naturally that long."

I had all sorts of arguments ready to spout at him. But then they deflated. "My eyelashes?"

"Yeah. You have beautiful eyes and I noticed your lashes frame them well."

I sat up a little straighter. "Thank you?"

"You're welcome." His deep voice had a new edge to it and I squirmed in my seat. "I really appreciate you getting there early and hitting me grounders. My coach expects me to be ready to start game one. The grounders help."

"Good. Not that I'm an expert or anything—which you *love* to point out—but you're not favoring your right leg anymore. You're remaining balanced."

"Thanks, CFD. Maybe you're not the worst."

"Don't make me blush, Gideon."

We shared a smile again before he leaned over on his knees. It brought him closer and words left me. His face in the firelight was bad, bad news for me. I could almost feel the inhibitions slide out of my body and I wanted to crawl into his lap.

"How's your drink?"

"Great," I managed to get out. "Yours?"

"Great."

Awkward. This was awkward. I took another sip and chose to look into the dark night. *What am I doing?* "I should—"

"I haven't gotten your goddamn body out of my mind. I'm having a difficult time letting you enjoy your drink in peace."

Yeah—I'm not going home yet. I eyed the glass, smirking at him before taking it all back in one swig. "Problem solved."

Chapter Twenty

Gideon

I didn't give a shit that Fiona had just taken a shot of whiskey that was balls expensive. Her throat worked to swallow the liquid and my brain had one thing to focus on — getting her naked. She pointed to the glass in my hand and I mirrored her action. The burn was some sort of foreplay and I was desperate. She tugged on the end of her shirt and tossed it to the side. Then came her bra.

Fiona sat in my backyard, shirtless with her perky tits on display. I bit my knuckle, saying, "God."

"Are we going to make it to an actual bed this time or continue our outside norm?" she asked, her nipples hardening in the cold air.

"Touch yourself out here. I want to watch," I commanded and gripped the edge of my chair so hard my fingers hurt. The thought came from out of the blue, but Fiona licked her lips and brought her fingers down to her perfectly pink nipples. She took them in her small fingers and pinched them, a small moan escaping her.

"Mm." She met my gaze and her pupils dilated. "I prefer your teeth on them, but I can continue."

"That'll come. Continue," I barked, then added, "Please."

She giggled and trailed down her toned muscles, slipping into the hem of her pants. She tugged them down to her ankles, her panties a deep red, and spread her creamy thighs open for me. *Fuck.* My dick strained against my pants and I was seconds from exploding. When had a woman been so carefree and sexy? *Jesus.* She propped her legs on the arms of the chair, leaving me with an entire view of her bare pussy. She brought her two longest fingers and spread open her lips, low groans coming from her throat. "Gideon. Do you like this?"

"Fuck, yeah," I replied in a haggard voice. I scooted my chair closer to her, getting a better view as she inserted her fingers in her cunt. The slim digits disappeared and her pussy swallowed them up. I gulped. I didn't have long.

She thrust in and out, arching her back against the chair, and each sound cut a string of my control. "Remove your fingers. Can I taste you?"

"Down there?"

"Please? I need to."

She nodded and spread her legs farther apart. Fuck the pain in my leg. I knelt on the concrete and gripped her thighs. I ran my nose down their length, breathing in her musky scent. The smell of her desire was hot as hell. "Your pussy is fucking perfect."

"Are you going to talk to it, or fuck it?"

"God, I love your mouth." I nipped at the spot where her leg met her hip and she jumped. *Good.* I dragged my tongue up her stomach, swirling it around her belly button before making my way down to her swollen clit. It throbbed against my mouth and I sucked it, switching between hard and soft. She bucked against me and fisted my hair. It stung, but I loved the fuck out of it. "Jesus. I could eat you for hours."

"Please."

I jutted my tongue against her clit, flicking it to the point she screamed and I would stop. I did it again, and inserted two fingers in her silky walls. She was soaked and I wanted her to lose herself entirely. In and out, bite and suck, and I pushed down on her lower abdomen when her legs began to tense. She tried to sit up as the pleasure hit her, but I kept her down. Lapping in the delicious cream from her orgasm, I wanted to see her explode again and again. "*Gideon.* God. Yes!"

I moaned into her when she said my name. She rode the last wave and relaxed into the chair after the first round of pleasure. One wasn't enough—I was a greedy bastard. I didn't give her time to recover before bringing my tongue to her wetness and starting again. She gripped my hair in her fingers, squirming against my mouth. Her desperation fueled me and before long, she bucked against me, saying my name as I brought her to orgasm. I kissed her nub, then her stomach and made my way to her beaded nipples. I used my teeth to bite down, a little bit too hard, but she just hummed in response. "You're so hot."

"I'm never complaining about your mouth ever again. Fuck me." She opened her eyes and they'd turned dark blue, her pupils dilated. "Kiss me."

I leaned over her, taking her mouth in mine. She clasped the edge of my shirt and clung to me. Her tongue clashed with mine in a fierce possession and I picked her up without breaking the kiss. She wrapped her bare legs around me and I carried her inside. "Finally making it to a bed. Thank Christ."

I chuckled at her desperation and groaned when she brought her mouth to my neck. She bit down and I smacked her ass. Hard. "Don't distract me. I might drop you."

"If you drop me on your dick, then I'm fine."

I laughed, but it hurt because my dick was burning to be inside her. I gripped the railing as I made my way downstairs to my room and threw her onto my mattress. I ripped off my clothes before grabbing a condom from the drawer and slipping it on. "I've thought for a while about you being in my bed. It's nothing like I planned."

"Rude!"

Her eyes flared but I shook my head. "No, this is better. Are you ready for me?"

"Check for yourself."

And I did. I spread her wide open, running my tongue down her and sucking her clit before biting it. She bucked, and I used that second to plunge into her. She gasped, digging her nails into my back. "*Yes,* Gideon."

I gripped her hips and slammed into her. Her tight walls were fucking heaven and I grunted in restraint— I wanted this to last. She squeezed her legs around my waist and lifted herself up, the angle having me go to the deepest part of her. I held her against me, thrusting ten more times. *I'm going to blow my load way too soon.* I slowed down, using my mouth on her neck, nipples and mouth. Our teeth clashed, our bodies at war for who would get more pleasure, and I pulled out. "I want you to ride me."

"I can't come that way."

"We can't have that, can we?" I flipped her over. "I can't have you not feeling fulfilled…how does this feel, Fiona?"

"Oh. Oh!"

I slid deep into her so my chest pressed into her back. I thrust slower, using my right hand on her clit to match my movements. She moaned and let out a cry when I picked up the pace. "Don't stop! Shit!"

I continued at the same speed, the build-up starting around my spine. It hit me too fast, the hot burst of pleasure spreading through my veins. I gripped her ass with my free hand, her name leaving my lips as I spilled into her. My ears rang, my feet and fingers tingling as though I'd been electrocuted. I collapsed next to her, my heart racing. I felt lightheaded and barely heard her when she said something. I waited until the weight on the bed shifted before opening my eyes. She gave me a sly look before pointing toward the bathroom door. "Can I use your shower?"

"Can I join you in a second?"

"Don't know if you can handle another round, gramps."

I snorted but she disappeared behind the door. I groaned — the adrenaline from the fuck had my knee aching. I shouldn't have carried her but it had been so worth it. I slipped off the condom and tossed it into the trash before going to the bathroom. I washed my face in the sink, grabbed some mouthwash and waited for Fiona to leave the shower. It felt too personal to join her.

We hook up. That's what we do. Fuck — that's all I'm capable of doing and she's an emotional wreck. Sex and orgasms with a little bit of baseball is the perfect combination. I smiled, happy with my self-talk, and froze when she opened the door. *Fuck, her body is perfection.* Water dripped over her magnificent chest, sliding down her smooth skin and landing in a small puddle on the floor. I handed her a towel and swallowed my comments. I wanted to take her — again.

"Were you afraid to come in or…?"

"Not afraid. Giving you space." *Shit.* My voice came out too rough. "Might hop in now."

"Cool." She brushed by me without giving me another look. I hesitated. Were we supposed to continue to hang out? Did I offer her another drink? I sighed, stepped into the spacious shower and ran soap over my face. I needed the cold water. I was a goddamn headcase. *Why am I fucking worried about her? She's damn well sure of herself and doesn't need me overthinking anything.* I quickly washed my hair and turned off the water. I'd offer another drink. That was it. It was simple and would give her the opportunity to say no and leave. *Perfect.*

I exited the shower and expected her to be waiting in the bedroom. She wasn't there, or in the basement or kitchen. "Fiona?"

No one replied and I took a quick look onto the porch. Her glass was gone, no sign of her anywhere. I walked to the front window and couldn't see her car either. *What the fuck?*

Gideon: Did you leave?

Fiona: Yup. Had things to do.

Gideon: At eleven at night…

Fiona: Yes. At eleven at night. See you tomorrow.

I read her messages again and frowned. I'd tormented myself worrying about what to do and she'd left without a goodbye. I should be relieved. I should be thankful I didn't have to fill any awkward chats. But I wasn't and *that* bothered me.

* * * *

Heavy metal music vibrated the walls of my weight room. The violent and aggressive beats fueled my blood and I gritted my teeth as I pushed through a workout. I had to be ready by February and I was done feeling sorry for myself. My muscles screamed in protest, but I continued with the squats and collapsed into a chair when I'd finished. Sweat poured down my face and I chugged water — then my phone rang. *Cheryl.*

"Yo."

"Gid." Cheryl's voice broke and I instantly sat up. "Are you free?"

"Yes. What's going on?" I stood and paced. Anxiety spread through my chest within seconds and I had the phone in a deathlike grip. "Is Quinn okay?"

"She's fine. We're fine. It's Vic. I heard from my lawyer, Sean. You know him. We have a court hearing at the end of this week. He…he wants supervised visits." She let out a pathetic cry and I leaned against the wall. I couldn't lose control — I had to remain rational for her and Quinn.

"Okay. It's better than custody. Supervised visits are every couple of weeks, right? Sean mentioned that, I think. Did you ask Sean who would be supervising? You know, as a worst-case scenario?"

"N-no. I d-didn't."

"Find out the worst-case situation and build from there. There's no evidence of Vic paying a dime for the past seven years and that's not in the best interest for Quinn. She doesn't know who the hell he is, couldn't pick him out of a crowd. He hasn't contacted you despite your attempts to find him. He doesn't have a leg to stand on, Cheryl. I don't see how this will work." *My gut tells me he doesn't have money, either.*

"There could be an error in the system or they could find out we were drunk and Mom and Dad —"

"Stop. *That* has nothing to do with it," I yelled at her. She sucked in a breath and I felt worse. "You're a great mom. End of story."

She remained silent for a full thirty seconds before she spoke in an unfamiliar soft voice. "I wish Mom and Dad were here. I need them, Gid. I can't do this alone. I just can't. Who's going to watch her? Who's going to tell her that the guy who left her wants to be her dad now? I can't. I refuse!" She sobbed and my eyes stung. "I'm losing my shit."

"I'll come over there. Help with anything you need."

"I appreciate that, but she's going over to a friend's after school today. The one day I wanted for myself, I'm a fucking mess and crying all over the place. I'm pathetic. I'm a sad excuse for a mom."

"Cheryl. You're… Stop. Quinn is the luckiest girl in the world because you're her mom. Look, why don't you come to the game tonight? Come help coach and be around teenagers. You'll get to see what you'll have to deal with when Quinn's old enough to date."

"She's not dating. I made her sign a napkin and got it notarized," she rambled and let out a snort. "I might. I need to calm down, eat ice cream, cry. Maybe drink a bottle of wine. But I appreciate you trying."

"I'll come over after the game regardless. Let me know what you need." I pulled on the neckline of my shirt and hated to ask her the finance question, but I had to. "If you need any...money to help pay for Sean, you'll let me know, right?"

"I can pay for my own lawyer, Gid."

"I understand. But I'm going to do whatever the fuck I can to protect Quinn. You must know that. It's not about you or your independence. It's about Quinn and keeping the three of us together."

She sighed and a little of the fight left her voice. "I love you, Gideon. I'm glad you're in our life."

"You too, sis. I'll see you later, okay?"

"Yeah, you will."

She hung up and I closed my eyes for a second. My first thought scared the shit out of me. Why would I think about Fiona after a family crisis? *Jesus.* Last night was fucking with me and it was best if I let it go. I shook my head, continued my workout and didn't count down the minutes until I had to leave for the game. I was *not* anxious to see Fiona.

Chapter Twenty-One

Fiona

Someone was in a mood. I sucked in my bottom lip as I wrote out the list of kids starting that game, sneaking glances over at Gideon and his tense shoulders. It had been two days since I'd left him after our intense hookup. Two days with an awkward sexual tension that was burning me up. I continued to watch him, a blush taking over my neck when my gaze went to his mouth. *God, he can use his tongue.*

"CFD. Why is Coach Titan disgruntled?"

I shook my head and hoped I didn't look embarrassed. I needed to control my thoughts.

"Disgruntled? You sound like a curmudgeon," I replied to Garth. He tilted his head and I snorted. "You can't use disgruntled and *not* know that curmudgeon is another word for grumpy old guy."

"Curmudgeon. I like it. Thanks for the new word, CFD."

"I do what I can," I said and snuck another glance at Gideon. *Is today the day to test him and place the kids where I think they're best? No. I shouldn't.* He didn't outright say he was pissed I'd just left, but there was a barrier in how he spoke to me now. Plus, our back-and-forth texts about practice plans didn't have their normal flirty inappropriateness. And that was okay with me. Barriers were good. "Coach Titan does look a little disgruntled, doesn't he?"

"Yeah. I looked up all his stats last night and spent time memorizing them, but when I told him, he made this grunt and that was all." Garth blew out a long breath of air and his shoulders sagged. I reached out and gave his shoulder a squeeze. *Gideon's being an asshole again.*

"I know he appreciates it, kid. He's having a bad day, so cut him some slack. This is a lesson — enjoy being a youth. Adulting is hard."

"Taxes and stuff, right?"

"You got it."

He gave me a nod and grabbed a handful of sunflower seeds before jogging back out to the field for warmups. I wrote the B team line-up since we were facing a weaker team and tore off the carbon copy to give to the umpire. I flicked Gideon on the arm when I walked by him, and ignored his pointed stare. He would absolutely be hearing about how he'd hurt Garth. I'd thought we'd made progress since the game where he'd lost his shit — but apparently not.

The opposing coach stood at home plate, shooting the shit with the umpire, and they both stopped talking when I approached. I gave them both a big smile and held out my hand. "Good afternoon, gentlemen."

"Hello to you, dear. How are you?" The coach slid off his sunglasses and gave me a long look. He had a salt-and-pepper thing going on and it worked well with his features. His lingering stare didn't quite bother me, and I waited for him to shake my hand. He did, but he cupped it with both of his, like I was fragile. *Weird.*

"I'm great. Here's our line-up. Do you have yours ready?" I asked.

"Not yet. I'll have our book lady bring it over to you. Where are you sitting, doll?"

Doll? Ugh. I fought the urge to roll my eyes. I'd despised the *doll* comments I'd gotten at IHOP and this nice-looking guy had just plummeted in my book. "I'll be on the base line. Coaching. You can hand it to me there."

His expression faltered for a second before he put the glasses back on. "How'd you get roped into coaching baseball? You filling in for somebody today?"

"Nope. I'm one of the coaches." I crossed my arms and met the gaze of the umpire. He looked uncomfortable as hell and I narrowed my eyes at him. He wasn't about to leave this riveting conversation.

"Interesting. Can't seem to see how. You certainly didn't play the sport. It's a man's sport, sweetheart." He gave me a snarky smile and smugness radiated off him.

The guy was a total sexist and I wanted to punch him. I twisted the end of my ponytail and pretended to pop my gum. "Are *you*, like, filling in for someone or are you, like, the real coach? I mean, if we're going to talk down to people, I want in on the fun."

His jaw tightened and he turned his entire body toward the umpire, cutting me out of the conversation. I clenched my hands into fists. "Thanks, fellas."

I did my best to keep my temper under control and went back to the dugout. I rubbed my temples as my blood boiled. *The nerve of that fucking guy.*

"Fiona, what's going on?" Gideon came into view and gave me a long look—the first time he'd acknowledged me since we got there an hour ago. Just add it to my list of guys being dicks. "What happened at home plate? Their coach is glaring over here."

"He's a sexist. I'm fuming right now," I replied and tried to stop my legs from bouncing up and down. "I need to walk or something."

"Explain what happened." He followed me out of the gate and onto the grass where the boys were throwing. "Your face is all blotchy and red. It's concerning."

"Thanks for your keen observation." I released breath after breath, trying my best to relax. "That guy was a total asshole and talked down to me for being a coach since I was a woman. Lots of doll, sweetheart and shit like that. I sassed him back and he just... God. It infuriates me when men think a woman can't do something, like coach. Jesus."

"Coach third."

"Excuse me?" I blinked at him, positive I'd misheard him. "Coach what now?"

"Forgive me, but you're a *bit* of a ballbuster. You're on my team. Fuck that guy. Coach third. Make all the calls and I swear we better fucking win the game."

I didn't even think. I jumped in the air, throwing my arms around his neck. I squeezed him in a hug and some unknown emotion had my chest feeling funny. I got warm and my rage instantly turned into joy. "I could kiss you right now."

"Best not with all the, uh, kids," he replied in a strained voice and pulled me off him. "Glad to help, though."

"I'm so geeked right now. I get to call the signs. Me. I get to do it. You trust me?" I grinned at him, my skin pulling tight at the gesture. I clapped a couple of times and some of the boys gave me weird looks. I was past caring. "Gideon Titan, you have officially shocked me. This is coming from the guy who told me baseball is for men. You. You're standing up for me."

"Calm down, Barbie. It's not that big of a deal."

At my nickname, I met his gaze and I swore his smile sent tingles down my body. It was the dimpled, sweet smile I didn't see often. He reached out, nudging me in the arm. "I take it you've already turned in the line-up?"

"Yup. We're good to go, Coach. Except." I paused and tried to figure where Garth was. He stood farthest away with his head hung low. "Apologize to Garth. He's upset that you didn't care about him memorizing your stats. He tried to impress you."

"Shit, I blew him off." He raised one of his sculpted arms and brought his fingers through his hair. "I had a hell of an afternoon. My family's…well…you're right. I'll make it up to him."

His expression changed to despair for a quick second and I desperately wanted to ask why or comfort him. *What's happening with Cheryl? Or Quinn?* He stood up for me… *I can return the favor, right?* "If there's anything I can do to help, let me know, okay? Apparently, we're a team."

"Yeah. We are." His gaze lingered on my face for another five seconds before he went back to the dugout.

We didn't talk for the rest of the warmup and I was okay with that. I had a game to coach and by god, I needed a win.

A couple of hours later, it came down to the last inning. "Listen up. Brad — I'm calling for a hit and run. You need to hit the ball in play and on the ground. Can you do that?"

"Yes, CFD." He nodded and we both looked at Chris.

"Chris — take off the second he goes into the wind-up. Get a good lead. Listen for my call if you head to third or not."

"Got it, Coach." He fist-bumped me and the three of us did a power clap before he ran back to first. Gideon met my gaze across the field and gave me a smile. We were down by one run in the bottom of the ninth, and I wanted this win more than I'd ever wanted anything in my life. My adrenaline pounded down my throat, my blood pumping with fire, and I hit Brad on the helmet.

"I trust you, Brad. Bat to the ball. You got this!"

He strutted back to the home plate, adjusted his helmet and kicked the dirt three times. The pitcher and catcher communicated about the pitch and the crisp fall air froze around me. The lanky kid on the mound began his wind-up — Chris taking off like a horse coming out of a gate — and I held my breath.

Brad double-pumped his arms, his left leg lifting as he twisted his body to meet the ball. The wooden bat cracked against the ball, the sound echoing inside my head. It hit the dirt — hard — and bounced past the second baseman into the outfield. I swung my arm around like a goddamn propeller and Chris rounded second and streamlined for third.

"Down! Down!" I screamed. The right fielder had an arm and threw the perfect relay to get it to the shortstop, the best player on the opposing team. He caught and threw it in one continuous motion and it was going to beat Chris to the base.

Chris dove head-first into the bag just as the third baseman caught it. I whipped my head toward the umpire and his arms were outstretched as though he was measuring his wingspan. "Safe!"

"Yes! Hell, yes! Keep it going!" I shouted and jumped up and down, high-fiving Chris and looking like a maniac. We had two baserunners on, no outs and our best hitter up. Garth. "Let's go, GT! Get some RBIs!"

The team all stood against the fence, every single one of them invested in their teammates. Pride blossomed through me and a wave of emotion had me blinking back tears. *Not the goddamn time.* "Wide gap in left center, Garth. Time the pitch and keep your arms right."

He tapped the edge of his helmet, our telltale sign that the message was received. I glanced over at Gideon and would've laughed if I hadn't been so stressed. He had his hands on his knees, his large frame leaning over with an aggressive expression on his face. He wanted this win, too.

The pitcher eyed the runners and went into his wind-up before—*shit!* He threw to the third baseman and Chris had too far a lead. *Shit. Fuck!* He was in a full-fledged pickle. He took three steps toward home, then third, then home as the defense did their best to get him out. But by god, their catcher—the son of the asshole coach, I'd learned in the first inning—overthrew the ball into the outfield and Chris easily scored.

That left Brad at second. All we needed was a single and we would have the game. I called time out and motioned for Garth to jog toward me. "Brad's out there for you. What do we need right now?"

"A hit, CFD. Just a hit."

"That's right. Don't worry about hitting a homerun or a rocket. We need contact on the ground that gets through the infield. Think you can aim for that?"

"You bet your ass, CFD. I want to beat this team so bad. I heard their coach badmouthing you and that pisses me off."

"First off, I love that you're standing up for me. Second, language. Third, get your ass up to bat and show us what you got, kid." I hoped I gave him a convincing grin. He jogged toward the batter's box and watched two pitches go by. *Hitters pitch. 2-0.*

"Believe, GT!" I shouted and almost lost my voice when he connected with the ball in a perfectly placed hard line-drive, straight into the outfield. We won. *Ohmygod. Yes!* I waved Chris to go home and the dugout exploded in cheers. It wasn't a big game, but we were acting as though it was. Our entire team jumped up and down, pairs of arms hugging me at all angles. It was in my top five favorite moments of my life.

"Gentlemen, please shake hands and sprint out to left field. Remember to always be good sports and exemplary athletes. Win or lose," I said between fits of smiles and laughter. Gideon came up behind me and put his hand on my shoulder. I tensed when his lips were inches away from my ear.

"Proud as shit of you right now. Try not to look too proud of yourself, though. Their coach might have a hernia."

I giggled. He gave me another squeeze and walked in front, letting me be the final person to shake hands. It was often reserved for the head coach and I held my head high when I shook all their hands. It was no surprise when the sexist man avoided my stare and my handshake, but I didn't let it fluster me. I loved our team, Gideon included.

"Nice win, Fiona. I'm proud of you."

Those words coming from Gideon would be forever cherished. I wanted to record him saying that and put it on a mixtape, just to listen to on sad days. He smiled at me, the warmth in his expression almost too much to handle. "Thank you."

"You're welcome. Now hustle out to the field. We need to do a post-game before getting a celebratory drink."

I laughed and enjoyed the post-game analysis. Gideon took the lead and it wasn't until Big Al spoke that I had to fight another fit of giggles.

"I heard him say to Coach Titan how could a man like him let a woman coach in front of him and I got so mad. CFD, I can't believe he said it!" Big Al almost shouted his words and I had to laugh it off. "But you should've heard what Coach Titan said."

"Yeah? What's that?" I slid my gaze toward the man in question and he gave me a shrug. *Interesting.*

"He said, and I quote, *'I'm sorry your dick's so small that she threatens you.'*"

"Oh my god. You can't...you can't repeat that." I wanted to laugh, cry and throw my arms around him again. But I needed to act like a coach.

"CFD, I'm in high school. I hear things that would make you cry. If anything, it taught me to always stand up for women when men are dick shits."

"*Language.*" I tried scolding, but the high of the win was too much. They all grinned at me, no sign of their teenage snark or attitudes. "Fine. Just know, I love the shit out of you guys."

"Love you too, CFD. Nice win!"

We all high-fived each other, Garth getting to pick the final cheer since he had the big hit. The punk chose *CFD for MVP*, and I fought back tears again as they all walked off the field. This was one of the best feelings ever. The best.

"I got an interesting email."

"I don't care. *Nothing* will ruin my moment right now. *Nothing*." I stuck my nose in the air. He matched my pace and let out a whistle. Uh-oh. It was too cheery.

"Okay. Well, just let me know what time you want me to pick you up Sunday to head to a boozy brunch. With your sisters and Jade. No biggie."

"What the hell did you just say?" I stopped walking and glared. *Jade found him? That traitor.*

"Does ten work for you, or did you want to get some foreplay in first?"

"I will hurt you one day, Gideon. Mark my words."

Chapter Twenty-Two

Gideon

Two wins later, one tearful lunch with Cheryl, and it was finally Sunday. I wasn't sure if what I felt was excitement or annoyance. It kept switching between the two. The thought of eating fucking brunch — *where they'd better have Bloody Marys* — with Fiona's family felt like I'd overstepped some boundaries.

Then again, Fiona was supposed to invite me and didn't, so irritating her ranked high on my list. I honked my horn twice outside her weathered apartment building and chuckled at her disgruntled expression. She'd opted for tight-fitting black jeans and a snug leather jacket. *Hm.* She looked good. Better than good.

"I don't understand how the hell you're invited. I chose not to ask you after she suggested it," she said the second she flung the door open. Her floral perfume flooded the car and it distracted me for a second. She smelled like a goddamn dream. "Explain."

"Ran into Jade at the stadium, next thing I know, I got an invitation."

"Jade? Jade just *happened* to run into you and invite you to the brunch with *my family*?" Her voice rose and she buckled herself in with a little too much aggression. "I'm calling bullshit."

"You seem worked up about it. You need something to relieve your tension?" I slid my gaze to her face and enjoyed her slight blush. "We can show up late."

"I'm game for a quickie," she deadpanned.

I burst out laughing at her expression — which slowly formed into a mischievous grin. "I knew I had game with the ladies."

"Fun fact, Gideon. If the bra matches the panties, trust me, it means I decided to have sex, not you."

"Well, do yours match?" My dick tingled at the thought of her in lingerie. *Get it together.*

"Behave today and I'll let you know," she replied with an annoying smugness to her tone. I adjusted my position in the seat and tapped the wheel. "Google says to turn right when you get to the main entrance to this neighborhood. We're heading north, I believe."

"You don't know where your sister lives? Aren't you close?"

"She moved recently. I haven't had time between school and baseball and, uh…things."

"Things like me?" I snuck a glance at her and enjoyed her clear discomfort. I was a sick bastard. "I can be distracting."

"Don't let your already inflated ego get bigger than it is. I can't take it." She let out a long sigh and crossed her legs. *Legs that I want to spread wide open.*

"Gideon? Did you hear me?"

"Uh, sorry. What?"

"Did Jade say what this was about?"

"She wants to talk to me about helping out with the charity and being a spokesperson. It's not publicly talked about, but I'm pretty into MADD and SADD." I stopped and cleared my throat. *Why is it awkward, telling her about the good parts of myself?* "My agent, Billy, always wants cameras there to film and capture my volunteer work but I refuse. My parents always told us to give back and yeah. I try. You probably don't believe me—"

"I know you do."

"Wait—how?"

"Curiosity got the better of me one night after a glass or three of wine. I looked you up. I can't say I'm surprised. You have your heart in the right place even though you come across as a total dickhole."

I swallowed down my emotions. So many thoughts crossed my mind. *She looked me up? My heart in the right place? Dickhole?* "I don't understand. You know I'm into the local chapter of the Boys and Girls club?"

"You like to give back to the community. It's all under the radar, though. I mean, shit, Gideon. You've donated back-to-school supplies to local kids, visited the after-school program and you've invited an entire club to a game. Plus, you're coaching a teenage baseball team and not a lot of people know. I assumed you would've blasted all your good-doings and shit the first time I met you."

I didn't respond. I wasn't sure how. If she knew I was into charity, why hadn't she said anything? It was something we both had in common—besides liking each other without clothes on. But our similarities ended there. My neck ached with anxiety and I used my free hand to rub the back of it. *Why does Fiona have this power over me?*

"In two miles, get on the highway and you'll be on it for a good ten minutes."

I nodded and tried to form my next words. After a few minutes of a stifling silence, Fiona reached out and put her hand on my forearm. I glanced at her touch—she rarely initiated contact—and ignored my body's reaction to her. "Gideon, relax. I'm not sure what's going on in that handsome head of yours, but chill. I never asked about the charity because it's not my business. It's yours. It doesn't affect our relation—situation. If you give it to me good and aren't a total dickhole to the kids, I don't give a shit if you donate millions or pennies to organizations."

My blood turned to ice. *Our situation? Doesn't affect her?* "Jesus. You're frustrating as hell, woman."

"So I've been told."

She let go of my arm and went back to closing off her body. I'd noticed it a week ago. She would cross her arms and legs and turn away from me whenever she said something intimate. Curiosity got the better of me, and I swallowed down my initial irritation. "It doesn't matter to you if I'm a good person or not. You only care about my dick and coaching the kids?"

"Pretty much. I mean... I didn't like you the first time we banged. I might dislike you less than in the beginning, but this isn't about our souls finding a match or shit like that."

"Hm." I blinked, trying not to be hurt at her words. I didn't do *hurt*. There was too much to do to worry about trivial things like feelings, but her words stung. *Interesting that the tables have turned.* I grew to not like, but respect and want to spend time with her while she used me for sex. *Fine.*

"I mean, I think it's absolutely awesome that you have this hidden side of you that no one knows about. You aren't doing it for fame and to get credit. I would've thought with the injury and meltdown from last year, you would want cameras everywhere."

"My personal choices don't have any play in my professional. Billy wants cameras and the whole shebang but I refuse. I hate my fame, but if I can use it to help kids, I will."

"That's good of you. I respect you a lot more."

"Thanks," I replied but hoped to end the conversation. It didn't sit well with me and the atmosphere in the car had got heavier. The rest of the drive was in an awkward silence, but I learned two things about Fiona that car-ride. *One — she doesn't acknowledge her feelings and if she tries, she turns into an asshole. Two — my charity work matters to her, she just doesn't know how to show it. She wants to keep it casual and all about the sex. I can play by her rules. For now.*

"Let's go meet the family. Big step for us," I teased after I parked the car on a long driveway. I needed distance between us. Fun and flirty distance, because we'd crossed a barrier we hadn't before — our morals and values in life. Fiona's entire body tensed and she gave me a tight smile, her disliking of my joke clear as day. I joined her as we walked up the paved path, shrubs and flowers lining it, to the door. Each step echoed on the cement and I swore Fiona's guard went up higher and higher the closer we got to the door. I stopped her, putting my hand on her shoulder. "Why are you so nervous?"

"I-I'm not."

"Liar," I replied, lowering my voice to try to comfort her. "We're a team, remember?"

"I'm not into team sports, Gideon. I do better at solo events." She shrugged my hand off and marched up to the front porch. Attitude, sadness and an independence that blurred into defense poured off her. My chest tightened and my stomach dropped at my thought.

I don't want her to be a team of one.

* * * *

"Tell us, Gideon, how is it working with my pain-in-the-ass sister?" Bea, the older version of Fiona, asked me after she'd refilled my second mimosa. I preferred a stiffer drink, but I didn't want to be rude. Champagne and orange juice it was, even if Amanda — the one with the annoyed expression permanently stuck on her face — gave me a scornful look.

"Challenging. An adventure. Frustrating," I replied and snuck a glance at my darling co-coach. The same co-coach who'd refused to look at me since her team of one bullshit a half an hour earlier. "How would you classify our time together, Barbie?"

"Jazzy. Just jazzy."

Jade and Bea snickered while Amanda still remained silent. I reached under the table to squeeze Fiona's knee. It got a slight reaction out of her — her cheeks blushing — but she didn't give me a smile. I wanted one.

"Now, the real reason I wanted to chat with you, Gideon — well, all of you — is about our first real charity event in March. We've reserved the venue, got an auctioneer and DJ — all that stuff is planned. We've invited all sorts of local Boys and Girls clubs, small organizations and big donors for our big event. We were hoping…" Jade gave Fiona a sweet smile.

"I was hoping to recruit you, Bea, to bartend the event and Amanda to help run registration. We couldn't pay you yet—we're still growing. But I know how important this group is to Fiona and thought you would want to help."

"Of course I'll help. Anything. Set up, take down. I'll do whatever I can," Bea replied and patted Fiona's arm. Amanda cleared her throat and both Fiona and Bea tensed. *Interesting.*

"Sure. I can help. Just give me the date."

"Great. Thank you, ladies. Now, Gideon, I'm hoping you'd be willing to be a keynote speaker. Could be an opening, a closing. Maybe just announcing. If you can't or would prefer not to, it's not a big deal. Fiona told—"

"Let him answer. He doesn't need an explanation," Fiona interrupted.

I gritted my teeth for a second, annoyed I didn't get to hear what Jade was saying.

"Are you in, or out?"

"Uh, let me hear more about it." I glanced back at Jade and fiddled with the silverware on the table. An uncontrollable urge to fidget took over. "What are the details? I would love to help, but the date makes a difference."

"It would be the second weekend in March. Not a huge commitment, maybe an hour or two tops. You could stay for the after-party and hang out, but the presenting would only be a small portion. All the donations go toward the TTL and funding more school counselors. That's our new goal this year," Jade said and puffed her chest out. It was clear how proud she was—Fiona too.

"You do amazing work. I'll have to check with my agent but, yeah, count me in." I held my hand across the table for a shake, and she gave me a firm grip. I wanted to ask Fiona about her flustered appearance or her sudden departure to the kitchen. "I'll be able to make a donation if needed. I'd love to help out with it. Fiona hasn't said much about it, but I've done some research."

"Hell, yeah. We'd appreciate it," Jade replied and held a fist-bump to me. We shared a grin and I cleared my throat to go check on my co-coach. "Don't worry about cleaning — we got it."

"No worries. I have manners, despite what the media says. You cooked, I'll help," I said but Jade gave me a sly smile. I shrugged and went behind the white swing door. Fiona was leaning against the counter with her fingers on her temples. My heart lurched. "What's wrong?"

She let out a long sigh and gave me a side glance. "Needed some space."

"Family too much?" I asked.

"No, you're too much." She crossed her arms and sucked her bottom lip into her mouth. Her pink cheeks and wide eyes gave me all sorts of mixed messages and I had no idea what to say. I blinked, hoping words would come together in my mind, but it remained blank. She studied me in silence, giving me an unreadable look. "Let's clean and head back, please."

"Okay. Yeah, let's clean." I joined her at the sink and we fell into a rhythm of rinsing and setting the dirty crockery into the dishwasher. Her hip hit mine and I splashed a little water on her. She laughed, and I did it again.

"Hey, man, I'm wearing a white shirt. You don't want my nips to perk up, do you?"

"I'm always wanting your nips to perk up, Barbie. They're fucking fantastic nips."

She chuckled and I enjoyed the pulse in her neck, our normal banter returning. I loved it—the jokes, the sexual innuendos and the insults. I ate it up, and I flicked more water at her.

"Asshole!" she screeched and retaliated. My cotton shirt had a huge wet spot on it and she held the sponge at me. "You messed with the wrong chick, Gideon."

"Don't I know it," I mumbled but gasped when she grabbed the rinser and blasted it on me. It was scalding hot and the smell of Dawn dish soap clogged my nose. Her little body slipped out of my hands when I reached for her, the curve of her mouth my undoing. "I guess I'll have to take off my shirt now and we both know you can't control yourself around me."

"Uh-huh, right. Try explaining that to Bea. This is her house *and* my potential boss is here."

"Fine by me." I lifted the hem of my shirt and got it to my neck before her small hands rested on my hips. "Oh, I like this."

"Keep it on," she growled.

"Nah, I want to embarrass you." I began taking it off again, but she jumped onto me. She wrapped her legs around my waist—my cock springing to life—and she pulled the shirt down. Her expression had my heart skip a beat. Her fierce blue eyes were almost clear, her lips parted, her eyes hooded, and I wanted her to be mine.

Like, really mine.

I cupped her chin with my right hand and kissed her. It was soapy, wet and tender. Our lips brushed against each other, her sweet taste and soft touch rocking me to my core. I swirled my tongue inside her mouth, tasting the remnants of the mimosa and her warmth. She groaned, rocking her hips against me enough to have all blood leave my brain.

No blood or rational thought remained. I would've taken her on the counter right there, but realization of where we were hit. Bea's kitchen. "Sweetheart, I need to stop."

She slowly opened her eyes, the passion and heat of seconds before still there. She wiped the back of her hand over her swollen mouth and slid down my body. Her neck was tinged red and she didn't say another word when she went back to finishing the dishes. I didn't either.

I wasn't sure what had happened, but something had changed. Her looks were a little longer. A little more tender. A little more scared.

And it didn't freak me out.

Chapter Twenty-Three

Fiona

My bottom lip almost bled from how much I bit it. I blamed Gideon—it was his damn fault with the *sweetheart* talk and sweet kisses. I didn't do sweet. Rough. Quick. Passionate.

Sweet? Jesus Christ. Sweet and feelings were too damn close for my liking. It didn't help that he was wearing tight workout pants and a pullover that left nothing to the imagination. Plus, I'd already seen all the tight muscles under the silky material. "CFD? Coach Titan said to pay attention to the game and not his muscles."

I made a scowl at Gideon, doing my best to tell him to *fuck off* with my eyes. "Thanks, Big Al. You don't need to be a messenger, though. Don't let him play you."

"I don't mind. You guys are funny. I caught him trying to sneak a whoopee cushion under you once, but it didn't work."

My mouth fell open. "The farting things?"

"Yeah. He showed me how it worked later. Gatorade came through my nose, I laughed so hard." He clutched his side and lost it into a fit of giggles. "Don't be mad, CFD. He picks on you because he likes you."

"Thanks for the advice, Al. I appreciate it."

He gave me a nod and walked to the on-deck circle. Quinn and Cheryl sat right next to our dugout and every time someone was on-deck, she stuck her little hand in the fence for a high-five. Any hope for humanity I'd lost was restored when every single grumpy, pimple-ridden teenage boy gave the sweet girl a high-five. Gideon and I shared a smile, but his disappeared real quick. We had been hot and cold since that *kiss* for no reason. Get *it together, idiot.*

It took every ounce of willpower to not talk about it, look at his mouth or stare at his ass when he bent over to pick up a bag of seeds. But I managed, and I was proud of myself. Plus, it helped that we'd played great and won the game.

"I need to talk to my sister for a second. Can you distract Quinn?"

"Sure." I gave him a long look, trying to figure out why he was scowling after our win, but I came up empty. *It could be the kiss, but that means I'm paranoid.* "Where you at, squirt?"

She ran up to me and demanded a gymnastics challenge. Some of the boys laughed at our cartwheels and handstands, but it brightened my mood. Garth challenged her to a handstand contest, and he let her win — the sweetheart — but Quin puffed out her little chest and ran toward the grass. I gave a sheepish smile in Cheryl and Gideon's direction and took off after her. My bones hurt and we made our way back to Cheryl and Gideon ten minutes later, after the boys had all left and my age had caught up to me. They were in a heated argument, words carrying over toward us. *Court. Custody.* I froze and grabbed Quinn's hand. "Do you think they would let us convince them to get ice cream?"

"I hope so. Uncle Gid is a softie for me. I can get him to do everything if I'm cute enough. That's what my mom says."

"I bet you're right." I cleared my throat and they both stopped talking. "Hi, guys. We were hoping we could go get ice cream. I can take her if you two need to clear up some issues. I don't mind—she's my new friend."

"What? No. We're...we're good. Thank you, though, Fiona," Cheryl replied and wiped under her eyes. "Come on, pumpkin."

"Okay. Bye, Fiona!"

"See you, monster." I waved and watched the two of them walk toward their car. I felt the rage coming off Gideon and I waited for them to leave before facing him. "Are you—"

He interrupted me with a frantic edge to his voice. "Can you watch her next Friday? It's a half-day at school and I have to be there for my sister. I can pay you. Anything. You're good with her and—"

"I meant what I said. Yes. I'll help any way I can." I reached out to touch him, but thought better of it. "Where?"

"My house. I'll make it up to you."

"No, we're even. Seeing that guy's face when a woman beat his team is enough to keep me smiling for at least two weeks." I gave him a smile and a wave. "See you tomorrow, muscles."

"Do you want to go out? Like, for food? Drinks?"

His sudden question startled me. He practically yelled it at me and I gulped. *Out? Like a date? Shit.* "I can't tonight. I have a huge assignment due tomorrow morning."

"Okay. Yeah, sure. See you."

He walked away without another look. Why did I feel like I just got dumped? I hadn't done anything wrong. *Jesus — this is why I don't do feelings. Fuck it.* "You can come over if you want. I don't mind the company."

What. Did. I. Just. Say?

He stopped walking, his tight back tensing even more. But then he turned and grinned. "Really?"

"I mean, if you want. I'm not exciting," I rambled and wished the ground would swallow me. "I do have work to do."

"I'll let you work. I prefer not to — well, thanks, Fiona. I'll follow you to your place."

I gave a brief nod and headed to my car with hundreds of questions. *Why am I nervous? Why is Gideon happy about coming over to just sit?*

And why is my heart racing?

The fifteen-minute drive seemed to go by in five seconds. I checked the rearview mirror every thirty seconds to see if his SUV was there — it was — and I gripped the wheel. This wasn't a booty call. Or maybe it was. "Shit. Shit!"

The bubble in my stomach grew and by the time we parked and his large frame towered over me at the door, I felt like I was on a goddamn date to prom. "I-I don't have any beer or anything."

"That's okay. If you hadn't noticed, I don't drink a lot." He held the door open for me after I unlocked it, and his faint cologne had me inhaling his delicious scent. "What's your project?"

"Business proposal with a set budget and list of employees, benefits, etc. Here, I'll make you a cup of tea. Let me get my computer started." I showed him the table, giving him the bright blue chair, and started the computer. I needed to keep my hands busy and ignored how the mugs clanked together after I'd heated up the water. *Chill the fuck out.* "I hope you like—"

"What the hell is this?" He squinted at my laptop with a huge, scary grin and I raced over to block it. Tea spilled onto my hands, but I ignored it. *What's on my screen?* "Are you… Did you seriously have a document filled with baseball knowledge?"

"Nope." I used my body to block it and I would strip to save myself. I would. I couldn't believe I forgot I left it open. *Fuck me.*

"Liar. I can't believe this." His grin stretched across his entire face and the dimples greeted me. *Damn, his perfect dimples.* I felt my resolve slipping.

"It's nothing, Gid." I began to take off my shirt—anything—to distract him. I got my sports bra off in seconds and sat there, topless, hoping it would work. It didn't. "Kiss me, Gideon."

"No, no, no." He reached out and put his hand on my shoulder, fits of laughter coming out of him. "I mean, yes. I will in a second. But, dear *Jesus,* this is golden."

I groaned into my hand and shoved past him to plop on the chair next to him. Modesty was never my thing and sitting there without a shirt didn't bother me. If it helped save me embarrassment, then I'd do what I had to. "Get it over with. Read it."

He remained quiet for five minutes, the only sign he was there an occasional chuckle, snort or head-shake. I'd made that before I knew I would be coaching with him. I'd reviewed it the night before and had forgotten to close it.

Because why would Gideon Titan be in my kitchen?

"Gideon. I refuse to be embarrassed."

"You wrote a definition of the Mendoza line. You're such a fucking dork."

I closed my eyes and tried not to think about all the blackmail he had on me. The chair creaked and I arched my back when warm wet lips closed down around my nipple. "Yes. *Finally.*"

"I'm going to test you over your ridiculous cheat sheet," he said between sucking and biting down on my exposed breasts. "Now, Fiona, what average is used to describe the Mendoza line?"

He dragged his tongue from my left to right breast, flicking the pointed tip and pausing. "Answer correctly, I'll continue moving down. Answer wrong, I leave."

"Two hundred, thirty-five," I moaned and lifted my back up, connecting my nipples to his mouth. "Please."

"Needy girl. I love it," he growled and cupped my breasts, squeezing and pulling the sensitive skin. Nipple play hadn't been a thing for me until the combination of his scruff and mouth. The hair rubbed against the skin, the rough feeling enhancing the pleasure. "I could taste you every day."

"I could let you," I replied with a raspy voice. I squirmed, trying to spread my legs for him, but he clicked his tongue. "Ask me another question."

"Not yet. Your body is gorgeous. I want to taste you a little longer."

Fuck. That was smooth. I remained speechless as he took his time licking up the center of my chest, trailing on my collarbones and the soft spot right below my ear.

I shivered. I fisted his hair and dragged his mouth to mine. *Fire. Heat. Tenderness.*

His tongue slipped into me with the ease of a lover, but ignited me inside out. I forgot about our rules, our short-term situation and the walls I fought to keep up. He cupped the back of my head, breaking the kiss for a second, and gazed down at me with the softest expression I'd ever seen on him. It was like the ground fell beneath me, and I almost stumbled.

"You kiss like it's your last breath. I fucking love it."

I grinned, bringing my fingers to the button of his jeans. "Life's short. Let's continue to enjoy the moment, shall we?"

He nodded and within seconds had me over his shoulder and I pointed him to my room. He tossed me on the bed and, after a quick strip-down, our naked bodies were pressed together. "I had more questions for you. You cheated."

"Slip inside me and you can ask me anything you want."

"God, I love your sassy mouth." He reached over to the side table and had the condom on in record time. I liked an overachiever.

I moaned, his cock filling and stretching me in the best way. "You feel so good, Gid."

He grunted, picking up my hips as he pounded into me. I held on to my sheets, their flimsy fabric not enough support. I closed my eyes, enjoying the pleasure rippling through me, but Gideon growled at me. "Keep your eyes open. I want to watch them as you come."

I blinked a couple of times and wrapped my legs around him, giving him access to my clit. He used his free hand and combined the thrusting with the right pressure on my swollen nub, and tingles began all over my body. They spread up and down my spine, the need for release so damn close. "Faster, Gideon. I need you."

"Fuck, yeah," he replied and kept his gaze on me. It was intense — his strong jaw clenched with passion and he continued to stretch my walls to new bounds. I swore he could see right through me, through my bullshit and terror. He pinned me down with his honey stare and I couldn't stop his name coming from my lips. "Gideon!"

"Say my name again."

And I did. I screamed his name as an orgasm unlike anything I had ever experienced rocked through me. My eyes watered when wave after wave of pleasure consumed me. Gideon held on to me the entire time, his muscles tightening. I arched my hips, allowing him to go deeper, and he quickened his pace. His gaze stayed on me, and when he said my name, spilling himself inside me, my throat closed up.

I must need water.

"Fucking hell, Fiona. My ears are ringing right now." He collapsed on the bed next to me, somehow managing to slip his arm under me. He cradled me, my head on the spot right between his neck and shoulder. I couldn't recall the last time I'd cuddled after sex. Panic began to rise in my throat, the need to run or make a joke overpowering. But he grabbed one of my boobs and gave it a squeeze, de-escalating the moment in his own way. "Best boobs ever."

I laughed and rolled onto my front, my hair hanging all over my face. I moved my hand to brush it out of the way, but he beat me to it. He gently brought his fingers to my face, pushing the loose strands behind my ear. I gulped, the entire lower half of my stomach mimicking a rollercoaster ride. "You have great hands. I'm pretty positive I could say best hands ever."

"I like a challenge, babe. I'll earn the title." He smiled at me, his expression soft, and warm tingles began in my chest. "Now, what does the expression 'a can of corn' mean?"

"Back to the document, huh? I thought the best sex ever would be enough to distract you," I replied and fought a smile. His happy, goofy mood was hard to not like.

"Excuse me, did you just say the best sex ever?" His voice rose.

"No. I said that for your benefit, not mine," I lied, dragging my teeth over my bottom lip. "And, it's when a pop fly is so easy, it resembles someone dropping a can of corn from the top shelf. Duh," I replied in an octave a little too high. He didn't laugh, though. He positioned himself over me again, his eyes all sorts of intense. I gulped.

"Not the best sex ever? I'd say it's pretty fucking fantastic. Do I need to use more tongue? Do you want me to bend you over the kitchen table instead? What's it gunna take to get that title, because in my book, you're the top, Barbie."

Words were too hard to form. His gaze darted to my lips, then to my eyes and back. His cheeky grin was too sweet, too flirtatious and too goddamn cute. I couldn't come up with a single comeback and he gave me a titty twister. "I call bullshit. You're never speechless. Now, I'll put clothes on so I don't distract you. Get your project done. I'll help you if I can."

And that was how I spent my night—Gideon trying to help me with a project he knew nothing about and me fighting off his *helpful* hints. He distracted me when

I got frustrated, looked up cheesy jokes to make me laugh and went and got takeout when my stomach growled. He fell asleep on the couch at three in the morning and I let him stay. I hadn't had that much fun with a guy, with clothes on, in...*years*.

And I never let them stay. But him, I did.

C h a p t e r   T w e n t y - F o u r

Gideon

Cheryl pushed the courthouse's glass doors open with so much effort they banged against the guardrail on the outside. She threw her hands up in the air, spinning around in a small circle before jumping onto me. I caught her, giving her the biggest hug I could. Pride, joy and a fierceness I didn't recognize went through me. She'd held her ground — and walked away without having to take anything to court. "Gideon, I'm amped up. Like, I need to fucking buy a lottery ticket or go run three miles. I'm so happy. God."

The tears started, not that I was surprised. My eyes had stung for a brief second when I'd watched the realization dawn over Cheryl's face when her lawyer said no custody would be awarded at all. "I'm happy, too. Quinn deserves the best, and Vic is a piece of shit."

"Sean had a theory that he was only after us to rope money out of you." She said the words so matter-offactly that I didn't have time to digest them. "I'm beyond pissed that any lowlife would do that to Quinn, make her a pawn in a money scheme, but no one messes with my family."

"We're a pack of wolves," I replied with a grin. My cheeks began hurting with all the muscles curving upward. "We can stop to buy some beer, cigarettes or your lottery ticket if you want. You deserve a treat."

"We should get back to Quinn and Fiona, yeah?"

"I think they can wait a bit more. What do you want, Cheryl?" I sent a quick text to Fiona with an update — *We won, but Cheryl needs a well-deserved drink.* "Champagne? Tattoos? Drugs?"

She laughed and her long hair shook around her with each chuckle. "I want one glass of Champagne. There's a place close to here that has great cocktails. You're right. We deserve one."

"You do. You're the best fucking mom I know. Quinn is lucky to have you," I said and squeezed her shoulder. I didn't have to say anything more — she knew the words I wanted to say but didn't.

She nodded and leaned into me as we made the short walk to a dive bar near the courthouse. It had a small sign on the front, but all locals knew about Fritzie's. A couple of walkers gave me a nod, but not one person had the crazy look. The look where they demanded autographs or selfies. I sent a quick prayer up — this was about Cheryl.

We entered the bar and found a quiet booth in the back. A server appeared in less than a minute and brought out the drinks right after. We clinked the fragile glasses and Cheryl only said two words. "To family."

I held her gaze, my emotion almost too much to handle. Our unique little trio had somehow survived unthinkable things. The abrupt death of our parents, Quinn's dad abandoning them after six months and my injury that could've ended my career.

But we were still there. "I feel like I've lost weight. Like, ten pounds of stress," Cheryl said after taking another long swig. Thankfully, the glasses weren't too large and there wasn't enough in there to get a buzz.

"No more stress. There isn't anything he can do to try again, right?"

"Not unless he makes up for six years of child support. My bet is he doesn't. No, not Vic. He couldn't bring himself to buy diapers for her. He's not going to weasel his way back into our life. Nope."

I nodded, making a vow to keep an eye on the asshole. If he came sniffing back around, I'd deal with it. "He sure as shit won't."

"Can we head back? I just want to hug my girl."

"Of course." I got the bill and we were on our way back in my SUV. The atmosphere differed from the car ride there in every aspect. She chatted almost nonstop about what she and Quinn were going to do and I relished her joy. I didn't realize how much her stress had wedged itself into my muscles, but now the situation had been dealt with, I felt free.

We parked in the garage and Cheryl didn't wait a second for me before heading into my house. I'd offered to have Fiona and Quinn stay here, a place they both were familiar with. I ignored the quickening of my pulse at the thought of seeing Fiona. I'd seen her the past three nights, and the past three mornings, but today was different. She'd done me a favor.

"Mommy!" Quinn's voice carried down the hall and I walked in just as she threw her little body at Cheryl. I instantly sought out Fiona, her blonde hair standing out in the foyer. She had it piled on top of her head in a ridiculous bun and wore tight yoga pants and an old sweatshirt. She had never looked so goddamn beautiful.

"How'd it go?" she asked and played with the end of her sweatshirt. "I've been anxious to hear about it. Cheryl looks happy, though."

"I'll tell you all about it. Let me get them going," I replied and reached out for her hand. I squeezed it and enjoyed the slow curve of her lips. It was one of her *sweet* smiles, where her skin crinkled around her eyes and a little dent formed beneath the left one. I adored that dent. "Quinn, are you going to give your second-favorite person in the world a hug?"

"Duh!" Cheryl passed her to me and I breathed in her kid-shampoo smell. My heart felt normal again and I gave her a noogie. "Uncle Gid! No! Fiona did my hair!"

"Did she now?" I set her down and raised an eyebrow at Fiona. She pursed her lips, looking way too smug.

"Yup. Come here, QT. I'll fix it." She got onto her knees when Quinn walked up to her. Fiona bent low, laughing as she brushed Quinn's hair out of her face. My entire face got warm, my body tingling at the sight of the two of them. I pulled on the collar of my polo and gulped. *Did they turn the heat on too high?*

"Thanks, Cool Fiona."

"You got it, girl. Anytime." Fiona reached her arms around my niece and her gaze met mine over Quinn's little shoulder. *Fiona would be a great mom.* I felt punched in the fucking chest. I blinked and went through the motions of walking Cheryl and Quinn out, taking my time before going in to face Fiona. *What the fuck happened? Thoughts of her being a mom? Jesus Christ.*

"Gid, I'm trying to be patient here, man, but I want the details."

I ran my hand over my face and collected my thoughts. We were co-coaches who hooked up. Maybe friends. I was unsure about that, but we had each other's backs and that was enough for me. "Sorry. Want a beer?"

"Nah, I'm good. I need to drive back soon anyway."

"We don't have a game tonight. We don't play until after the holidays."

"I know. I want to enjoy my free night," she replied and rolled her eyes. She hoisted herself up onto my island counter and continued to stare at me. "What's wrong? You have that haunted, I'm-becoming-an-asshole look right now. It either means you're horny or pissed. What is it?"

I laughed. I didn't want to, but her candor amused me. Her expression warmed and I moved to stand between her legs. "I'm always horny when you're around."

"You're insatiable." She giggled when I ran my hand up and down her leg. "But get to talking. I want to hear all about it."

"Want to sit outside or in the bean bag room?"

"Need you ask? Bean bags, please." She jumped off the counter and led the way into the basement. I watched her ass the entire time and didn't feel the pinch in my knee once on the way down. *Hell, yeah.* "If I ever need extra money, I'm selling pictures of this man-child room to the tabloids. I'm giving you a heads-up to prepare for the backlash."

"You wouldn't dare," I threatened, but without real force. Her teasing meant she cared and I'd grown to love her little quips. "If you're going to sell anything, I can pose nude for you. That'll get you at least a couple of grand."

"You're right, maybe some calendars. Holy shit! Yes. Can we make a sex calendar of you and get profits for the charity?" Her voice rose two octaves too high and she clapped her hands like a fool. Her joy was contagious, and I smiled too.

"Hm. I'm going to say a hard no, but I'll pose for you anytime."

"You know, I think you're the first person I've met who has my libido. Honestly, the most productive thing I've done today was fantasize about you being naked." She smiled and I felt it in my chest. *Huh.* "Well, besides hang out with your niece. That was fun, but enough sexy-talk. Tell me everything."

She plopped onto her stomach and grabbed a pillow to support her head. She glanced up at me, patting the spot next to her, and another emotion went through me. *Longing.* I longed to be with her. "Come on, big guy. Get comfortable."

Clearing my throat, I joined her and lay on my side to face her. "Okay. Vic is Quinn's father who abandoned her after six months. He came sniffing around wanting to get custody, after years without paying child support. It was settled today and he gets no time without Cheryl's permission and paying all the support he owes."

"Good lord, that's great news." She closed her eyes with a slight tremble to her lip. "I'm happy for Quinn and Cheryl, but did he express any interest in seeing Quinn?"

"No," I replied and my tone darkened. "That's what pisses me off. That piece of shit doesn't care about his daughter. We had a feeling he wanted to get a paycheck or blackmail from me. He kept looking at me in the meeting and it creeped me the hell out. He's not getting shit from us, ever."

"Fuck that. God." She paused and clenched her hands into fists. "I'm sorry you had to go through that. But I'm so glad Cheryl and Quinn have you. You're a good man."

"Thank you." I stared at her mouth. It still shook a little. "Are you okay?"

"I can't forgive someone who leaves a family behind. It's the worst thing a parent can do. I get this rage-fueled emotion inside my chest when I think about it, but also an innate sadness that is bone deep. My dad left us, but I was old enough to remember time with him. He, uh, has a new family now. I think I told you that after that shit-storm of a night."

"Have you talked to him?"

"I tried. I called him a bunch afterward, but he never returned my calls and they became less frequent. My mom would scream at us when we tried contacting him, and that's not the worst part." She hesitated and I took her hand. Her sad gaze met mine for a second and I wanted to turn every one of her bad memories into good ones. I would've agreed to anything to help her. "My mom knew he had a new family, wife, house, daughters and she didn't want Amanda, Bea or me to know. But I went behind her back and found out when I was fourteen."

Jesus. "Does your mom know you found out?"

"Yeah, but we've never talked about it. Amanda...probably. But I'm not sure. Bea knows too, but he's just a topic we shove under the rug. It's so fucked-up." She wiped her eyes and I forgot about our rules. I just wanted to take her sadness and fill it with joy. I pulled her to me, enclosing her body with mine.

"He missed out. He missed out on everything, Fiona. That's on him, not you. He doesn't get to see the amazing, beautiful, talented and ass-kicking woman you are." She blinked up at me, tears welling in her eyes again, and I kissed her.

Her lips were softer than normal. I slowly brought my tongue to hers, taking my time to speak without words. She opened her mouth, arching her neck so I could deepen it. We started out slow, an agonizing dance of give and take, and that shook me to my core in every way. She let her emotions come into the kiss, not holding anything back. She was sad, and I did my best to change that. I cupped her face, dragging my lips across her jaw, up to her ear and back to her mouth. "His fucking loss, Fiona. You're helping change the world."

The smallest, almost inaudible whimper left her and it broke my heart. I rolled her on top of me and slid my hands down her sides. God, I wanted all of her. Her joys and pain. But she stopped. She sat up, wiping the back of her hand on her mouth.

"I'm on my period so I should go soon."

I froze. *Wait, what?* "Uh, I don't care if you're on your period."

"You're into that sort of thing?" She scrunched her nose and gave me a weird look. There was no more tenderness in her gaze. No more sadness or vulnerability. The fiery glint that I loved on the field was in her eyes, but why was I a game to her? I shook my head, becoming more annoyed at her direction of her conversation.

"No. I'm saying, we can still hang out if you're on your period. I grew up with a sister. I understand what it means."

"We can't hook up, though. That's sort of what we do," she mumbled and avoided my stare while she got off me. My muscles tightened again and my stress came back. "I should go anyway. I'm so happy for your family, Gideon."

She didn't wait before leaving the room and it took me ten seconds to get my wits about me. *What did I do?* "Fiona! Wait."

I jogged up the stairs, wincing at the top step since I took it a little too fast. "What the fuck just happened?"

"N-nothing. Nothing happened. I need to go." She was already heading toward the front door and I ran up to it, putting my hand on it to prevent her from opening it.

"Look at me," I commanded.

She slowly turned her head but masked her face. It was unreadable. "What, Gideon?"

"Did I do something wrong? I'm at a loss right now, Fiona. We had a serious conversation and I kissed you. Now you're leaving."

"That's the thing, we aren't supposed to do serious conversations." She crossed her arms and clicked her tongue. "You didn't do anything wrong."

I squeezed the back of my neck, anger flowing through me. Why was she too fucking stubborn in refusing to admit there was something more...some connection we shared? "Fine. Run away. At least let me give you your Christmas present."

"Present?" she squeaked and jumped away from me. "You...got me something?"

"Foolishly, yeah. Fuck." I groaned into my fist and grabbed the bag I'd kept on the foyer table for the past week. I felt like a goddamn idiot and I threw it at her. I didn't wait to see what she did. I marched down the hall and slammed the door to my office, but not without shouting at her one last time, "Merry fucking Christmas, Fiona."

Chapter Twenty-Five

Fiona

Michelle had checked on me twice already—asking me if I needed a stiff drink, a sedative or a slap in the face. I appreciated her effort, but I shook her off. I had to deal with my own shit alone. *Fucking Gideon.*

His gift sat on the kitchen table, remaining unopened in the white tissue paper I tore apart. That wasn't true, I'd touched it countless times that first time. But I couldn't bring myself to actually open the journal. *What if he wrote in it?*

"Gah!" I hit the table and paced the kitchen. This was why I always had jobs on top of school. I needed constant distractions or I got lost in my thoughts. I'd aced my finals weeks ago and had no homework to occupy my brain power. He'd gotten me a goddamn journal. A journal to write in when I'd finished the other one. It was the most thoughtful gift I had ever received in my entire life and I hated it.

No, I loved it.

But I hated how it made me feel. I hadn't talked to him in two days and my conflicting thoughts confused the hell out of me. I reread the card for the umpteenth time and rubbed my temples.

Fiona,
I can't imagine all the things he's missed. When you run
out of room in your other journal, use this one.
Gideon

So simple. I pinched the bridge of my nose and counted to three. Then I picked up the journal. The smooth brown leather felt like butter—I dragged my fingers over the material and breathed in the scent. It reminded me of shoe stores and baseball gloves. The hard journal fell open and creamy the white pages were in front of me. The pages were thick enough to write with my favorite heavy pen and not bleed through. It was the best journal I had owned and I wanted to write in it right then.

My favorite ink pen was at the bottom of my backpack and I found it within seconds. My heart raced with a need to write, and I began with Gideon. I wrote about coaching the baseball team, how hard it was without Justin this year, especially with the decision about joining TTL in the air, but also how the players reminded me of him every day. I wrote about my conflicting feelings about life and the joys it was supposed to bring. Sadness had a place in life, and I understood it. But happiness was scary. Because if I was happy, it could just get taken away.

The fear. I stopped writing and clutched the pen. The fear of what? Not being happy? I leaned back into the chair, not far enough to tip over, but so far it wiggled and my heart lurched in my throat. I yelped and Michelle ran out of her room.

"What the hell is going on?"

"I almost fell. I stopped it, though."

"Girl, you're acting nuts. I don't know if you're into *Harry Potter* and shit, but that journal is not a goddamn horcrux."

Her joke was not lost on me and I laughed. We shared a long belly-laugh and she joined me at the table with nothing but concern on her face. "I am acting nuts. I'm sorry."

"Don't apologize. If you need to talk, I'm here."

"This is a step in our relationship."

"We already live together. I'm too broke to cause a scene or move out, so you can trust me." She gave me a smile and put her hand on my arm. "We're a lot alike, Fiona, and I have a feeling we're better at giving other people advice than taking our own."

I rolled my eyes but relaxed with her presence. She wasn't entirely wrong. "Go on. You have my attention."

"Gideon is messing with you. Justin and the charity are messing with you. Neither is related to the other, so what consumes your mind more?"

I frowned, tracing the edge of the journal with my pointer finger. "Both. Neither. I'm not sure."

"When you're driving or falling asleep at night, what do you think about? Justin? Gideon? We all drift off into our thoughts when we're not too busy, and you've been not busy for almost a week now without classes. You've been acting different that whole time. So, what is it?"

"Decisions. I have so many decisions that I can't be expected to make and ensure they are the right ones. This job…what if I hate it and I can't quit when it's for Justin? What if it hurts too much and it destroys me?" I avoided her stare. I looked at my fingers and twisted them into each other, playing with the silver ring I had on my thumb. "I know it's irrational, but it's a big decision."

"You're not irrational, Fiona. Don't think about a forever job. Think about five years. Could you learn and grow and even enjoy the job for five years? Dedicate yourself to getting it running and doing a kick-ass job at it, then think about leaving? You love working with the kids and you can make sure you do a school visit once a week."

I nodded and dared to meet her gaze. Her stare bored into me — not in an intrusive way, but in an *I get you* way. It reminded me of Jade. And Gideon. "Coaching this team has been so rewarding. I didn't think it would be like this."

"The charity is to help kids be aware of the dangers of texting and driving. I think that answers itself. Not many twenty-somethings can say they helped a charity grow across states."

"You researched Texting Too Late?"

"Of course. You're my friend and I want to help once you accept this job." She grinned and a weight the size of a truck lifted from my chest. "Now, about Gideon."

"One issue at a time, please. I can't believe I made the decision. I'm doing it. I'm going to accept it for five years. Then I can re-evaluate. Fuck yeah. Holy shit… Michelle. Thank you."

"You got it. We don't have to talk about Gideon if you don't want to, but that gift isn't casual. Neither is dropping you off, picking you up, standing up for you on the field and saving you from a drunken date." She stood, squeezed my shoulder and left me to my thoughts. I took a long, calming breath, picked up my phone and called Jade. She answered on the first ring and I didn't even greet her.

"I want the job."

"Wait, really? Hold on. Mom—get over here!" She shuffled the phone around and my heart hammered in my chest. "I'm so happy. I just knew it!"

I let out an awkward chuckle and a cry as Diane—the president of TTL and Jade's mom—got on the phone. "Hi, Fiona. I hear you'll accept the position full-time?"

"Yes, Diane. Year by year contract, I will sign."

"You're perfect for this, Fiona. Your dedication to volunteering, coaching and candor when speaking about Justin…the experience you bring is crucial. I might've acted all confident and told Jade to act like it isn't a big deal, but I can't imagine this team without you."

"Yeah, I love this team. Sorry for being a pain in the ass about it. Send over the contract whenever you can and I'll get it back to you."

"Will do. Here's Jade again."

"Oh my god. Girl, I'm so happy for you. For me. For us," Jade said.

"I love you and your mom rocks. You're weirdos, but my kind of weirdos."

She agreed and hung up. I couldn't describe how the weight had lifted off my shoulders. Diane and Jade had lost a son and brother to texting and driving, and the vice president had also lost a loved one to it. They were a core group of strong women and I felt a little foolish that it had taken so long to decide. But I had and I was happy with it.

I eyed the journal again before moving on to my next issue. The guilt from how I'd left Gideon. Shame consumed me. I hadn't gotten him a gift that clearly had effort and he deserved better from a co-coach. No...friend. We were friends. How did I start this conversation, though? I couldn't just apologize like a crazy person. I needed to hook him. *Sex!* Yes. I would sex my way in.

Fiona: I wish you were inside me right now.

Fiona: Oops. Autocorrect. I meant good afternoon.

Gideon: Send nudes.

Gideon: Oops. Autocorrect. I meant, hey.

I giggled. This was normal banter. I relaxed into my chair and swore tension rolled off me. Psh—I had been worried that he hated me.

Fiona: I have news. Want to meet for a drink?

Gideon: Can't until Christmas. Took Cheryl and Quinn up to Flagstaff. After?

Fiona: Sure. Have fun!

It shouldn't annoy me, or make me sad that I couldn't see him. But my feelings didn't quite listen to my brain and I frowned. Two more days...I could wait that long. That gave me time to come up with a gift.

* * * *

The jersey material was stiff and uncomfortable, but my last name and favorite number stood on the back with the red embroidery. Yeah—the gift could be a total bust between the signed jersey from the kids and my autograph. But I hoped it would make him smile, at least. I rearranged the tissue paper in the bag about six times, smoothed down my hair three times and adjusted the hem on my slim black sweater dress. Bea had gotten it for me the day before and it fit me in all the right spots. Amanda had gotten us mace keychains—practical, but not a fun Christmas present. *Whatever.*

I wasn't trying to impress Gideon. No. I wasn't. Nor did my palms sweat and my heart race. The café was just too hot and I'd had too much coffee. My watch read ten minutes past our meeting time, and a ripple of panic went through me. *What if he stands me up?*

The bell rang at the front of the store and his large, perfectly toned frame appeared. I gulped and ran my teeth over my bottom lip when he actively searched for me. The smile that greeted me went straight to my heart, shooting through my veins into my toes. *God, he's beautiful.* "Hey, muscles."

"Barbie," he replied and ran a hand over his jaw. It tensed but his smile broke out again. "You're a sight, I tell you."

"A good one, I hope?"

"Yes, Fiona. A very good one." He walked to the other side of the table and bent low, his face inches from mine when he stopped. Instead of greeting me with the lips I craved, he just gave my hair a tug. "You look happy. Did you have a nice holiday?"

"I took the job!"

"Wait, really?" he shouted. "Fiona! That's fuck—that's amazing!" He winced and lowered his voice. "Tell me everything."

His genuine interest about did me in. I told him about Michelle's conversation—leaving the part about him out—and he leaned closer to me with each word. His eyes warmed over and he gripped my hand the entire time. I had never felt so supported. "I knew you'd take it."

"Yeah? How so?"

"He'll always be a part of you. Your story. Your puzzle. We're all made of pieces and each one keeps us together. He's at least three or four of them. You'll miss a piece of yourself without him."

I blinked, replaying those words in my head. "That was beautiful, Gideon."

"I have my moments." His gaze went from my eyes to our joined hands. "I'm proud of you. Not that you took it—I knew you would—but that you figured it out. It's not an easy decision, but I think you'll find happiness there."

"Thank you," I replied and hoped my shaky voice wasn't too apparent. I took a swig of water and looked at the beige carpet for a couple of seconds. "I got you a gift."

"Oh? I hope it's not just a guilt gift. Those are the worst," he groaned and the familiar sound made me grin. I preferred grumpy Gideon. I knew how to deal with him. Sensitive, thoughtful and sweet Gideon...hell, no.

"Okay. It's not a guilt gift. One is important...the other is for fun."

"You didn't have to get me anything, you know. I didn't expect it. I found that journal when I was out with Cheryl buying some weird-ass book about organizing her life. I just thought, you're going to run out of paper at some point. It wasn't that big of a deal."

"No. You're wrong," I raised my voice to the point a couple near us gave us speculative glances. "It meant a lot to me. I never got to thank you. So, this is me, thanking you in my awkward way."

"Fair enough. Now, where's my gift?" He clapped his hands and gave me the goofiest grin I had seen. He rivaled a little kid and it was fucking cute. "Quinn got me socks and Cheryl bought a world's best uncle mug. I love the two of them, but they are the worst."

I chuckled and handed over the bag. The second it left my fingers, nerves danced down my throat. *What if he hates it? Laughs at it? Throws it at me?* I deserved it after I'd left his place last week. "Ah, can I... Never mind."

"What?" He stopped opening it and gave me a concerned look. "Why are you pale? Oh my god. You're nervous. Fiona, I'll love it."

"I'm not sure. Just, get it over with please." I clenched my eyes shut and waited as the paper shuffled. The café smelled of bacon and grease, but it wasn't enough to distract me from my inner turmoil. I waited, and he finally made a sound.

"Holy shit."

"It's just a joke—" He had his jersey, the one with all the kids' signatures on it. He was supposed to open that one second. His entire face froze and his gaze moved all over the jersey and he held it up higher. The white material danced across the table and twenty miserable seconds went by. "Gideon. Do you like it?"

"I love it." He spoke with such confidence and determination, I sat up straighter. "I'm getting a frame and hanging this up in my favorite room of my house."

"The basement?"

"Ha, no. The kitchen. I spend the most time there. This is my favorite gift. Thank you, Fiona. Wow." He looked at it again and stood.

"What are you—"

He kissed me. Right in the middle of the café, people around us and the smell of burning hash browns clogging my nose. I sighed his embrace, his soft lips welcoming me home. He squeezed my hip and ended the kiss sooner than I wanted. "Thank you."

I blinked back emotion at the tenderness in his voice. He would break me and I was almost okay with it, as long as I got more time with this interesting man. I took another drink of water and waited until I could mask my face better. "I'm so glad you like it."

"You didn't sign it, though?" he asked, tracing the signatures like a kid getting his favorite athlete's autograph. "Where's your name?"

"Well, that's the thing. You were supposed to open the other gift first and end with this one. Now, it's all messed up and the other gift will be really stupid." I groaned and bit the end of my knuckle. "Let's just forget about the other one?"

"No chance in hell." He clapped his hands again, folding his jersey into a nice square and setting it gently on the table. "What did you do, Barbie?"

I didn't answer and waited when he pulled out another jersey. This time, my name was on the back. "It's fucking stupid."

"Did you...did you sign this?" Humor laced every word and I tried to think of any excuse to leave. Anything. "*Fiona.*"

"Fine. Yes. I signed it. I thought it was funny. You know, when I'm a famous person, you can sell it for money." I buried my head in my hands and mumbled to myself, "Dumbass."

"I stand corrected. This is the best gift. I'm getting two frames now. Both of these are going in my kitchen. Treasures, Fiona. These are fucking treasures," he spoke between bouts of laughing and snorting.

"You're laughing your ass off at my expense. Not really sure I trust your words."

"I swear it. Best. Gifts. Ever." He grinned at me, grabbing my hand one more time. "I'm so glad we're coaching together."

"You know, I am too. I know it's short-term, but we sort of work together, don't we?" I asked the question without thinking, and I instantly regretted it. His entire face fell, my chest hurting for reasons I couldn't quite decipher.

"Short-term?"

"Yeah," I stuttered and blinked way too fast. "Like, the season ends in six weeks, then what? It was a given this was short-term," I said and hated myself. I hated his reaction, the feeling in my chest, but I couldn't take them back. "Right?"

"Sure," he replied but his shoulders tensed and the warmth that had been there seconds ago was nowhere to be found. "I report back to workouts the second week in February."

No more Gideon after February. The thought didn't sit well with me, but I didn't think about it. I dove into a pathetic, word-vomit babble that would have had any sane man running in the opposite direction. "Do you think you'll be ready? We can train more. I'll hit you grounders or help you stretch or go jogging with you. I'm a shit jogger. Bea bitches at me when I try to run with her because I either talk the entire time or fall into the grass every five minutes. Maybe we shouldn't go running together. I can bike? You run and I ride a bike. Yes. We can do that. Or—"

"Babe, calm down." The sparkle came back into his eyes, the dimpled grin not at all matching his mood of seconds ago. He had to switch moods like I changed the radio stations. "Yeah. I'd like your help."

"Perfect. Cool. Just, tell me when. I'll pencil you in." *Fuck me. Why do I sound like a twat?* "I'm not really hungry. The coffee was fine. Want to head out?"

"No way. I haven't seen you in five days. Your insults are good for my ego," he said without breaking eye contact. "Unless you have somewhere to be?"

How can I say no to that face? "No. I don't."

"Good. I kind of like your face. I want to see more of it...plus I have a date—er, activity planned for us." He ran his hand over his forehead and leaned closer to me.

"Yeah?"

"Escape the room. Just us. Whoever gets more clues wins. Loser has to walk around naked the rest of the night. You in?" He wiggled his eyebrows and I stood no chance against his charm.

"With you? Yeah. I need more opportunities to snap pictures of you naked. You know, to start that calendar. Let's go!"

Chapter Twenty-Six

Gideon

"Get that woman off the field, man. She doesn't know shit about the game," a drunken, sloppy masculine voice carried across home plate. I heard it. The team heard it. Fiona damn well heard it and it pissed me off beyond measure. No one talked about her like that when I was around. No one.

Yeah—my thoughts were a bit irrational, but in the past two weeks Fiona had somehow wormed her way into my mind, body and goddamn soul. Fuck the short-term bullshit. I cared about her. Plain and simple. I glanced over at her, her blue eyes dimmed and her posture a little less tall. Nope. I needed to talk to this guy. "Hey, buddy. Come here."

I wiggled my fingers at the older guy and he pointed to himself right in the middle of the chest. *Jesus.* "Yeah. You."

"The Gideon Titan wants to talk to me. Holy hell. Take a picture, Marge." He slurred his words and moved to the area right beyond the chain-link fence. I swore I could feel the gaze of all the members in the dugout, but I put my back to them.

"Stop being an asshole."

"That chick sent the runner and she shouldn't have. This ain't softball girl leagues."

"Thanks for pointing out that obvious fact. Yes. I coach a baseball team, but so does CFD. Clearly, you aren't rehearsed in plays. I called for a hit and run. That's why Brad took off. The boys know they run if they miss a sign."

"You sent him, then? Not that blonde girl?"

"Yes. I'm not repeating myself. Sit and watch the game—don't make an ass of yourself or you'll be banned from the field." I laced each word with venom. I had no idea if we even had the ability to ban anyone from the field, but he backed away looking terrified. I gave him one more glare before releasing a long sigh. Fiona chewed on her bottom lip and closed the distance between us. "You okay?"

"Fine, yeah."

"Fuck that guy."

"Gideon. Kids are around," she said with her eyes widening. "But yeah. Fuck him."

I gripped her shoulder, giving her a squeeze, and glared at the asshole one more time. My pulse raced and I prayed he left the game as soon as it was over. I wasn't sure who he was there to see, but I felt bad for the kid who was related to him.

"Coach Titan. Are...are those your teammates?" Big Al asked, his voice going an octave higher. I followed his pointed finger and grinned when Tate and Brigham nodded at me. *They came.*

"They are." I opened the side gate and let them into the small dugout. We were on defense, Chris pitching quite well for the third inning, and I clapped my teammates on the back. "I didn't know you were stopping by."

"We didn't either. Got bored. Wanted to see you in action. The team looks good. That hit and run didn't work out, though. The catcher has a hell of an arm. You should've known that, Titan," Brigham said, but his smile balanced out the sting. Their presence here meant a great deal and the conflicting emotions were hard to grasp. "Hey, kid. Where do you play?"

"I like to play second base. What do you play?"

"Hey, that's my spot, too. Maybe Coach will put you in and I can give you some pointers." Brigham raised his eyebrows at me and I nodded. I guess I had to put Big Al in the game. "You're not a teenage boy."

"You're observant," Fiona quipped back. Her tone rose, the flirtation easily coming off her. Brigham and Tate gave me sly grins before ignoring me entirely. Great.

"Are you the one assigned to coach with this clown?" Tate asked, elbowing my ribs. I shoved him away and scooted closer to their conversation. I didn't appreciate the way Tate's gaze went all the way down to her legs, or the fact that Brigham left mere inches between them.

"Yup. That's me. He's only moody half the time, though."

"Funny. What's your name?"

"Guys—she has a team to coach," I replied, hoping they would get the hint. Brigham ignored me and I swore he got closer to her.

"Fiona Davis. You're Brigham Donahue and Tate Monaghan. I dislike both of your walk-up songs, but the promo you did arguing over the fact that a hotdog is not a sandwich is hilarious."

"Jason Aldean is great."

"Country is not a baseball song. It's not motivating."

"Country is as American as baseball, sweetheart. You should know that if you're trying to coach it," Brigham fired back. Fiona got that glint in her eyes and my chest tightened. She was about to lay into him and it pleased me to no end.

"Sweetheart my ass, pretty boy. Your hitting slump in July stopped when you switched your song, *sweetheart.*"

Brigham blinked in response, Tate smothering a laugh. I had to chuckle — she was my little ballbuster. "You're feisty."

"So I've been told..." She slid her glance my way, winking, and patted Brigham on the shoulder. "Feel free to gossip. I'm going to coach...you know, the reason why we're here."

She left us at one end of the dugout and went to watch near the entrance. Big Al leaned against the fence, cheering on his teammates when Fiona ran out and called time. She didn't discuss the move with me, and I realized I trusted her. I'd stopped trying to overanalyze moves she made on the field because she'd more than proved her knowledge. She leaned down, whispering something to Big Al, and sent him to second base. Cory, the kid who started almost every game, sprinted back into the dugout with a huge grin. She gave him a high-five and a huge smile, and I felt it in the center of my chest. *Love. Warmth. Longing.*

Brigham had to ruin it. "I like her."

"Nope," I replied with a smack to his head. "Nope."

"You hitting that, Titan?"

Anger shot through me and I wanted to punch him, but Tate read the situation with the ease of a natural leader and stepped in. "Brigs, keep it in your pants. Teenagers, man. Come on."

"Shit, you're right. I just liked her attitude. The sassy ones are always more fun."

"Yeah. Are you staying for the whole game? Maybe watch from the stands?"

Tate gave me a small smile before nodding. "Yeah. We'll catch up with you after. It's good to see you, man. You look happy here."

"I am."

He led Brigham to the bleachers and I sighed in relief when Fiona joined me a minute later. Her floral scent met my nose and a calm flowed through me. She was with me, not them. "I hope that's okay I put Big Al in. I heard him talking to Brigham—"

"I trust you, CFD. It was a good call." I jutted my chin over to Cory and pride filled my chest. The kid cheered on the smaller player, slamming his fists against the fence when Big Al scooped up a routine grounder. "You did that."

"No. We did." She hit her hip against mine and gave me one of her smiles. Her blue eyes turned into pools of water, swirling with secrets and hope, and I was gone. She had me completely. My pulse quickened when she reached over me to grab a bag of seeds and a sliver of her skin showed. Questions flew through my mind.

Do I love her?

Do I want this to last beyond the season?

What will she say if I tell her?

"Gid, did you hear me?"

I stared at her, not really hearing anything besides the rushing of blood into my ears. I had to blink a couple of times before focusing. "Hm?"

"You're such a boy. God, I was just asking. Never mind." She made a goofy face at me and walked away, completely unaware of the turmoil going on in my head. I hoped she hadn't said anything important because my world had shifted.

Not to be dramatic, but it felt like how I imagined earthquakes would feel. I stumbled a bit to the bench, taking a long drink of water and channeling my game-day focus. *Baseball.*

That was my life. *Baseball.*

The sounds, the sweat, the swings. I didn't have room for love, did I? No. That was silly…so it shouldn't bother me when my teammate asked about her. Nor when Fiona stated we had five weeks left of the season.

God, I'm a shit liar.

* * * *

"God, you guys are fucking gross," Fiona shouted across the high-top table later that night. We'd won the game and Brigs and Tate had demanded we get a beer to celebrate. It'd annoyed me because I much preferred to be alone with Fiona…since we only had five more weeks together. But she'd gladly accepted their invitation.

"We're athletes. It's what we do."

"Uh, I'll check with my boss's brother. He either shielded me from this sick side of being a professional, or you're nasty. Throwing used jockstraps at the newbies? Monsters. Did you do that, Gideon? Please say no."

I sucked my lip into my mouth, unable to prevent a smile. She threw her hands in the air and let out a drawn-out groan. "Sorry, Barbie. It's true."

"I need to go wash my hands or something. Anyone need a beer?"

"I'll go with you. I'll get the next round," Brigs replied and got off the bar stool so fast I didn't have a chance to protest. I clenched my jaw to prevent a negative comment from coming out, but Tate remained behind. His easygoing smile reminded me of our unfinished conversation all those weeks ago and I calmed myself down. I wasn't jealous. That would be ridiculous.

"Do you think you'll be ready by February? I'm counting on you being on the field, man. If Brigs gets moved to short, I'll never hear the end of it."

I snorted. "He'll never move there. He's a headcase."

"You ain't kidding," he replied and jutted his chin at the bar. Brigs had all the moves, the ones I'd used once upon a time. He leaned over Fiona, dragging his fingers over her arm and probably telling her all sorts of fucking jokes. Tate tapped the table with his fist and laughed. "Damn. She's something, huh?"

"Yeah. She is. Brigs has me feeling murderous again."

"He's harmless. Don't even worry. She's not biting at all. This is highly entertaining. I've been trying to get to know the younger guys on the team, but those assholes like to stay out all fucking night and hit the high-end clubs. He lays on his ridiculous charm and leaves with a different girl every night. It's good to see him go up to bat and strike out. His ego was getting a bit too much." He sighed and ran a hand over his face. "I used to be like that, but not anymore. I don't know when I got old, but I'm there."

"You still got plenty of years left in you, Tate." I patted his shoulder but continued to check on Fiona every couple of seconds. He wasn't lying—she wasn't leaning into Brigs, or turning her body toward him at all. I smiled. My girl wasn't into Brigs.

"We'll see. This might be my last year. Enough about me, though. You going to be in or not? I need to know so I can start planting other ideas in Coach's ear."

"I'll be ready." I rubbed my knee, confident in my answer. "I can take grounders without flinching and can jog at a steady pace. Doc says I'll be cleared for full activity soon, but the thought of running and sliding freaks me the fuck out. That's where I'm afraid I'll damage it more, you know?"

"Trust your body. That was the best advice I ever had. Your body will tell you what you feel. Don't be a dumbass and ignore it. Look, they're finally coming back. I was getting thirsty."

His words repeated over and over in my head, their meaning hitting me hard. Trust my body. Did that mean feelings, too?

"Here you go, gentlemen." Fiona set down a beer in front of me and slid back onto her bar stool. Her legs bumped into mine, and I snuck my hand down there and placed it on her thigh. She didn't try to move, nor did she give anything away. But it pleased me how a slight blush showed on her cheeks. "Brigs was telling me that you guys have team-bonding days in the clubhouse where the coach brings all sorts of weird things. Care to share about them?" We all shared a look and shook our heads. Those were secret for a reason.

"Come on. I'll tell you something embarrassing if you do."

"Unless you made out with a girl or ran through a crowd naked, then it won't be that interesting," Brigs replied to her, looking all sorts of an asshole.

"Fuck off, Brigs. I'm not giving you any material for your spank bank."

I choked on my beer, the carbonation burning my nose. "Fiona. *God*."

"Just being honest." She pressed her legs together, communicating with me under the table. I gripped tighter and enjoyed the shocked expression on Brigs' face. "Anyway, Brigs, to finish your question, yes. I am a Soles fan. I'm a native to Arizona. Shocking, I know."

"How did you get paired up with this grump?"

"My boss's brother works for them."

They accepted her answer and Tate went into a series of stories from his youth that had us all cackling. Fiona cried, she laughed so hard and I relaxed when she leaned over and whispered in my ear, "I only got five more weeks left of you. Let's get out of here."

I chugged the rest of my beer and took her hand. To hell with Tate and Brigs. The meaning of her words hit me, as hard as a punch to the gut, and I decided I wasn't going to waste a second of time with her. Five weeks left. I'd make them worth it.

Chapter Twenty-Seven

Fiona

My core throbbed with need as soon as we got into the car. We drove together—not my best decision because I would need to find a way back to my house that didn't involve an Uber, but that was too far in advance. Rationality had no place with my nervous, horny energy. It had been a while since I'd had him inside me, and I craved him. *Missed him. Needed him.*

He started the car and didn't say a word for the first ten minutes. He let out a couple of grunts, sliding his gaze to me before looking back at the road. *Interesting.*

"You okay, Gid? Seem tense. Like you need a rub-down."

"I am tense."

"Why?" I reached over and ran my fingers up his leg. He jerked and sucked in a breath.

"I get jealous when someone else has your attention. Makes me feel a little violent. And predatory."

My heart lurched at his words. Not the aggressive ones. The *jealous* comment. We didn't talk about that shit, but my face warmed. "Brigs? I wasn't flirting with that clown. He was over the top and way too much."

"Yeah. He was. But he stole too much of my time with you." He gripped the wheel a little tighter and the cutest line formed on his forehead. I chuckled and ignored the odd sensation in my stomach. "Why are you laughing? I'm hurting over here. I only have five weeks with you and Brigs took up most of the night I could've been inside you. Tasting you. Pleasuring you. I'm pissed and fucking turned on. It's not a nice combination."

"False. That first time on the motorcycle, I was pissed and fucking turned on. It has its moments."

"Yeah." His tone darkened, and moisture pooled between my legs. "I'll be fine when you're naked. Distract me until we get home."

Home. His word choice shouldn't have caused an array of emotions to flow through me—but it did. It was his home, not mine, and we weren't going to his home as a couple. It was…as fuck-buddies who were friends. Yeah. That was it.

"You're cute when you're jealous, Gid. I'm all yours. Tonight." I knew I'd said the right thing when he reached out and took my hand. My words were meant to settle down the moment, break the tension that wound its way around my throat. But it backfired.

I couldn't recall the last time someone had held my hand. Sure, in bed to restrain me, but like this? As if we were lovers? I gulped and tried to focus on anything but the way his large palm covered mine. He dragged his thumb across the delicate skin on top and let out a deep hum. God. He confused the hell out of me.

Sweet. Hard. Rough.

Five more weeks. I had him for thirty-five more days and I didn't need to waste time thinking about feelings that scared me. I should focus on this man, this troubled yet wonderful man.

We drove in silence the rest of the ride and he parked in his large garage. I passed the bike — the one that had sparked our first fuck — and wiggled my eyebrows at him. "Want to go down Memory Lane?"

"No. I want you in my bed. Shower. Floor. Kitchen…you name it. Watching you waltz around in those pants almost killed me. I had to hide my goddamn boner at the game."

"Mm. That would've been awkward, huh?" I leaned against the door, taking my time looking him up and down. "You seem to have a bulge in your pants now."

"Yeah. Wanna help a guy out?" He caged me in, his minty breath hitting the skin under my ear. I shivered, leaning in to him to get as much as I could from him. I wanted to feel his lips on me, his rough beard rubbing against my skin. I grabbed his face, dragged my teeth over his bottom lip and kissed him. He'd stood up for me that night and words weren't enough to thank him.

I wanted to show him. He opened my mouth with his tongue and gave me a soul-crushing kiss. It was deep — as if our tongues had been lovers in our past lives and were reunited for the first time. My body felt electrified, parts of me I kept hidden coming out. My heart raced, but it was different. It was a rhythmic beat, matching his.

"Gideon," I moaned his name, not quite asking for anything, but he answered anyway. He picked me up, not breaking contact, and opened the door. There was a rush, but not a frantic urgency. It was a sweet rush, like each breath we shared had a countdown. He gripped a little tighter, kissed a little deeper and held my gaze a little longer.

I ground into him and enjoyed how taut his body got. I did that to him. I wanted to continue. He made the trip to his room in record time, his hands never leaving my body. "I want to lick every inch of you, but I can't wait anymore."

"Agreed, I need you inside me now." I bit down on his ear and gasped when he tossed me onto his bed. "Hot, Gideon. You look hot as fuck right now."

His eyes burned for me. The dark orbs danced with promises and he whipped off his shirt so fast I barely had time to register the muscles I loved to look at. He stalked to the bed, gripped the edges of my yoga pants and ripped them down my legs. "One day, I'm going to stay right between your legs for hours. But this will work for now."

I gripped the sheets when he brought his tongue down on my swollen clit. I was soaked, my lips throbbing with need. He didn't give me any warning before slipping two fingers inside me, and I clenched my teeth. The warm buzzing began, but it was too soon. He had me so fired up, it wouldn't take more than a couple of seconds. "Stop."

He froze, worry etched into his beautiful eyes. "What's wrong?"

"I'm so close already, I want to come with you."

His expression softened and he leaned over me, pressing kisses along my ribs and up my chest. He removed my shirt with ease and brought a possessive grip to my side. He didn't need to talk. He slipped out of his pants, put on a condom and lowered himself onto me. "You're fucking beautiful, Fiona. So fucking beautiful."

He slid inside me, his length the perfect size. I arched my back, moaning in pleasure. I dug my nails into his muscles when he thrust ever so slowly into me. He wasn't in a hurry, and I relished his touches.

He brought his lips to my neck, my mouth and my eyes. I almost broke, that gesture so outside my comfort zone, but he stopped. He slid out of me and rolled me over. "I need to see you ride me, sweetheart. Can you do that? I want to see you lose control."

I grinned at the encouragement in his voice. His pulse raced in his neck and I grabbed his shoulders, sliding down onto him. The position filled me, stretching me farther than before, but I rocked against him. I was drunk on power—the way he gazed into me and gripped my hips like a lifeline, or the way he said my name right before his legs tightened.

He lifted his hips just enough so the right pressure built around my core. I moaned, pushing myself to get the right angle, and I shook as a small explosion began in my lower stomach. It spread down my legs, through my toes and back up again. I cried, tears leaking out of my eyes when I rode out the best orgasm I'd ever had. Gideon bucked, digging his fingers into my skin when he shuddered against me. "Fiona, *fuck*."

My entire body hummed when he gently set me on the bed next to him. *Wow. That was the best…everything.* I closed my eyes, listening to the sounds he made shuffling around the room and cleaning himself up. The bed dipped when he returned. "You're fucking amazing."

"You too, Gid," I said without opening my eyes. He dragged his fingers across my peaked nipples, carefully trailing them up and down my body until they landed on my hip.

"Stay with me tonight." He gripped my hip tighter and that small gesture changed everything. Suddenly, I wanted him for more than just a release. He'd become someone I cared about. I wasn't sure how or when, but it was more than I'd ever experienced and it scared the hell out of me. "I'll make you breakfast in the morning. Let me enjoy you when you're with me, okay? I want you here."

"Sure," I replied with a tight throat. My body burned with desire and the urge to bolt out of there. But his eyes warmed when he looked at me, and the crook of his arm was perfect to slide into. "I'm staying for breakfast. That's it. For food."

"Of course. Food is the way to your hea—stomach. Food is the key. I get it now."

"I'm a simple creature."

"False. Now, get your cute ass closer to me." He pulled my body toward him, giving me a clever grin. God, he was adorable. If I got any more involved with this man, I wouldn't want to leave. I fought every urge I had to bolt and scooted closer to him. He enveloped me in his arms, his warmth radiating throughout my limbs. Our heartbeats matched rhythm, the deep vibration of his chest hitting my back. For one moment, however brief, I didn't think about the next day. I didn't think about my next course of action or the downfall.

I enjoyed the attention of a guy who understood me.

* * * *

Coffee…pancakes…music? I bolted upright in a bed that wasn't mine and searched my surroundings. Dark walls, huge bed, woodsy scent. *Gideon.* I was at Gideon's. My body relaxed but my brain spun out of control, with thoughts whipping by so fast I couldn't grasp onto one. I stretched, my naked body a little sore from the second round in the middle of the night. My entire face warmed at the memory—it was sweet how he'd woken me up by pressing his lips down my bare spine. Yeah—I liked sleepy sex. I'd never had that before and I envisioned more of that in the future. A crash sounded from upstairs, and I found the first shirt of Gideon's I could from a drawer. I padded up the stairs, skipping two at a time, and entered the kitchen. "Gideon. Everything good?"

"Hey." He froze, the spatula in his hand stopping when he gave me the softest smile I had ever seen. My breath caught in my throat, the warmth and emotion in his expression not part of the deal. "You look really fucking good in my clothes."

I blinked. I fidgeted with the end of the shirt, hating how easily I blushed at his words. "I heard a crash."

He jutted his chin to the pan on the floor. "I got fancy. Dropped it. Have a seat. Coffee is ready. Almost done with pancakes. Do you prefer chocolate chips in yours or no?"

"Clown question. Yes to the chocolate. Always yes. I'm surprised a health freak like you would allow sugar to be in the house."

"I'm not a robot. I need my fix from time to time. Kind of how I feel about you."

"Fair enough. Let me know when you need another hit." I winked at him and plopped down on the high-top stool.

He responded with another panty-dropping smile and slid a chipped mug over to me. It had *world's best uncle* and an old picture of Quinn on it. "This is cute."

"It would be cute if I didn't also have a plate, mouse pad, and sweatshirt with the same picture. Little nugget has her face all over my stuff."

"You're a good uncle, Gideon. She's lucky to have you."

His face softened. "I'm lucky."

That expression. The world didn't get to see him this way—shirtless in a massive kitchen with coffee mugs with his niece's face on it. It fucked me up. I had only ever been on a rollercoaster once, when I was a kid, but I remembered the feeling. Right as we'd approached the top of the arch, there'd been a pause. A second where time froze, where everything was at peace before crashing back down to earth. I was at peace. It was terrifying. I collected myself when I poured a cup of coffee. I preferred it black but put in three packets of sugar. *The extra release has to help my inner turmoil, right?*

"Mm. You in my kitchen…in my shirt. I wouldn't have such a hard time waking up if this greeted me in the morning." He ran his nose down my neck and squeezed my hip. "How do you smell so good?"

"Naturally gifted." He trailed his lips up to my jaw, my eyes almost rolling back in my head. He had no idea what his words and touch did to me, there was no way. "Speaking of hard…"

He chuckled and pressed his aroused length into my back. "I can't help it when you're around."

"I need to remove your batteries. Where do you keep them?"

He threw his head back and laughed. It was a heavenly sound. "I can bend over and show you."

"No, just, no." I shoved him in the chest, my smile stretching my skin. I hardly recognized the asshole from that first day, months ago. So much had changed. "I'm a little hurt. You told me you would hang those jerseys in your kitchen and I don't see them. Liar."

"Watch the pancakes. Flip them if they get too brown." He took off toward the main foyer. I frowned. I hadn't expected him to run on the tile, but curiosity got the better of me. I flipped the pancakes and waited another couple of minutes before he came back with two large frames, at least three feet long.

"Well, fuck. You kept your word."

"Sure did. I got them both framed. After breakfast, help me hang them up?" His tone rose at the end, and the sound went right to my chest. "Scratch that. If you lift your arms up, I'll get distracted by your skin. Next time, you'll see them, though."

"Next time, eh?" I walked toward him and ran my fingers down his chest. His grin was infectious. His mood was infectious, and I knew the peace wouldn't last long. I wanted to bury myself in it. "Getting cocky again?"

"I was going to bring it up after I fed you, but might as well now. Fiona." He paused and cupped my face after setting the posters down on the counter. "I have an idea. It benefits us both. You ready?"

I gulped before nodding.

His gaze darted back and forth between my eyes and the charcoal color lightened. "I vote you come here every night after a game. I have three reasons why."

"I'm listening." My ears pounded with my pulse and I swore my palms sweated.

"One. Post-game analysis would be a hell of a lot more fun here. We could be naked. Doing stats naked sounds way better. Two. Sometimes, I wake up horny dreaming of you and it would be easy if you were already here. And three. I like seeing you in my kitchen. What do you say? For the rest of the season, you stay here with me."

His eyes pleaded with me. The hope in his voice about did me in and I could think of a million reasons why I should say no, but none made sense. *Peace.* I needed to enjoy the peace. "Hmm. I'll have to get back to you on that. Check with my people."

"You don't have people, Barbie." He tugged on the end of my hair before lowering his mouth to mine. "It'll be fun. Just say yes. We can sleep on the bean-bag floor every night."

"Christ. You had me at bean bag. Yes. I'll stay with you after every game, but just until the season ends."

Chapter Twenty-Eight

Gideon

"Three more to the left. Don't puss out. Come on, man!"

"Fiona. I'm not pussing out," I fired back—Fiona had had a stick up her ass since she arrived and seemed hell-bent on taking it out on me.

"Then take more grounders. Backhand."

She didn't wait before rocking a one-hop grounder to me. I bounced, scooping it up without issue. Something was different about her today. Sure, it was our last game, but we'd grown into a routine that worked.

Almost every night, she went to bed with me. Sometimes we got naked, sometimes we talked about the future. Sometimes we passed out after playing video games until the morning hours. We were in a relationship. She just didn't know it. "CFD, are you trying to hurt me?"

"Nope."

She hit another grounder, harder than the last one, and I barely stopped it. After three more attempts at killing me, she dropped the bat and marched into the dugout. *Okay then.* I wiped sweat from my forehead and stretched before going to find her. We got here earlier than the kids most games and she had no need to be in the underground dugout. "Fiona. What's wrong? Pissed I beat you at Mario Kart still?"

"No." Her voice was too tight and high-pitched. That didn't sit well with me and I put a hand on her shoulder. She stiffened at my touch. That was new. My stomach clenched but I shook it off. "I'm fine, Gideon."

"I know I'm a guy, but I'm not an idiot. You're not fine. What gives?" I tried touching her again, but she shrugged my hand off her and turned to stare at me. Her crystal-blue eyes weren't warm or tender. She narrowed her gaze at me and tapped her foot. Her gaze slid to her backpack for a second—not enough to stop conversation, but I caught it. The journal I'd gotten her peeked out of the corner and I ran my hand over my mouth. *She uses the journal.* It made me inexplicably happy. "Well?"

"Just tense, I guess. Didn't have a great day. Cleaning. The upcoming charity event. That sort of thing."

"Fair enough. Are the plans all coming through? I've worked on my opening speech. Thought about talking about setbacks. We all have them, but we can't let them define our future." I kicked the dirt, hoping like hell she'd appreciate what I had in mind. Her face remained emotionless. For someone who always had a comment, she stayed silent. "I didn't want to approach the topic of texting while driving specifically, but the desire and the guilt. I can relate to that…and, well, I'm nervous."

"That's great, Gideon. Your story will resonate with a lot of teenagers. I have no doubt your speech will be amazing," she said without changing her bleak expression. "You turned in your rough draft to the email I gave you, right?"

"You mean your email?" I wiggled my eyebrows at her, hoping it would ease some of the stifling tension. Superstitions were a waste of time, but my gut told me something was wrong. "I wanted to attach a picture to it for you to enjoy. But since it's housed at the charity, I made the more mature decision. Be proud of me."

"Anyone can access that email account. It's not mine." She straightened her posture and twisted her neck, causing two loud cracks. She rubbed the back of her head and sighed, directing my attention to her obvious discomfort. "Don't put my job in jeopardy by sending pictures."

"You're joking." I laughed, hoping it sounded sincere instead of angry. Her words irritated me. "I would never do anything to put your job in jeopardy. I would think you knew that."

"Yeah, I guess." She bit down on her lip and avoided my gaze like we were meeting for the first time and I'd run over her foot.

"Did I do something to piss you off?"

"No, stop asking. You're fine," she replied in a nasty tone and rubbed her temples. "I'm sorry. I'm stressed out about the event. It's ten days away. Ten. I've worked with the freelance designers and the program isn't done. It had to get to the printer yesterday and on top of that, the picture we wanted to use of Justin isn't the right size for the poster and I tried resizing it, but it looked pixelated. Jade hired two marketing interns and a fucking event planner without my vote and we agreed we would always vote as a council—she didn't keep her word. She said I was too busy and she didn't want to overrun me, but it's going to be my job. I should have a say on who will be working with me in the shitty office." She spoke the words so fast, they blurred together and I almost didn't catch the blip in her voice. "I'm disappointed. I counted on her and…well, she didn't follow through."

She deflated. Her shoulder slumped and all the feisty energy I loved left. Fuck the need to suffer alone. I put my arm around her and dragged her to my chest. "I'm sorry. That's shit. From what you've told me, you're on the council of four and you all vote, right? How did it go through?"

"She had everyone else there for the interviews. Three voted yes. My opinion wasn't needed." She spoke with her face pressed against my shirt, and the muffled sound almost made me grin. It was cute. "Thanks for the support, Gid."

"Anytime." I rubbed her back, giving her neck a little squeeze. "I know just the thing we can do after the game that'll help you relax. One hint—bubbles."

"Right." Her tone changed back to the hardened, almost unrecognizable one. Then she pushed off me and slammed her lips together. "I'm going to get started on the line-up. I researched that this team isn't very talented and we can start the same guys for the first two innings, but I vote we rotate them all in. It is their last game."

"I'm on board with that. I'll get the field ready, I guess." I paused at the gate and gave her one more look. "Are we okay?"

"Why wouldn't we be?"

Great question. I scratched my head and found the device used to chalk the diamond. Her mood swings were erratic. I knew the littlest thing could have her go on a rant about anything, but I didn't understand the hostility in her gaze toward me. I wasn't someone who'd let her down. Nope. She'd spent all last night with me, waking me with her mouth around my cock. It had been a hell of a morning and she hadn't walked away without three orgasms. We were fine, but she made me feel as if it was my fault. I gave her another long look and did my best to forget about it. It wasn't easy, but when the first kid arrived — Big Al — I gave them all my attention. It was our last game and I wanted to enjoy every second.

* * * *

We won the game. Our last game of the season. Pride filled my chest when I studied each of the fifteen teenagers I'd spent four months with. I high-fived every one of them, an unknown emotion crawling up my throat. I would miss them. I would miss the team and I wasn't sure I was ready to stop coaching.

I damn well knew I wasn't ready to be done coaching with Fiona. My gaze slid to hers and my breath caught in my throat. She was gorgeous. She was a mess, but each one of her flaws made me love her a little more. Yeah. I loved her and didn't have a fucking clue what to do about it. Every single time I brought up anything beyond the timeframe of the season, she changed the subject or distracted me. If I even said the word relationship, she laughed or made a joke. She had relationship issues. I understood that. But we had a friendship and she owed me a goddamn conversation about it.

"Coach Titan! We gotta get a picture!" Garth shouted over the cheering of the team. I whistled and called everyone over to home plate. Fiona chose to stand on the other side of the group—right by Big Al—and didn't meet my gaze. It bothered me. She had been weird since our conversation and it had gotten worse. We didn't stand side by side against the fence, nor did we compare notes on the pitcher. Those were some of my favorite parts, hearing her take on a game. But she didn't grant me any of those little joys. She tried to stay as far away from me as she could, and despite my selfish need to confront her, I knew. I knew in my gut that she was pulling away.

I didn't have a chance to catch her after the picture. Parents, kids and even news outlets circled me after our team photo. Some wanted pictures, others wanted quotes, but Fiona was nowhere to be found. Anger crept its way into my bones. *Is she going to run away without a word?* Worry continued to grow in my gut and I had to force an excuse to remove myself from the lingering parents. It was at least an hour before I broke free from their questions. I hadn't felt dread like this since the call. I jogged toward the dugout, searching for her. Her bag was gone. *Fuck.* I squinted into the parking lot and relaxed when her blonde hair stuck out. She sat on the hood of her car with her head down. *What the hell?*

I shouldered my bag and made sure we left the place clean, an odd sense of nostalgia clouding my thoughts. My coach had been right. Coaching this team had reminded me of a lot of things about the world.

Being part of a team was indescribable.

Loving a game I was lucky enough to call a career was rare.

Finding a partner who wasn't complacent and challenged me brought me to life.

It was done and I wished it wasn't. I hit the side of the brick wall one last time and made the trek to the parking lot. My entire body tensed with anticipation of the conversation — my hair stood on end and I swallowed down my nerves. "Hey, CFD. Nice season."

"Yeah. I can't believe it's over." She still hadn't looked up from her crossed legs. I gritted my teeth to prevent myself from yelling. She was being fucking frustrating and needed to be an adult. "It went by quicker than I thought."

"Look at me."

She did and her big eyes were expressionless. Gone was the girl I'd kissed hours ago. Gone was the spunky, feisty co-coach who I'd hoped to continue being with. I rubbed the back of my neck and let out a cuss word. "What's going on? Why are you looking at me like that?"

"It's over. The season. Us. It's all done. You're ready to head to spring training and you can barely tell you had an injury." Her voice remained monotone and her goddamn eyes had a blank stare to them. "Thank you, Gideon, for everything. This — "

"Are you fucking kidding?" Shit, I winced when I spotted other people leaving the park. I stepped closer. "What the fuck are you doing?"

"Saying goodbye." She tilted her head and let out a small laugh. "I thought that was obvious."

"Why? Why does it have to be goodbye?" My voice almost cracked at the end, but I coughed to cover it up.

My neck stiffened and the rage I'd felt all last year came back in small stages. "This is it for you?"

"It was a fling. We had fun. That's what it was, right? We agreed five weeks. We never made promises for more." She blinked three times before turning her attention to the sky. "I was a challenge to you. It's dumb to think we would continue to...to what? Fuck? Hang out? We were forced to see each other six days a week. We won't be around each other anymore."

"We can still make time for each other, Fiona."

"How? You'll be traveling for baseball and I'll be consumed with graduating and my new job. I can't miss out on big decisions being distracted. Plus, we weren't in a relationship. Sure, we agreed not to be with other people, but I do that with all my hookups."

"Do you really mean that?" I dropped my hands, taking a step back. My voice was calm and laced with venom. My breathing hitched and my heart raced like hell. *How can she say those words to me?* "It didn't mean anything to you?"

"No, yes...I don't know." She put her head in her hands and let out a hiccupped sigh. Tension clawed in my chest. It was like there was an itch inside my ribs and I couldn't scratch hard enough to get it. "We weren't more than two adults enjoying each other's naked bodies."

"Wrong. It was more than that." I took another step toward her and lifted her chin in my hands. Yeah, my hands shook, but I didn't give a damn. "We could be more."

She blinked at me. That was her goddamn response. I waited. The crisp air stilled between us—laughter carried over from the remaining players and it clashed with every emotion inside me. Her jaw trembled but then she shook her head. "I should go."

"So, this is it?"

"Yeah. I don't see how it could be more."

I clenched my fists — anger and despair combined into a lethal combination and I had to get the fuck out of there. She wiped her eyes but it didn't faze me. Not at all. Fuck her. I stormed away but shook my head and went back. She slid off the hood and had her keys in the door, and dropped them when I yelled at her. I couldn't control it. My voice trembled, the new, raw emotion pouring through me.

"This is total bullshit. I know you have a fear of relationships. We all do. You're not the only one to lose someone, *Fiona*. What we had was real. Fuck you for not being decent enough to admit it to me. Yeah, there's no guarantees in life but when you find someone who gets you, you make an effort."

Her mouth opened, but I raised a hand to stop her. She didn't deserve to hurt me anymore. "No — I'm not done. I wanted it all. With you. But you're scared. I gave you time." My goddamn voice broke and I swore I felt my heart break. With one last look at her, I lowered my voice and said, "Grow up, Fiona."

Chapter Twenty-Nine

Fiona

Michelle warmed up yet another cup of tea and set it on the coffee table. She lingered. She'd begun doing that for the last week and would walk into the room I was sprawled out in, leave and come up with an excuse to come back in. It annoyed me and charmed me. I thanked her and brought the hot liquid to my lips. "You don't have to babysit me."

"I'm not. Trust me." She frowned and tidied the books on the table. They were straight enough. I waited her out for about thirty seconds before she put her hands on her hips and glared at me. "Fine. I am. But I don't understand what's going on with you. You're sullen and nothing like the spunky chick you were weeks ago. We don't talk about your past, or Gideon or feelings. I get it. I really do." She paused and ran her hand through her hair. It was long and hung down in waves. *When did her hair get so long?* "My dad cheated on my mom six times. She forgave him every single time he came crawling back. I get shutting yourself down. I do. But this isn't you. What happened? Did Gideon break it off? Did he ghost you without an explanation?"

I rubbed my eyes with my palms and let out a long breath. The mention of his name was like a pair of scissors digging into my chest. I missed him and the foreign feeling kept me up at night. I crossed my arms and relaxed further into our weathered couch, hoping the squishy seat would bring me comfort. "The baseball season came to an end."

"Okay?"

"We hooked up because we were together all the time." I winced as soon as the words left my mouth. "Okay, not true. But we didn't break up. We weren't together."

"Fiona, you spent the night at his place most of the past month. I'm going to call major bullshit. What's holding you back? Is it fear? Grow up, girlfriend. Can't let the fear of striking out keep you from playing the game."

"Did you just use a baseball quote at me?" I snorted, but hated how her words made sense. She was the second person to tell me to grow up. Gideon...those were the last words he'd said to me eight days ago. His crumpled face, tortured words and anger were how I'd left it with him. My eyes stung again and a panicked desperation took over.

"Oh, I quote it at you. Get in the batter's box. Take charge. Lead the team to victory. Don't watch a pitch go by. Let—"

"Stop." I held up my hand and laughed. Her brave attempt at pulling me out of my misery helped a little, but the sorrow I carried around felt like a part of me now. "No more baseball talk."

"Then spill it. I don't have to work for another hour and I've had enough of your walls. I'm tearing them down." She took the seat next to me and gave me such a pointed stare I almost winced. Almost.

I told her everything. The fear of having him disappoint me after almost everyone I knew had. My dad. Justin. My sisters. Jade. My chest hurt and I couldn't prevent the tears. I cried. She put an awkward hand on my back and tried to comfort me, and her kindness made the sobs come out. Grief. Guilt. Awareness.

"I'm so fucking sorry I lost it." I wiped my eyes and sniffed. "Jesus."

"It's not healthy to keep all that shit locked up."

"You're one to talk," I fired back and regretted it. She had been nothing but a good friend. "Shit. I'm being an asshole. Thank you for listening."

"Of course. What are you going to do? You realize this is fixable, right? He isn't Justin. He's not your dad and he certainly isn't your crazy family. What has he done that broke your trust?"

Not a thing. I gulped a couple of times before nodding. "It is fixable. I owe him an apology…more than that."

"It's never fun when we fuck up and have to apologize. It'll suck. But you need to do it."

My gaze went to the phone, but she shook her head. "In person, Fiona."

"What if he doesn't want to chat? He was pissed." *What if it's too late?*

"Well, he said he wanted more, and you didn't acknowledge it." She raised her eyebrows and gave my back another pat. "I have about twenty minutes to get ready, but call me if you need anything. I'm not a fan of how this happened, but I'm glad we took a step forward. We're all sorts of fucked up, aren't we?"

"Yeah." I sniffed again and thought she might hug me. She didn't and I relaxed. "Thank you."

She smiled and disappeared into her room. I was left alone with my thoughts—and they weren't a great place to be. *Trust.* My issue was trust. I didn't have enough of it for most people, let alone men, and it wasn't fair to put Gideon in the same category as the ones who'd hurt me. The picture of Justin and me mocked me and I grabbed my phone. The tipping point was Jade and the job. Using the excuse that she was too busy to include me wouldn't fly. She'd looked me in the eye and said I was a part of the team. She'd let me down and I needed to talk it out with her. I stared at the old picture of me and Justin, embracing the waves of emotion going through me.

She answered on the second ring. "Lo? What's going on, Fiona?"

"Ah, well… Are you busy?"

"I got ten minutes. What's up?"

I rearranged the knick-knacks on the table and decided to cut the bullshit. "Why did you interview and hire employees without including me?"

"The schedule didn't work out between my crazy life and your coaching. It wasn't intentional—"

"Yes. It was, Jade. We made the board of four so we all could vote. Diane *and* you thought I should be on the board. I wasn't there." My voice remained leveled and focused despite my knee bouncing up and down and my heart beating against my ribs to the point of pain. "I've signed the contract already, but it makes me nervous. You broke my trust and I have no idea how to handle it."

"Fiona, I'm sorry." She hesitated. "Why didn't you say anything sooner?"

"Because I've got my own shit going on. Plus, the event is in two days and we've all been finalizing the details. I couldn't keep it in anymore. I want to know why."

"I told you. It wasn't intentional. We knew you had a game and I thought we were doing you a favor…listen, I swear. I would never leave you out of anything. Justin, well, you were the biggest role in his life. I know what this group, him, all of it means to you."

The part right between my eyes began throbbing and another wave of emotion hit me, almost making me hunch over. "Don't leave me out of anything. If I'm too busy or can't make it, then fine. But leaving me out of three hires, *three* of them, Jade, feels like a goddamn slap in the face."

"It won't happen again. I promise." She cleared her throat and spoke in a softer tone. "I'm having a hard time balancing running this, some family stuff going on that I'll tell you about later… Little things are falling through the cracks and this was one of them. I've never let you down, Fiona, and it's not going to be a habit. It is a relief knowing you'll be full-time soon. Trust me, okay?"

Tears slid down my cheeks and I nodded. *Shit. She can't see me.* "Okay. Don't do it again…I'm not a forgiving person."

"Yes. I know," she mumbled. I gave a strangled laugh at her tone.

"I'll see you later. We're still meeting at the venue by Camelback tomorrow to go over placements?"

"Yup. Don't wait so long to call if you need to yell at me. I can take it."

She hung up and it was as though a small weight had lifted off my chest. She'd made a mistake. That was it. Gideon would probably say a couple of cuss words and move on with his day.

God, just the thought of him had my entire body tense. The urge to call him hit again, and I scrolled through my phone. I about screamed when a text from him came through.

Gideon: Can you give me Jade's number? I need to prepare for the TTL event.

Fiona: She's swamped. What's your question?

I stared at his message with my heart in my throat. I set it on the table and ran through every scenario and how it could end. Would he call? Did I want him to? God. I did. I missed his deep voice and stupid jokes. My throat constricted and I waited for the phone to ring. The vibration echoed on the table as it bumped against the white dish holding our coasters. I snatched it, hitting hello before the first ring ended. *Desperate, much?*

"Hello?"

"I never got the agenda for the event."

He didn't greet me, acknowledge me or anything. Nerves bounced in my stomach and I clutched a pillow in my lap. "Okay. I can send it to you. Were you sent parking arrangements?"

"Yes. Southeast lot." His voice—the one I'd spoken to every day the past four months—sounded like a stranger. I hadn't had a breakup before, but this was miserable. I wanted to ask him how he was doing, how his ACL felt, spring training, his family, but my throat remained tight. "If I want to bring guests, who do I contact?"

Who is he bringing? God – another woman? It couldn't be. "Uh, Bethany. She's the event planner they hired. I'll text you her number."

"Thanks. See you there."

"Wait." I froze. He hadn't hung up yet, but I didn't know what to say. Everything? Nothing? My eyes stung and I scrambled for anything. "Uh, the banquet."

"What banquet?"

"For the baseball team. Have you thought about when you'd like to have it? I know spring training started this week, but what date works for you?"

"I'll have to check."

"Okay. Just, uh, let me know." I gripped the phone, hating the tense situation. It was worse than I'd imagined. Helpless. I felt helpless being so far away from him. "How've you been?"

"Let's *not* do this. I gotta run."

Click.

I fell onto the couch, riding the wave of misery. The ironic thing was that not four months ago, he'd hung up on me and I'd almost been in tears. *This time it's my fault.* A wave of self-pity hit me – I deserved this. The feeling of helplessness clogged my throat and lungs.

Why couldn't I apologize to him? Tell him I felt *whatever* it was, too? I sat up. I could tell him. I would tell him. At the banquet, I would eat crow and own up to everything. It couldn't be too bad…at least not worse than this.

* * * *

"Fiona! Registration needs help. The system broke down," Jade's voice crackled through the headset.

"On it." I turned, mid-step, toward the entrance and smiled as guests filled the small reception hall. We'd chosen a hotel that overlooked the valley and had mountains. It was beautiful—the perfect spot for our first run at a gala. Amanda had ended up being fantastic with setup and Bea had a huge line at the bar already. She'd even told me every tip she made that night was going to be donated in Justin's name for me. I made a note to try harder to see Bea—she was a good sister. I headed toward their direction and spied Bethany, who had red spots on her cheeks and her black hair waving everywhere. "What's going on?"

"The app we downloaded won't work at check-in. It's not accepting guests."

"Do you have a paper copy as a Plan B?" I scanned the tables and fought a sigh when I didn't spy any back-ups. "I'll run into the hotel and try to print them. Just write down the names and their pledge if they're donating. Assign different bidding numbers. We can add them all later."

"Are you sure? Where's Jade? I can't believe this failed!"

"Jade—what's your twenty?" I gave Bethany another long look. A twinge of *told you so* went through me, but I didn't let it stay. The event was the focus, not the beef I'd already settled.

"Silent auction. Everything good?"

"Issue with the app. Going to the hotel to try and print the guest list. Also, hey—tell Bethany I invited the baseball team. She needs to give them the farthest table in the back. Tell me if there are problems." I hoped I looked composed. My pulse raced and sweat dripped down my back as I weaved through guests. Gideon wasn't expected to arrive for another hour, but that didn't stop me from searching for his tall frame every couple of seconds. Tonight was the night. I was going to tell him everything.

"Ma'am. Do you need help?" A concierge winced at my expression and I responded with one word.

"Printer."

"This way." He led me across the tiled entrance and my heels clacked against the floor. Time seemed to stop. Gideon stood there, dressed in a sleek, form-fitting black tux, with perfectly styled hair and his jawline had me weak at the knees. My heart skipped a goddamn beat and my entire body heated over. My nipples tightened into beads and I was sure anyone around me could tell — but the overwhelming feeling in my chest startled me.

"Ma'am, are you all right?"

"Y-yes," I stuttered. I took another step, still trying to get my fill of Gideon and — *crash*. "Shit!"

The column must've come out of nowhere and I now sat on the cold tiled floor, my dignity long gone and any chance of not having to talk to Gideon with it. His loud, recognizable footsteps marched toward me and I did my best to lift myself up. The poor concierge gave me a pitying look, perhaps checking out the long slit in my dress and the way my legs tangled in it. "Ma'am, the printer is just through there. Are you sure you're fine?"

"I'm okay, Chris. Just emotionally bruised." My ass throbbed, the dull ache in my elbow not pleasant either. I slid my gaze toward Gideon and sucked in a breath. *I miss those eyes.* "Mr. Titan. I hope you found the parking accommodations suitable."

One side of his mouth quirked up, but just for a second, before his gaze slid all the way down my body. I shivered. The decision to go braless because the back of the dress was open had not been the best idea. I crossed my arms, hoping to hide my attraction, but his smirk told me otherwise. "Sure. Are you good?"

I nodded. "Peachy." *I hate myself. Peachy? Of all the things to say, I went with that.*

"Your cheeks are a little red and you got this wide-eye thing going on. You sure?" He reached out his hand, but didn't quite touch my face. The longing in his eyes disappeared as quickly as it had got there, and his expression turned to stone. "Well, I'll see you in the ballroom."

"Can we talk? Like, later? I mean, if you're not busy. I think we should. I, uh…would like to say things to you." *Oh my god.* I closed my eyes, the shame of my rambling and idiocy almost too much to bear. His minty breath hit my face and I forced myself to look at him. "If not, we can totally do it later. If you have time with baseball-y stuff."

"Baseball-y stuff." He ran a hand over his jaw, covering his mouth. The suit moved with him, the material clinging to every inch of his hard body that I'd explored countless times. Moisture pooled in my panties and I crossed my legs. *Jesus.* "What do we need to talk about?"

"That last conversation we had—" I froze. A woman waltzed up next to Gideon, her gorgeous dark hair and perfectly done makeup making me feel like a teenager playing dress-up. Her manicured nails matched her deep green dress, and I had to fight from throwing up. *He brought her.*

"Hannah, this is Fiona Davis. One of the board members of Texting Too Late," Gideon said, putting his hand on the small of her back. He didn't mention coaching, further implying he was dating her. *In ten days... God, I'm replaceable.*

"Oh, wow! Fiona, it is so nice to meet you. I've heard a lot about this charity. You're doing amazing work in the community. It's an honor to be here," Hannah replied in a singsong voice that sounded like honey. I ground my teeth together and hoped I didn't look like I was falling apart.

"Nice to meet you too, Hannah." I shook her hand — soft and not sweaty like mine — and avoided Gideon's glare. "I hope you both enjoy the event."

"I have no doubt I will. I'm hoping to score something nice in the silent auctions. Someone mentioned there were private whiskey tours. If that doesn't have my name on it, I don't know what does." She laughed, knocking her hip with Gideon's. "I'm going to go check in. I'll see you upstairs in a minute?"

"Sure." He gave her a small smile, and watched her walk away.

My entire body shook and my tears were going to ruin my makeup, which Jade had paid to get done. *He has a room with Hannah. He's going on a whiskey tour with her.*

"Gideon. I-I..." I couldn't stop staring at the girl as she waited by the elevator. She was stunning — perfect lips, hair, smile. She didn't look like she had baggage that clogged her brain at night, whispering what ifs about the worst-case scenario. My heart couldn't take any more. It broke in two. "I should go. I have papers. The copies. I have to get copies."

"What did you want to say, Fiona?" His eyes hardened and the line of his jaw stiffened. Every cell in my body was telling me to abandon my mission. He had a date. He'd moved on. He'd forgotten about me. I blinked back tears and shook my head. *He'll leave eventually.*

"Thank you for...everything. Have f-fun." I took a step back.

"Everything we've been through, you want to *thank* me?" He tilted his head and snarled. "Speak your mind, Fiona. What did you want to say?"

"I need to go. Registration had issues and..." I eyed the small office to the right. "Goodbye, Gideon. Good luck with everything."

Chapter Thirty

Gideon

I gritted my teeth, taking a deep breath and counting to ten. It was better than the alternative. *I don't need another social media scandal.* "That girl is hurting, Gideon. I was all for playing the part for you, but damn." Hannah returned from 'checking in'. I ran my hand over my face and tension coiled itself down my body. "I'm pleased to attend, but you should go talk to her. I don't mind, really. This is a huge favor for me, being here."

"I owed Tate," I barked out. Fiona's face was burned into my mind. Her crestfallen expression, the slight shake of her chin... *Why couldn't she say what she wanted to?* "Would you mind going to check us in at the registration table?"

"Not at all. Go talk to her. I'll meet you inside."

I nodded, pinched the bridge of my nose and entered the business center of the elegant hotel. It amused me —

the image of Fiona wearing a lethally sexy midnight-blue dress with her crazy blonde hair hanging in waves and sitting next to a relic of a computer. She tapped the machine with her hand, yelling at it, but nothing happened. She let out a small groan and pressed a button on the side of her headset.

"Yes, *boss*. I am working on getting the hard copies. Also, fuck you for not telling me Gideon brought a date. No. No. You're dead to me. Dead. D-e-a-d."

If I wasn't so pissed at her, I would've laughed. She flipped off the computer, letting her limbs fall at all angles. It was as if the air had completely left her body and she spoke in such a soft tone, I had to lean forward to catch it all. "Obviously, I have feelings for him, Jade. It just took time for me to accept it. I was too late. He has a new sidepiece. I'm not doing this feel-y shit with you right now. The computer isn't letting me log in for the originals. Let's just have the attendants write the information down by hand and get it to the tech guys to program into the system. It'll be fine."

She paused, snorting at something Jade said, before she stood. "You want me to let Gideon know where to go? How about hell fucking no. I'll check in with the silent auction. I'm turning this thing off if you think I'm going to talk to—"

"To me?"

She gasped and spun around so fast I swore she pulled a muscle in shoulder. "I gotta go, Jade."

I gestured to the headset and couldn't hold back my grin. "You can tell Jade not to worry about finding me."

"Thanks for pointing that out." She bit her bottom lip, her gaze darting at everything but my face. A small blush crept up her neck, enflaming her face. Her eyes were bluer than I remembered, and a sharp reminder of how she'd left everything between us. "How much, er — what did you hear?"

"Oh, the entire thing." I stepped closer and enjoyed the way her chest heaved with each breath. It pleased me to hear she had feelings for me, but I wasn't about to make it easier for her. I crossed my arms and did my best to remain expressionless. "Are you mature enough to talk like real adults?"

She blinked, her hands forming two fists at either side. *Good. Maybe she hurts like I do.* "It doesn't matter."

"It all matters, Fiona."

"I have to run back and help," she stuttered and tried to move past me. I blocked the exit and let myself enjoy her perfume for a couple of seconds. "Gideon, please."

"No. Look at me."

And she did. With her trembling bottom lip, wide, scared eyes, and chin jutted out, she met my gaze. All the air left my lungs at her beauty — I needed her back in my life and I wouldn't let her leave until she told me. I knew she felt it. I had done back when she crushed my heart, but I understood her.

We had no chance if she wasn't the one to take the first step. It had to be her and waiting sucked. "What did you want to tell me?"

She ran her tongue over her mouth, her back straightening. My chest tightened when I watched her walls fall down. "I-I… It was real. For me. Everything."

"What was real?"

She swallowed quite loudly, her throat bobbing. "What's the point? I need to protect myself here, Gid."

"Isn't that what you did ten days ago? Protect yourself from getting hurt, by ignoring the truth. This isn't different. I put it all on the line for you." My pulse raced and I swore my adrenaline had never been this high before. I took her hand and put it on my heart. "I'm not going to give you another shot. I need to think about myself, too."

She dug her nails into my chest, her cherry-red lips pursing twice before opening. "I want to try. You and me. Being together. I'm a mess. I'll scream and fight with you—relationships aren't my thing. But, Gid—" She paused and glanced over my shoulder. "You're here with an-another woman. I shouldn't be saying any of this."

"Yes. You should. It's perfect."

I cupped her jaw with my left hand, bringing her mouth to meet mine. I didn't wait another second before kissing her. Her arms wrapped around me, her heartbeat pounding into me. She tasted sweet, her tongue greedily trying to get inside. I obliged and deepened the kiss, tipping her head back. She moaned and all the pieces inside me fell back together. "I missed you," I whispered between kissing and caressing her sides. "Hannah is a friend. I promise."

Fiona shoved my chest away and her swollen lips sent a wave of desire through me. It had been too long and my cock tightened against my pants. "You're not sharing a room with her?"

"Hell, no." I chuckled and pushed a strand of her hair behind her ear. The silky blonde hair was soft and I wanted it spread across my bed. "I may have insinuated it just to rile you."

"Excuse me? You did *what*?" She took a step back and stared at me with a bemused expression. "You asshole. Look who's immature now."

"I'm not ashamed. It got a reaction out of you, and yeah. I wanted to hurt you. You let me walk away in that parking lot without a word. Never again. Okay?" I cupped her face and pressed a soft kiss on her mouth.

"Okay."

"It's only been you." I traced a finger down her face, ending on her collarbone and taking my time admiring her outfit. "You're stunning."

"I'm scared." Her lip trembled again and I would've done anything in the world to protect her. "There's so much hurt at stake."

"I know it's going to be hard. You drive me fucking crazy in the best way possible and I want to be there when you fall apart a little bit. You're the missing piece. I didn't know I needed it, but I want to be yours. Life is way too damn short to not enjoy every moment of joy we find. You're my joy, and I think I can be yours, too."

"God, that was good." She sniffed and hope blossomed in my chest. She leaned into me and I held her tight against me. She fit there. "I wish I didn't have to work the event. I thought — well, I planned to find you afterward. I have a room. Two-twenty."

"Was that an invitation?"

"Yes." She kissed me again, gripping each side of my jacket. "Fuck, yeah it was. I should go. Jade's probably losing her shit."

"Okay. I'll walk you there, plus, you need to show me where to go." I placed my hand on the lower part of her back and guided her out of the door. It was going to be a long night before I could have her to myself, but it would be worth it.

* * * *

One look. That was all it took. Fiona ran her fingers over her bottom lip, pausing to say something to Jade before she joined me in the archway. She took my breath away—her speech about the dangers of texting and driving, and her battle, the fact that she'd invited the entire baseball team here and given them a shout-out, her inner beauty that drew people to her and her eyes... They heated every time she looked my way. Fuck. I loved the shit out of this girl. "You ready to go, Barbie?"

"Am I ever." She took my outreached hand, intertwining our fingers and dragging me toward the garden. "I have to help at the after-party, but I have an hour. So, use those sexy long legs for something and follow me."

Follow her? "An hour?"

"Yes. Keep up, Gid. I need you naked as soon as possible. We're going to my room."

Blood slowly left my brain, traveling down to my cock. Her hips swung with each step and I would've followed her off a bridge if she'd asked me to. We approached an elevator, but she darted right. "Convinced the suckers to give me ground floor."

"Thank god for small miracles." I meant the words. My body throbbed with need for her and I couldn't control it much longer. She fumbled with the keycard and I pressed a kiss behind her ear. She practically melted into me, and I moved my length against her. "Open the door, Fiona."

She did. I didn't wait for her to shut it before picking her up and shoving her into the door. I attacked her mouth with so much passion, I couldn't see straight. Her exquisite taste drove me wild. A mixture of wine and *her.* She rocked against my hips, moaning my name over and over. Hearing my name from her lips got me wild. "Fuck. I need you inside me, Gideon."

Best. Words. Ever. I threw her onto the bed, using one hand to slip off her panties. Yeah—I knew she had an event and didn't want to totally embarrass her. "How does this dress come off?"

"No time. Here." She hoisted the beautiful material up over her hips, exposing her freshly shaven pussy. *Christ.* "Mm."

That one-syllable moan almost killed me. She defined desperate—crazy eyes, legs spread wide with evidence of her moisture pooling around her core, and slight movement of her hips. "What do you want from me, Fiona? Say it."

"I want you inside me. Fuck me, Gid."

I undid my pants and barely tossed them onto the dresser before I froze. "I don't have a condom, Fiona. Shit!"

"I trust you. I'm on the pill," she replied, her voice husky and all sorts of sexy. I slipped into her after hearing those amazing words. Pleasure unlike anything before flowed through my entire body as her tight walls stretched to fit me.

She gripped my ass, digging her nails into the flesh as I pounded into her. I wouldn't last long, and positioned us so my fingers could reach her swollen, needy clit. "I'm wound tight. Jesus, pinch my clit."

I obeyed, using two fingers to pinch and swirl around her lips, flicking the hardened clit and moaning right along with her when she fell apart. She did something different, too. She held my gaze with each ride of her orgasm, her blue eyes turning darker than I had ever seen. "Jesus, you're fucking beautiful."

"So are you," she panted. "So are you."

I about lost it at the tender expression on her face. I tightened my hold on her hips, tilting them so each thrust put pressure right where she craved it. She arched her back, her body clenching while I picked up the pace. My legs tightened, my spine tingling as an orgasm built. I held off as long as I could, ensuring she got another one, but it happened simultaneously. I spilled into the girl I loved while her body trembled all around me.

My ears rung, but her throaty voice pulled me back. "Amazing. You're amazing, Gideon."

I kissed her lips, then her cheek, then her eyes. "As are you." I cupped her face, admiring the extra length of her eyelashes. They looked good, but I preferred Fiona just the way she was. My chest tightened, the flutters in my stomach unlike anything I'd experienced. But fuck it all to hell—I was going for it. "I love you. I'm ridiculously, annoyingly in love with you. All of you."

She blinked, her blue eyes lightening and filling with moisture. Her entire body tensed and I swore her bottom lip shook. I laughed, bringing my fingers to her mouth. "Babe, don't worry. There's no pressure. That wasn't a caveat. I feel it and I want to say it to you. I know what we have is real and one day, you'll be ready."

"You... You're okay with...me not returning it?" She sniffed and tilted her head at me. I nodded.

"With you, yeah. I understand you. I'll just keep working at it until you do." I snuggled her into my arm, pulling her weight against me. "Who would've thought one baseball season would change our lives?"

She ran her hand over my chest, humming into my side. "I'm not good with words, but I'm fucking glad. Did I ever tell you...? No. This is embarrassing."

"Nice try. Spill it."

"I had a poster of you in my room, until that first phone call. You were such an ass, I swore to hate you forever."

"Wait—what? Used to?" I lifted my head and forced her to look at me. "You threw it *away*?"

She laughed. She snorted and did the charming belly-laugh that had intrigued me in the beginning. "Sure did, hotshot. I love how that's what you're focusing on, not the hate comment."

"Like, did you crumple it up or carefully set it in a dumpster somewhere?" I teased, loving getting reactions out of her. It worked. She groaned and rolled her pretty eyes.

"You're annoying."

"But you like me."

"Yeah. I do. Guess that means I'll need another one, huh?" She wiggled her eyebrows and pointed her gaze toward my cock. "We could have fun creating some?"

Hell, yes.

Want to see more from this author? Here's a taster for you to enjoy!

Classic Curves: Whiskey Surprises
Jaqueline Snowe

Excerpt

Fern

It didn't matter how many damn to-do lists I had, or how many of those items I checked off—I could never sleep the night before the big event. My Rusty Nail, the best drink ever created, burned my throat in the perfect way and the adorable bartender slid me my second glass. He defined eye-candy with his plucked eyebrows, chiseled jaw and styled hair, a bit too young for the looks he was throwing my way. I had no issues with being a cougar, but there were lines I wouldn't cross. He was one of them.

He flipped the towel in a dramatic fashion and I hid my snort. In a practiced move perfected by long nights with big tippers, he leaned over the bar onto his strong arms and batted his long lashes. He dipped his head slightly to the side and met my gaze. "Mama, what's a pretty thing like you doing sitting at a bar alone?"

"Drinking. Strong, independent women are the new wave." I scanned for a name tag and not at all over his uber-defined pecs. Tony grinned but leaned closer and crooked his finger for me to lean in. I wasn't rude, so I appeased him.

"You must have a lot of confidence to sit alone."

I tilted my head to the opposite angle and added a bit of attitude to my voice. "Incorrect. I have a lot of desire to *drink* alone." I held up the glass. "Cheers, Tony."

He got the hint and took his charm elsewhere. I closed my eyes and hummed in pleasure at the rich taste of Scottish whiskey and Drambuie. The honey and citrus combination almost calmed the nerves dancing around in my belly. Some people handled pressure fine. I did not. Stress began in my gut and spread throughout my limbs, making me second-guess every decision I had made regarding the event. *Every* decision. Like, why didn't I order red polo shirts for the staff? Did I bring enough socks for the week?

Right, it didn't matter. But my nerves got the better of me and whiskey was the answer to any question. I took another sip, the pain in my chest growing at the severity of my situation. I pinched the bridge of my nose, hoping to relieve some of my tension, but failed. I continued to replay my boss's words. If I said them enough, then maybe they wouldn't be true—if we didn't make our threshold in revenue this year, then I wouldn't have a job.

Being single at thirty-two when every goddamn person I knew had two-point-five kids and a house with four dogs and a partner was annoying. I loved my friends, coworkers, family—the whole lot of them. Even my younger brother who rarely showered had found a human who wanted to spend his life with him. I could handle their jabs about my personal life and if I was confused. But being single *and* unemployed was not a route I wanted to head down. *Nope. No thank you.*

It wasn't as if I was awful or un-dateable. I took care of myself, ate healthily, worked out and had a normal amount of confidence and above-average conversational skills. I just didn't like wasting time on small talk when I had to help run a multimillion-dollar Silvas car show. *Ain't no time for relationships when a wild ride in the sack suffices.* Plus, why force a relationship if I knew it wasn't going to work?

"You look like you're trying to solve all the world's problems," someone said next to me. The voice was deep, a guttural masculine rhythm. It startled me a bit and I set my glass on the bar before giving the stranger my attention.

"Try again."

"Excuse me?" His deep voice drew me in, instantly sending heat all the way down to my core. It made no sense to have this reaction to a voice, and I had to see if it matched his face.

I bit back a groan. It matched. *Good god.* Testosterone and sex just oozed off him in waves. *Delicious* waves. His jet-black hair went well with his soft hazel eyes and tan skin. Lines appeared on the edges around his eyes — a sign he lived a happy life. His jaw was sharp and defined, and his day-old beard didn't hurt either. I grinned and adjusted my position to face him. His gaze moved from my face down to my legs. His nostrils flared twice and awareness burned through me while he continued his perusal back to my mouth.

Ten points to me for shaving and wearing the summer dress. Maybe it was the spark in his eyes that challenged me. *Well, could be my feisty personality.* But instead of going easy on the handsome man, I slowly ran my tongue over my teeth and tilted my head. "I said try again. That line you used is not original. I've heard it an obnoxious amount of times."

He bit down on his bottom lip, doing nothing to hide his amusement. He raised his eyebrows and leaned an inch closer. "Do you find yourself at a bar alone drinking a gentleman's drink often?" He transformed that smirk into a lazy smile that showcased two dimples. The goofy grin clashed with his broad shoulders and intimidating suit and tie but I sure as hell wasn't complaining. Dimples were my kryptonite.

"I prefer to not classify drinks by gender. I drink what I like. We all should do what we like. Life is too short. But to answer your question, yes."

He nodded and didn't ask before sliding onto the bar stool next to me. His cologne teased me, the masculine scent like leather and mint and something…woodsy. I wanted to scoot closer and drag my fingers over his firm pecs, but refrained. I wasn't sure I liked the guy, but my body didn't care. He ordered an Old-Fashioned and winked when he held up his glass. "Clearly, we have great taste in drinks. To the whiskey of the world."

We clinked glasses and he held my gaze throughout the entire sip. His throat moved and desire shot through me. It was such a simple gesture—a man taking a drink. But he did it so much better than all the other men I'd met at bars. He held it up, taking his time smelling the rich liquid, releasing a small moan. His long fingers made the glass seem so much smaller and ideas flew through my head as to what he could do with those hands… I cleared my throat and took another sip.

I didn't have time for commitments of any kind, not with the Silvas car show lasting the next five days, but a fling with a stranger could help with the stress. It had been at least a month since I'd had an orgasm not produced by yours truly, and before I could rationalize my thoughts, my skin tingled in anticipation. I readjusted my legs, crossing the right over the left, and enjoyed his reaction. He followed the motion with his eyes and ran his tongue over his bottom lip, his mouth a little slack. Yeah, I had nice legs and was proud of it. I opened my mouth to speak but he beat me to it.

"You're direct. I appreciate that." He grinned again, the heat in his eyes unmistakable.

"Why waste time on small talk and fake conversations?" I pursed my lips at him and took my time studying every feature on his handsome face. The strong forehead, the slightly crooked nose, the dusting of gray around the temples giving him a beautiful silver fox look… My nipples tightened with need when he leaned closer — not enough to touch me, but enough for the air around us to ripple with tension. I ran a finger down my neck, drawing his attention to the low dip of my dress. He hummed in approval and I swore his cologne got stronger.

"Can I walk you back to your room when we finish our drinks? I know you're independent, but I'd like to offer my help removing your dress."

I smiled, held up my glass and downed the rest of the amber liquid. "How about I walk you back to your room and I help you remove *your* clothes?"

His eyes lit up with delight and he mirrored my action. Not two seconds later, our glasses were empty and I slid off the tall bar stool. He requested our drinks be charged to his room and he put his hand on my lower back to guide me toward the elevator. I was tall for a woman, two inches shy of six feet, but the handsome stranger still had half a foot over me. My limbs trembled at every small gesture. When he dug his fingers into my lower back, I felt it in my toes. He carefully brushed my hair off my shoulder and when the pads of his fingertips touched my skin, electrifying tingles broke out. My body was a puddle of hormones and lust.

"How long are you in town?" His throaty voice sent chills down my back as he pressed his lips against my ear. He had a commanding tone, strong and deep in timbre. I had no doubt he'd have a wildly successful career as a phone sex worker.

"Five more days," I replied when the elevator doors pinged, announcing its arrival. My speech wasn't recognizable with its hoarse tone. I cleared my throat. "You?"

"Same."

The air stilled when the door shut. It was just the two of us in the small hotel elevator, my pulse racing as anticipation built inside me. My panties were soaked and I wanted nothing more than to have my way with the handsome stranger. "What floor should I push?"

"Tenth." He brought his fingers to my neck and eased my long blonde hair off my shoulder. He trailed the delicate skin behind my ears, down my neck and the exposed part of my back. I shivered when he pressed his lips right where my spine met my neck. "Mm. Your skin is beautiful."

He tightened his hold on my hips and pulled my back flush against him, his beard tickling me while he continued kissing tender parts of me. He brought one of his hands around and cupped my breast, pinching my taut nipple. "Braless?"

"It's summer. Too hot to tame them."

"Sexy. I love that." He pressed the tip between his strong fingers and bit down on my ear just as the doors opened. "After you. Third door on the right."

I strutted in front of him, ever so thankful for my long stride, and led us to his room. He didn't rush, and my impatience grew. I was hot, horny and ready. He took his time getting out his key and slid his heated gaze my direction "What's your name?"

"We don't need to do this part, do we?" I tilted my head at the question. There were no misconceptions here. This was a hookup, a way to relieve stress and enjoy a hot night with a stranger. Names weren't necessary.

"I want you screaming my name each time you come. So, yeah. We do need to do this." His rough tone turned me on and my stomach swooped. "I'm Rylan."

"Fern."

His eyes twinkled and he repeated my name. I moaned at hearing it coming from his lips and he finally opened the door. He let me go in first but gave me no time to take in the surroundings. He picked me up, spreading my legs around his waist, and slammed my back into the door. Rough hands went around my hips and he brought his mouth to mine.

God, he kissed like a fucking summer storm. No warning. *Aggressive. Powerful. Magical.* The burn of the whiskey combined between us as we explored each other's mouths. I arched my back when he bit down and sucked on my bottom lip. It gave me a moment to look into his eyes and the intensity there sent another wave of desire through me. It was electric.

Dirty. Animalistic.

I couldn't satisfy my need to have him. I attacked his mouth, trying to taste all of him in that one kiss.

He groaned and brought a hand to my neck. He squeezed the skin where my collarbone met my shoulder and continued down my body until he got to my breasts. Without missing a beat, he brought his mouth down to my chest and pulled the fabric aside. His breathing got heavier with my breasts exposed, the hitch in his breath causing all sorts of sensations in my core. "Gorgeous. Just gorgeous."

He sucked the sensitive nipple into his mouth, swirling his tongue around it. I jumped with pleasure and fisted his hair. "Yes, use your teeth."

He hummed and bit down, mixing the point of pain and pleasure. He repeated the action on my other breast and I bucked against him. "I love your reactions."

I used his break to slide down his body, enjoying his erection bursting to get out of his pants. Size was so *not* an issue. "Lose the clothes, Rylan."

"Yes, ma'am." He smiled and set me on the ground. It was a highly intimate moment between strangers, but I didn't give two shits. My body was alive. I whipped off my dress and removed the thin black panties that were already ruined. I stood there, naked and needy, and admired the curves of his muscles. His pecs were defined, but his abs and arms were just as impressive. "I'm having a hard time focusing with your fine ass watching me, Fern."

"I didn't take you for needy," I goaded him. His eyes changed from light to a darker hue, now almost green, and his arousal grew. Drunk on power, I undid his belt buckle and helped slide his slacks off. His cock sprang free and my core throbbed with need. I desperately wanted to feel all of him inside me, stretching me thin and making me forget my name.

"You're licking your lips looking at my dick. My self-restraint only has so much control." His voice came out huskier and I grinned.

"It's a nice dick. I want to ride it." I reached out and wrapped my fingers around it. I felt his heartbeat in his swollen cock, the head displaying a small bead of moisture. My hand almost covered half of it and I gave him a couple of pumps. He shook at my touch but I didn't get more than ten strokes before he picked me up and tossed me onto the bed. "Woah!"

"You're sexy as hell," he said, his tone exciting me. His face had a predatory smile and I was into it. *Really into it.* He didn't wait for me to respond before kissing and sucking the sensitive skin around my neck and down my ribcage. He brought his fingers to my clit and swirled around it, inserting two fingers inside me. "You're soaked. All for me. Mm."

"Go faster," I said into his neck. The faint scent of sweat mixed with his cologne and it made me drunk. He finger-fucked me to the point I was desperate, seconds away from exploding, but he removed them. "I'm desperate. Don't stop."

"I can't watch you scream my name like this." He slid down the bed so he kneeled on the floor. I thought he was about to go down on me, but he spread my legs apart and used two hands. Ten digits. It was too much. My legs tightened. A burning hot wave of pleasure started in my clit and spread to my limbs. He increased the pressure on my swollen clit and explored the rest of my folds, letting me ride out the wave.

"Rylan, fuck. Yes!" I arched my back and screamed. My legs shook as the orgasm settled down, but he didn't give me any time to recover.

"I can't get enough of your reactions. You're dynamite."

"It's your touch," I replied but grabbed a pillow to muffle my response when he hovered over me and put his teeth down on my nipple. He used one hand to stroke me while giving me the perfect combination of pain and pleasure. He worked me right to the point where the teasing became too much, and I moaned when a second orgasm took control. I yanked his hair and dragged his face to mine, desperate to taste him again.

This kiss was just as aggressive, but there was warmth in his eyes when I glanced at him. Our bodies clung together, the heat building between us until a dull ache began in my core. I wanted all of him. Reading my needy moans, he pressed one last kiss on my lips before getting off the bed. He sheathed himself in a condom from his wallet and gave me a long look. "You're sure?"

A part of me appreciated the gesture, the last question. But my pussy throbbed and I was going to die if he didn't enter me soon. "One thousand percent. Get inside me, Rylan."

His grin was the perfect answer. He held on to my hips and thrust into me in one swift motion. I swore I saw stars. I gripped the sheets around us while he groaned in pleasure. It was intoxicating, knowing he enjoyed it. But the position wasn't doing enough for me. I motioned for him to go to his back and he obeyed.

"God, you're a sight Fern," he breathed. His voice dropped an octave lower, his pupils almost blocking out the green orbs. I slid down onto his cock, releasing a long growl when he stretched me further than I had been in a long while. "*Jesus*, you feel amazing."

I grinned and pushed his hands above his head, pinning them down. I rocked my hips, perfected by years of doing Zumba, and he lost control. He slammed his mouth to mine, our teeth clashing as I rode him. Our bodies blended into one and sweat dripped down my spine. He broke free of my restraint and squeezed my ass.

A third orgasm was close. I could feel it, my stomach muscles clenching when we found our rhythm. He read me like a goddamn book and brought his thumb to my clit. I dug my nails into his firm skin and quickened my pace, leaning forward. The pressure was perfect and I clung to him, screaming his name, riding out the orgasm. He tightened his hold on my hips when he tensed.

"Say my name when you come, Rylan," I commanded with the little voice I still had. His eyes lit up and he obliged. My name left his lips as he did three final thrusts before the sexiest sound came from his mouth. It was a growl and a moan and *fuck* if I didn't want to keep it.

"Christ," he said between pants. "Incredible."

He picked me up like I weighed nothing—and I was a curvy woman—and set me on the bed next to him. He patted my ass and gave me a swift kiss on the shoulder. "Let me clean up. Stay put."

I always appreciated hook-ups where the stranger gave me the needed recovery time. I could catch my breath without worrying about what was next. My body was flushed, my legs shaking from the strong orgasms. I didn't have time to get up before he came out of the bathroom and plopped back on the bed.

"You can stay if you'd like." He leaned on his elbow and my heart lurched. He looked so perfect with his lone curl escaping in the front. I never stayed but I almost thought about it with him. *Almost.*

"Can't. I have a huge event tomorrow. My job may or may not be on the line."

"I have every confidence in you."

"Thanks, handsome." I re-dressed quickly, forgoing my panties. The stress of the event came back despite the three orgasms and I gave Rylan one more glance. "You know...I wouldn't be opposed doing this again while you're in town."

His entire face lit up in a grin and he grabbed a hotel key from his nightstand. "Five more nights here. Come in any time after nine."

"Awful trusting of you, just meeting me," I said, looking at the white key card in my hand. The gesture moved me…it was too trusting. But I couldn't stop the excitement at the thought of seeing him again.

"Sweetheart, I've just been inside you and made you scream my name three times. I'm game if you are, but the ball's in your court." He relaxed into his pillows, his entire body loose and on display.

I licked my lips and gave him another glance. "Then I guess we'll see what happens."

"Can't wait."

Then I left the amazing specimen of a man in the room and went to obsess over the car show that could very well be my last one.

Home of Erotic Romance

Sign up for our newsletter and find out about all our romance book releases, eBook sales and promotions, sneak peeks and FREE romance books!

About the Author

Jaqueline Snowe lives in Arizona where the 'dry heat' really isn't that bad. She enjoys making lists with colorful Post-it notes and sipping coffee all day. She has been a custodian, a waitress, a landscaper, a coach and a teacher.

Her life revolves around binge-watching Netflix, her two dogs who don't realize they aren't humans and her wonderful baseball-loving husband.

Jaqueline loves to hear from readers. You can find her contact information, website details and author profile page at https://www.totallybound.com